Phillips Brooks

Phillips Brooks Year Book

Selections from the writings of the Rt. Rev. Phillips Brooks

Phillips Brooks

Phillips Brooks Year Book
Selections from the writings of the Rt. Rev. Phillips Brooks

ISBN/EAN: 9783337385996

Printed in Europe, USA, Canada, Australia, Japan

Cover: Foto ©Andreas Hilbeck / pixelio.de

More available books at **www.hansebooks.com**

PHILLIPS BROOKS YEAR BOOK

SELECTIONS FROM THE WRITINGS

OF THE

RT. REV. PHILLIPS BROOKS, D.D.

BY

H. E. S. AND L. H. S.

"The thought is stronger for us because he has thought it. The feeling is more vivid because he has felt it. And always he leads us to God by a way along which he has gone himself."—PREACHING, p. 119.

NEW YORK

E. P. DUTTON & COMPANY

31 WEST TWENTY-THIRD STREET

1895

Press of J. J. Little & Co.
Astor Place, New York

NOTE. - — References to the Works of Bishop Brooks have been added, with the thought that some might like to turn to the context. They are respectively as follows : I., II., III., IV., V., to Vols. one, two, three, four, and five of the Sermons. "Influence" to "The Influence of Jesus." "Preaching" to the "Yale Lectures on Preaching." "Tolerance" to "Tolerance."

PREFACE.

TO the friends of Bishop Brooks this little book will come as no stranger. His sermons have had such living qualities in them, that they are read and re-read by many a one who never came under the influence of his marvellous personality. Their quality will be still farther tested, it seems to us, by this separating process of presenting their thoughts in fragments. If in this way the thoughts do not lose in suggestiveness, in vividness, and in strength, it will be a new testimony to the fact that the sermons are among the immortal few, which are for all time and not for one special age alone.

The aim of the book is to group together cognate thoughts in sequence of time, as well as to represent fairly this man of large love for humanity and of absolute surrender to his Master.

That he found a place for such books is sympathetically shown by his preface to a

volume of selections published some years
since. In this preface he says: " The most
notable quality of such books is their suggestiveness. . . . It is not the fulness of their
hands which makes them welcome. It is the
delicacy and discrimination of the finger which
they lay upon some spring in us and set some
of our nature free. . . . Some suggestive word
out of this book will fall upon a score of lives
some morning, and will touch the key of each.
Each will be better for it, but how differently!
One will do better trading; another will do
better teaching; another's household life will
be more pure and lofty."

To those who have known Bishop Brooks in
the past, and looked to him for guidance in the
upward way, these daily thoughts from him
will surely come with the added joy of memories which are very precious. "In the old
days it was strength to be with him; in those
to come it will be strength to remember
him."

THE EDITORS.

Brethren, the time is short.—I. COR. vii. 29.

THE shortness of life . . . spreads the feeling of criticalness all through life, and makes each moment prepare for the next — makes life prepare for life. This is its power. Blessed is he who feels it. Blessed is he in whose experience each day and each hour has all the happiness and all the solemnity of a parent towards the day and the hour to which it gives birth, stands sponsor for it, holds it for baptism at the font of God. Such days are sacred in each other's eyes. The life in which such days succeed each other is a holy family, with its moments "bound each to each by natural piety."

I. 328.

Sail fast, sail fast,
Ark of my hopes, Ark of my dreams ;
Sweep lordly o'er the drownèd Past,
Fly glittering through the sun's strange beams ;
Sail fast, sail fast.
Breaths of new buds from off some drying lea,
With news about the Future scent the sea ;
My brain is beating like the heart of Haste,
I'll loose me a bird upon this Present waste ;
Go, trembling song,
And stay not long ; oh, stay not long :
Thou'rt only a gray and sober dove,
But thine eye is faith and thy wing is love.

SIDNEY LANIER.

Ye have not passed this way heretofore.

JOSHUA iii. 4.

IT is good, then, for a man to come to a future which he does not know. It is good for you if God brings you to the borders of some promised land. Do not hesitate at any experience because of its novelty. Do not draw back from any way because you never have passed there before. The truth, the task, the joy, the suffering, on whose border you are standing, oh, my friend, to-day, go into it without a fear; only go into it with God — the God who has been always with you. Let the past give up to you all the assurance of Him which it contains. Set that assurance of Him before you. Follow that, and the new life to which it leads you shall open its best richness to you.

V. 305.

Grow old along with me!
The best is yet to be,
The last of life, for which the first was made:
Our times are in His hand
Who saith, " A whole I planned,
Youth shows but half; trust God; see all, nor be
    afraid."

ROBERT BROWNING.

[The shepherds] made known abroad the saying which was told them concerning this child.

LUKE ii. 17.

THE tale the shepherds tell fits the world we know — a world which has God in it, and yet in which even God works under the limitations of humanity, and where the power which is divine yet lingers and must slowly grow. Surely this is our world to which the Incarnation perfectly corresponds.

Sureness and patience — sureness because it is God; patience because it is a child. Sureness and patience! Oh, my friends, if you and I could catch them both from the shepherds' story, how clear this world would grow to us, and with what calm and faithful energy we should work away at it in these few years in which God has appointed us to work; . . . satisfied, perfectly satisfied, if we can help the new Incarnation of Christ (which is the gradual embodiment of His divine soul in the life of a regenerated world) toward its completion, as Mary and Joseph tended and taught the Divine Child who was in their humble house. Can we picture a life more soberly enthusiastic, more patiently devoted — a life more truly " without haste and without rest " than that life must be ?

CHRISTMAS SERMON, p. 20, 21.

Beloved, now are we the sons of God, and it doth not yet appear what we shall be : but we know that, when He shall appear, we shall be like Him ; for we shall see Him as He is.   And every man that hath this hope in him purifieth himself even as He is pure. — I. JOHN iii. 2, 3.

NOT merely, I shall grow so that I shall be able to understand vastly more of what God is and of what He is doing. God also will be ever doing new things. He is forever active. He has purposes concerning me which He has not yet unfolded.   Therefore each year grows sacred with wondering expectation. Therefore I and the world may go forth from each old year into the new which follows it, certain that in that new year God will have for us some new treatment which will open for us some novel life.

IV. 363.

For lo ! in hidden deep accord,
The servant *may be* like his Lord.
And Thy love, our love shining through,
May tell the world that Thou art true,
Till those who see us see Thee too.

A. L. WARING.

There were two thieves crucified with Him.
MATT. xxvii. 38.

THE Saviour had left behind heaven; He had left behind even the little heavenliness which He had found upon the earth. All the disciples had forsaken Him and fled. The little flicker of sympathy which He had seen upon the face of Pilate He had lost now. He had come to the company of robbers. There were two thieves crucified with Him.

That is the sight which we behold as we look at these three crosses standing out sharp and terrible against the sky. Into the darkest of earth's darkness, into the deepest consequences of sin where it was possible for innocence to go, the Incarnate One has gone. Our Immanuel, our God with us, is with the worst of us in His most awful misery. No child of God shall know any suffering which this love shall not fathom to its depths with him.

I. 197, 198.

Nay but thou knewest us, Lord Christ, thou knowest,
    Well thou rememberest our feeble frame,
Thou canst conceive our highest and our lowest,
    Pulses of nobleness and aches of shame.

Then tho' our foul and limitless transgression
    Grows with our growing, with our breath began,
Raise thou the arms of endless intercession,
    Jesus, divinest when thou most art man!

FREDERICK W. H. MYERS.

I am the Light of the world. — JOHN viii. 12.

CHRIST is unspeakably great and glorious in Himself. The glory which He had with His Father "before the world was," of that we can only meditate and wonder; but the glory which He has had since the world was, the glory which He has had in relation to the world, is all bound up with the world's possibilities, has all consisted in the utterance and revelation and fulfilment of capacities which were in the very nature of the world on which His Light has shone.

V. 4, 5.

Tell us, thou clear and heavenly tongue,
Where is the Babe but lately sprung?
Lies He the lily-banks among?
Or say, if this new Birth of ours
Sleeps, laid within some ark of flowers
Spangled with dew-light; thou canst clear
All doubts, and manifest the where.
Declare to us, bright star, if we shall seek
Him in the morning's blushing cheek,
Or search the bed of spices through
To find Him out.
    Star. — "No, this ye need not do;
But only come, and see Him rest,
A princely Babe, in's mother's breast."

Come then, come then, and let us bring
Unto our pretty Twelfth-tide King
Each one his several offering.

HERRICK.

Wist ye not that I must be about my Father's business? —LUKE ii. 49.

AS Mary went back with her Son, realizing out of His own mouth that He was not only her Son but God's ; as she settled down with Him to their Nazareth life again, must not one single strong question have been upon her heart, "What does God want this Son of His to be? Oh, let me find that out, that I may work with Him." And as you go into the house where you are to train your soul, realizing, through some revelation that has come to it, that it is God's soul as well as yours, one strong and single question must be pressing on you too, "What does God want this soul of mine to be? Oh, let me find that out that I may work for Him." . . . The Son of Mary was a revelation to the mother in whose care He lived. So a man's soul, his spiritual nature which is intrusted to his care, is a perpetual revelation to him. If you can only know that your soul is God's child, that He is caring for it and training it, then it may become to you the source of deep divine communications. God will speak to you through your own mysterious life. He will show you His wisdom and goodness, not in the heaven above you, but in the soul within you. He will make you His fellow-worker in that which is the most divine work of His of which we can have any knowledge, the training and perfecting of a soul.   IV. 40, 41.

WHAT will God do this year? How will He come near to man? It may be, oh, that it might be! that He will break up this awful sluggishness of Christendom, this terrible torpidity of the Christian Church, and give us a great, true revival of religion. It may be that He will speak some great imperious command to the brutal and terrible spirit of war, and will open the gate upon a bright period of peace throughout the world. It may be that He will draw back the curtain and throw some of His light upon the question of how the poor and the rich may live together in more cordial brotherhood. It may be that He will lead up from the depths of their common faith a power of unity into the sects of a divided Christendom. Perhaps He will smite this selfishness of fashionable life, and make it earnest. Perhaps by some terrible catastrophe He will teach the nation that corruption is ruin, and that nothing but integrity can make any nation strong. Perhaps this! perhaps that! We make our guesses, and no man can truly say. Only we know that with a world that needs so much, and with a God who knows its needs and who loves it and pities it so tenderly, there must be in the long year some approach of His life to its life, some coming of the Lord!

IV. 364. 365.

Give ear, O Shepherd of Israel, Thou that leadest
  Joseph like a flock;
Thou that dwellest between the cherubim, shine forth.
Before Ephraim and Benjamin and Manasseh, stir up
  Thy strength,
And come for salvation to us.

Ps. LXXX. 1, 2.

WHAT bulwarks have you, rich, luxurious men, built up between yourselves and the poverty in which hosts of your brethren are living? What do you know, what do you want to know, of the real life of Jesus, who was so poor, so radical, so full of the sense of everything just as it is in God? You tremble at the changes which are evidently coming. You ask yourself, How many of these first things, these fundamental things, are going to be disturbed? Are property and rank and social precedence and the relation of class to class going to be overturned? Oh, you have got to learn that these are not the first things, these are not the fundamental things! Behind these things stand justice and mercy. Behind everything stands God. He must speak to you. He will speak to you. Oh, do not try to shut out His voice. Listen to Him, that you may live. Be ready for any overturnings, even of the things which have seemed to you most eternal, if by them He can come to be more the King of His own earth.   V. 87.

Cry unto Jesus, our Brother born to save us:
    O come, Son of Mary,
    Jesu, our Redeemer,
O come, King triumphant, and reign on earth.

SELWYN IMAGE.

I know how to be abased. — PHIL. iv. 12.

POVERTY seems to men to be like the old
fabled sphinx, — a mysterious being who
has in herself the secrets of life, but who holds
them fast, and tells them only in riddles, and
devours the brave, unfortunate adventurers
who try to guess at the wisdom she conceals,
and fail.   The result is that few men seek her
wisdom voluntarily.   V. 160.

> From street and square, from hill and glen,
>   Of this vast world beyond my door,
> I hear the tread of marching men,
>   The patient armies of the poor.
>
> Not ermine-clad or clothed in state,
>   Their title-deeds not yet made plain,
> But waking early, toiling late,
>   The heirs of all the earth remain.
>
> The peasant brain shall yet be wise,
>   The untamed pulse grow calm and still ;
> The blind shall see, the lowly rise,
>   And work in peace Time's wondrous will.
>
> Some day, without a trumpet's call,
>   This news will o'er the world be blown :
> " The heritage comes back to all !
>   The myriad monarchs take their own ! "

T. W. HIGGINSON.

*If I then, your Lord and Master, have washed
your feet, ye ought also to wash one another's feet.*
　　　　　　　　　　　　JOHN xiii. 14.

STRANGELY, on that solemn night the disciples had fallen into an untimely quarrel which of them should be the greatest, and then the Lord Himself rose from the table and tied the towel round His waist, and went from one wondering disciple to another and washed the feet of all. Did Jesus compare Himself with each of those disciples, and own Himself the inferior of each? He only said by His exquisite action that there was something in every one of them, in serving which even His divinity found no inappropriate employment. It was the truth of His whole Incarnation wrought into a homely picture.　　I. 346.

I saw a Saint. — How canst thou tell that he
　　Thou sawest was a Saint? —
I saw one like to Christ so luminously
　　By patient deeds of love, his mortal taint
Seemed made his groundwork for humility.

And when he marked me downcast utterly,
　　Where foul I sat and faint,
Then more than ever Christ-like kindled he;
　　And welcomed me as I had been a saint,
Tenderly stooping low to comfort me.

Christ bade him, " Do thou likewise." Wherefore he
　　Waxed zealous to acquaint
His soul with sin and sorrow, if so be
　　He might retrieve some latent saint:
" Lo, I, with the child God hath given to me! "
CHRISTINA ROSSETTI.

"FOR their sakes I sanctify Myself," said Jesus; and He hardly ever said words more wonderful than those. There was the power by which He was holy; the world was to be made holy, was to be sanctified through Him. I am sure that you or I could indeed be strengthened to meet some great experience of pain if we really believed that by our suffering we were to be made luminous with help to other men. They are to get from us painlessly what we have got most painfully from God. There is the power of the bravest martyrdom and the hardest work that the world has ever seen.

I. 17, 18.

Live thou deeply and wise;
Suffer as never before;
Know joy, till it cuts to the quick;
Eat the apple, Life, to the core.
Be thou cursed
By them thou hast blessed, by the sick
Whom thou in thy weakness nursed.
With thy strength the weak endue;
Be praised when 'twere better to blame;
In the home of thy spirit be true,
Though the voice of the street cry shame.
Be silent till all is done,
Then return, in the light of the sun,
And once more sing.
Oh, then fling
Into music thy soul! . . .
Tell the skies,
And the world, that shall listen at last.

RICHARD WATSON GILDER.

Ye shall be witnesses unto Me both in Jerusalem, and in all Judea, and in Samaria, and unto the uttermost part of the earth. — ACTS i. 8.

YOU know the venerable argument, which was never very strong, and which halts and stumbles now from age and long dishonorable service : " The heathen in Boston ! " we are told. " Look how poor a thing our home religion is ! Shall we not make our own religion strong, convert our own masses, conquer our own sins, before we go around the world to preach our yet unappropriated Gospel to the heathen ? " It is not always those who are most earnest or active to complete our home religion who use such an argument. . . .

Probably it is not an argument with which it is worth while to argue, but we cannot help thinking where, with such an argument in force, would have been the richness of Christian history ! If every land must for itself have made the very best and fullest use of the Gospel before it could offer it to any other land, how the great work would have halted and stayed in its first littleness ! Still, on the desolate fields of Galilee, or amid the ruins of Jerusalem, a few disconsolate and hopeless Jews would be telling to-day to one another the unbelieved and unused story of the cross. The earnest heart and manly intellect of Paul, full of the spirit of his Master, soon broke the spell of such a sophistry as that, and Europe saw the light through the dim medium of a Judaism which was itself still more than half darkness.   IV. 187, 188.

The earth is the Lord's, and the fulness thereof; the world and they that dwell therein.

Ps. xxiv. 1.

IT is not the desire to enforce the argument of a Foreign Missionary sermon, it is the sincere and deep conviction of my soul, when I declare that if the Christian faith does not culminate and complete itself in the effort to make Christ known to all the world, that faith appears to me to be a thoroughly unreal and insignificant thing, destitute of power for the single life, and incapable of being convincingly proved to be true. . . . The opened world— the simplified faith! Surely this of all times is not the time to disbelieve in Foreign Missions; surely he who despairs of the power of the Gospel to convert the world to-day, despairs of the noontide just when the sunrise is breaking out of twilight on the earth. . . . Distance has ceased to be a hindrance. Language no longer makes men total strangers. A universal commerce is creating common bases and forms of thought. For the first time in the history of the world there is a manifest, almost an immediate, possibility of a universal religion. No wonder that at such a time the missionary spirit which had slumbered for centuries should have sprung upon its feet, and the last fifty years should have been one of the very greatest epochs in missionary labor in the whole history of the world.

IV. 166, 169, 190.

I CAN conceive that Joseph and Mary may have wondered why those Gentiles should have come out of the East to worship their Messiah. But very soon the enlargement of their faith to be the world's heritage proved its power by making their faith a far holier thing for them than it could have been if it had remained wholly their own. Christ was more thoroughly theirs when through them He had been manifested to the Gentiles. And so always the enlargement of the faith brings the endearment of the faith, and to give the Saviour to others makes Him more thoroughly our own.

II. 164.

Then I preached Christ: and when she heard the
   story —
  Oh, is such triumph possible to men?
Hardly, my King, had I beheld Thy glory,
  Hardly had known Thy excellence till then.

  .   .   .   .

Oft when the Word is on me to deliver,
  Opens the heaven and the Lord is there;
Desert or throng, the city or the river,
  Melt in a lucid Paradise of air, —

Only like souls I see the folk thereunder,
  Bound who should conquer, slaves who should be
    kings;
Hearing their one hope with an empty wonder,
  Sadly contented in a show of things.

Then with a rush the intolerable craving
  Shivers throughout me like a trumpet call, —
Oh, to save these! to perish for their saving,
  Die for their life, be offered for them all!

F. W. H. MYERS.

OUR ordinary life with one another, what in the language of the world we call *society*, has so left and lost the spontaneousness of natural impulse and so failed to attain the highest conception of itself as the family of God, it so hangs fast in the dull middle regions of conventional propriety and selfish expediency, that it becomes not the fountain, but the grave, of individuality.   INFLUENCE, 99.

> Duty — 'tis to take on trust
> What things are good, and right, and just;
>   And whether indeed they be or be not,
>   Try not, test not, feel not, see not:
>   'Tis walk and dance, sit down and rise
>   By leading, opening ne'er your eyes;
> Stunt sturdy limbs that Nature gave,
> And be drawn in a Bath chair along to the grave.
> 'Tis the stern and prompt suppressing,
>   As an obvious and deadly sin,
> All the questing and the guessing
>   Of the soul's own soul within:
>   'Tis the coward acquiescence
>   In a destiny's behest,
>   To a shade by terror made,
>   Sacrificing, aye, the essence
>   Of all that's truest, noblest, best:
>   'Tis the blind non-recognition
>   Or of goodness, truth, or beauty,
>   Save by precept and submission;
>   Moral blank, and moral void,
>   Life at very birth destroyed.

ARTHUR HUGH CLOUGH.

Lo, a great multitude, which no man could number, of all nations, and kindreds, and people, and tongues, stood before the throne, and before the Lamb, clothed with white robes, and palms in their hands; and cried with a loud voice, saying, Salvation to our God which sitteth upon the throne and unto the Lamb. — REV. vii. 9, 10.

To him that overcometh will I give to eat of the hidden manna, and will give him a white stone, and in the stone a new name written, which no man knoweth, saving he that receiveth it. — REV. ii. 17.

NOWHERE do we find on earth that picture of society reconstructed by the idea of Jesus, society around the throne of God, which shines out upon us from the mysterious promises of the Apocalypse ; the glory of which society is to be this — that while the souls stand in their vast choruses of hundreds of thousands, and all chant the same anthems and all work together in the same transcendent duties, yet each bears the sacred name written on the flesh of his own forehead, and carries in his hand a white stone, on which is written a new name which no man knoweth saving he that receiveth it. It is individuality emphasized by company, and not lost in it, because the atmosphere in which the company is met is the idea of Jesus, which is the fatherhood of God.

INFLUENCE, 99, 100.

And thither thou, beloved, and thither I
May set our heart and set our face, and go
Faint yet pursuing home on tireless feet.

CHRISTINA ROSSETTI.

JESUS did not spend His life in trying not to do wrong. He was too full of the earnest love and longing to do right—to do His Father's will.

And so we see, by contrast, how many of our attempts at purity fail by their negativeness. . . . I do think that we break almost all our resolutions not to do wrong, while we keep a large proportion of our resolutions that we will do what is right. Habit, which is the power by which evil rules us, is only strong in a vacant life. It is the empty, swept, and garnished house to which the devils come back to hold still higher revel.

I. 183.

> Time was, I shrank from what was right
>   From fear of what was wrong ;
> I would not brave the sacred fight,
>   Because the foe was strong.
>
> But now I cast that finer sense
>   And sorer shame aside ;
> Such dread of sin was indolence,
>   Such aim at heaven was pride.
>
> So when my Saviour calls, I rise
>   And calmly do my best ;
> Leaving to Him, with silent eyes
>   Of hope and fear, the rest.
>
> I step, I mount where He has led ;
>   Men count my haltings o'er :
> I know them ; yet though self I dread,
>   I love His precept more.

JOHN HENRY NEWMAN.

OH, the freedom with which the gates of the divine forgiveness are thrown open ! The Bible trembles and burns and overruns with offers ! They crowd on one another. Not waiting to be asked, not giving it reluctantly, but following to tempt them with it, in His open hands, the eager Saviour brings His free forgiveness. — The great wonder of the Incarnation was the great miracle of that free pardon. — As if sin, with all its enormity, had yet this accidental glory, almost transfiguring it, that it gave a new license of utterance to the unutterable love. The Forgiver stands upon the heights of the great human tragedy and summons man to be forgiven.

Mss.

Even with so soft a surge and an increasing,
   Drunk of the sand and thwarted of the clod,
Stilled and astir and checked and never-ceasing
   Spreadeth the great wave of the grace of God.

Bears to the marishes and bitter places
   Healing for hurt and for their poisons balm,
Isle after isle in infinite embraces
   Floods and enfolds and fringes with the palm.

F. W. H. MYERS

We love Him because He first loved us.

I. JOHN iv. 19.

JOHN the Disciple had learned from Jesus, his Master, the truth of the priority of God — the truth that before everything is God. . . . It is as when up the morning sky, all coldly beautiful with ordered ranks of cloud on cloud, is poured the glow of sunrise, and every least cloud, still the same in place and shape, burns with the transfiguring splendor of the sun. So is it when the priority of existence is seen to rest in a Person, and the background of life is God. Then every new arrival instantly reports itself to Him, and is described in terms of its relationship to Him. Every activity of ours answers to some previous activity of His. Do we hope? It is because we have caught the sound of some promise of His. Do we fear? It is because we have had some glimpse of the dreadfulness of getting out of harmony with Him. Are we curious and inquiring? It is that we may learn some of His truth. Do we resist evil? We are fighting His enemies. Do we help need? We are relieving His children. Do we love Him? It is an answer of gratitude for His love to us. Do we live? It is a projection and extension of His being. Do we die? It is the going home of our immortal souls to Him.

Oh, the wonderful richness of life when it is all thus backed with the priority of God! It is the great illumination of all living.

V. 41, 45.

I am He that liveth. — REV. i. 18.

THAT word, "liveth," is a word of continuous, perpetual life. It describes the eternal existence which has no beginning and no end; which, considered in its purity and perfectness, has no present and no past, but one eternal and unbroken present — one eternal now. It is the "I Am" of the Jehovah who spoke to Moses. "He that liveth" is the Living One; He whose life is The Life, complete in itself, and including all other lives within itself. My dear friends, if anything has come to us to make us feel what a fragmentary thing our human life is, I think there is no greater knowledge for us to win than that the life of one who loves us as Christ loves us is an eternal life, with the continuance and the unchangeableness of eternity.

I. 212, 213.

Strong Son of God, Immortal Love,
  Whom we that have not seen Thy face,
  By faith, and faith alone, embrace,
Believing where we cannot prove!

Thine are these orbs of light and shade;
  Thou madest Life in man and brute;
  Thou madest Death; and lo! Thy foot
Is on the skull which Thou hast made.

Thou wilt not leave us in the dust;
  Thou madest man, he knows not why;
  He thinks he was not made to die;
And Thou hast made him: Thou art just.

TENNYSON.

Are they not all ministering spirits, sent forth to minister for them who shall be heirs of salvation?

HEB. i. 14.

TO him to whom life is but an episode, a short stage in the existence of eternity, who is always cognizant of the great surrounding world of mystery, grief comes as angels came to the tent of Abraham. Laughter is hushed before them. The mere frolic of life stands still, but the soul takes the grief in as a guest, meets it at the door, kisses its hand, washes its travel-stained feet, spreads its table with the best food, gives it the seat by the fireside, and listens reverently for what it has to say about the God from whom it came. . . . I beg you, if God sends you grief, to take it largely by letting it first of all show you how short life is, and then prophesy eternity. Such is the grief of which the poet sings so nobly, —

           Grief should be
Like joy, majestic, equable, sedate;
Confirming, cleansing, raising, making free;
Strong to consume small troubles : to commend
Great thoughts, grave thoughts, thoughts lasting to
    the end.

But grief, to be all that, must see the end ; must bring and forever keep with its pain such a sense of the shortness of life that the pain shall seem but a temporary accident, and that all that is to stay forever after the pain has ceased, the exaltation, the unselfishness, the mystery, the nearness to God, shall seem to be the substance of the sorrow.   I. 326, 327.

Phillips Brooks entered into Life, 1893.

Ye, like angels, appear
Radiant with ardor divine.

.   .   .   .   .

Ye alight in our van !   At your voice
Panic, despair, flee away.
Ye move through the ranks, recall
The stragglers, refresh the outworn,
Praise, re-inspire the brave !
Order, courage, return ;
Eyes rekindling, and prayers,
Follow your steps as ye go.
Ye fill up the gaps in our files,
Strengthen the wavering line,
'Stablish, continue our march,
On to the bound of the waste,
On to the City of God !

MATTHEW ARNOLD.

THE relation between preacher and congregation is one of the very highest pictures of human companionship that can be seen on earth.   Its constant presence has given Christianity, much of its noblest and sweetest color in all ages.   It has much of the intimacy of the family, with something of the breadth and dignity that belongs to the State.   It is too sacred to be thought of as a contract.   It is a union which God joins together for purposes worthy of His care.   When it is worthily realized, who can say that it may not stretch beyond the line of death, and they who have been minister and people to each other here be something holy and peculiar to each other in the City of God forever?   PREACHING, 216.

Thy brother shall rise again. — JOHN xi. 23.

MEN'S souls leaped to that word because they wanted to believe it, and had not dared wholly to believe it till He showed them that it was true.   And now if we believe in Him, we do believe it, and death is really changed to us, and the dead are really living by the assurance of the living Christ.   In those moments when Christ is most real to me, when He lives in the centre of my desires and I am resting most heavily upon His help, in those moments I am surest that the dead are not lost, that those whom this Christ, in whom I trust, has taken He is keeping.   The more He lives to me, the more they live.

I. 225, 226.

Do we indeed desire the dead
  Should still be near us at our side?
  Is there no baseness we would hide?
No inner vileness that we dread?

.   .   .   .

I wrong the grave with fears untrue:
  Shall love be blamed for want of faith?
  There must be wisdom with great Death:
The dead shall look me through and through.

Be near us when we climb or fall:
  Ye watch, like God, the rolling hours
  With larger other eyes than ours,
To make allowance for us all.

TENNYSON.

DO we not all feel the change that had come between Paul crying submissively "Lord, what wilt Thou have me to do?" looking to an outside Christ for commandment, and the same Paul crying "Not I live, but Christ liveth in me!" rejoicing in the inspiration of an inward Saviour? This was the perfect victory after which Paul was always longing so intensely. It did not come perfectly to him in this world. It cannot to any of us. Dependent as it is upon the knowledge of Christ by the soul, it cannot be perfect till the soul's knowledge of Christ shall be perfect in heaven. . . . The great privilege of the Christian is deepening personal intimacy with Him who is the Christian's life, the Lord Jesus Christ. All comes to that at last. Christianity begins with many motives. It all fastens itself at last upon one motive, which does not exclude, but is large enough to comprehend, all that is good in all the rest, "That I may know Him." Those are Paul's words. How constantly we come back to his large, rounded life, as the picture of what the Christian is and becomes.

II. 50, 51.

Christ! I am Christ's! and let the name suffice you,
 Ay, for me too He greatly hath sufficed:
Lo with no winning words I would entice you,
 Paul had no honor and no friend but Christ.

. . . .

Ay, for this Paul, a scorn and a reviling,
 Weak as you know him and the wretch you see,
Even in these eyes shall ye behold His smiling,
 Strength in infirmities and Christ in me.

F. W. H. MYERS.

The things which are seen are temporal; but the things which are not seen are eternal.

II. COR. iv. 18.

THE Incarnation is the perpetual interpretation of our life. Jesus cries, "It is finished," on His cross, and at once it is evident that that finishing is but a beginning; that it is a breaking to pieces of the temporal, that it may be lost in the eternal! That cross is the perpetual glorification of the shortness of life. In its light we, too, can stand by the departing form of our own life, or of some brother's life, and say, "It is finished," and know that the finishing is really a beginning. The temporary is melting away like a cloud in the sky, that the great total sky may all be seen. The form in which the man has lived is decaying, that the real life of the man may be apparent. The fashion of this world is passing away; the episode, the accident of earth is over, that the spiritual reality may be clear. It is in the light of the cross that the exquisite picture of Shelley, who tried so hard to be heathen and would still be Christian in his own despite, is really realized:

> The one remains, the many change and pass;
>   Heaven's light forever shines; earth's shadows fly;
> Life, like a dome of many-colored glass,
>   Stains the white radiance of eternity,
> Until death tramples it to fragments.   I. 331, 332.

Lord, for the erring thought
Not into evil wrought :
Lord, for the wicked will
Betrayed and baffled still :
For the heart from itself kept,
Our thanksgiving accept.

For ignorant hopes that were
Broken to our blind prayer :
For pain, death, sorrow, sent
Unto our chastisement :
For all loss of seeming good,
Quicken our gratitude.

W. D. HOWELLS.

O LORD, by all Thy dealings with us, whether of joy or pain, of light or darkness, let us be brought to Thee. Let us value no treatment of Thy grace simply because it makes us happy or because it makes us sad, because it gives us or denies us what we want; but may all that Thou sendest us bring us to Thee, that knowing Thy perfectness, we may be sure in every disappointment that Thou art still loving us, and in every darkness that Thou art still enlightening us, and in every enforced idleness that Thou art still using us; yea, in every death that Thou art giving us life, as in His death Thou didst give life to Thy Son, our Saviour Jesus Christ. Amen.

V. 323.

That light
Fringing the far hills, all so fair, so fair,
Is it not dawn?   I am dying, but 'tis dawn.
" Upon the mountains I behold the feet
Of my Beloved : let us forth to meet " —
Death.
   This is death.   I see the light no more;
I sleep.
   But like a morning bird my soul
Springs singing upward, into the deeps of heaven,
Through world on world to follow Infinite Day.

DINAH MULOCH CRAIK.

HOW shall I bind myself to eternity except by giving myself to Him who is eternal in obedient love?   Obedient love!   Loving obedience!   That is what binds the soul of the less to the soul of the greater everywhere. I give myself to the eternal Christ, and in His eternity I find my own.   In His service I am bound to Him, and the shortness of that life, whose limitations in any way shut me out from Him, becomes an inspiration, not a burden to me.   Oh, my dear friends, you who with Christian faith have seen a Christian die, tell me, was not this short life then revealed to you in all its beauty?   Did you not see completely that no life was too long which Christ had filled with the gift and knowledge of Himself; no life was too short which departed from the earth only to go and be with Him in Heaven forever ?

I. 332.

OUR souls are sick with the sight of hunger and nakedness and want. . . . Cannot He who fed the hungry Jews feed these hungry Americans? We are ready to doubt the old story of His mercy, or to think He has forgotten to be gracious and ceased to care for these modern nations whom He has not "chosen." And then, just as we are ready to give up to despair in one or other of these forms, we catch a glimpse of something better, of something which makes us see that the manna and the miraculous loaves and fishes, made perpetual, would be demoralizing and degrading. Some light comes on the necessity and nobility of struggle. We see the greater glory of the new miracle—the miracle of the advancing civilization, whose purpose is not to do away with struggle, but to make the conditions of struggle fair and the prospects of struggle hopeful. Into the spirit of that miracle we cast ourselves, not expecting to see the world's misery suddenly removed, but sure that at last the world, in and through its misery, will triumph over its misery by patience and diffused intelligence and mutual respect and brotherly kindness and the grace of God.   V. 30, 31.

> I have considered the days of old —
>   The years of ancient times.
> Will the Lord cast off forever?
>
> .   .   .   .
>
> Hath God forgotten to be gracious?
>   Hath He in anger shut up His tender mercies?
>   And I said, This is my infirmity;
> But I will remember the years of
>   The right hand of the Most High.

Ps. LXXVII. 5-10.

MEN say, "The world has been disturbed before. Classes have clashed with one another. Governed and governors, employed and employers, rich and poor, have come to blows in other days, but things have always adjusted themselves again. The stronger have grown kinder ; the weaker have grown humbler ; the paternal governor has grown more fatherly ; the obedient subject has grown more filial, and things have gone on again as smoothly as before." "So shall it be again," men say. That is what they expect as the outcome of all this conflict. But other men see clearer. . . . It is not going to be enough that the strong should once more grow kinder and the weak grow humbler. The balance and distribution of strength and weakness is being altered, must be altered more and more. The sources of artificial strength and artificial weakness are being dried up. Governors and governed, employers and employed, are coming to be coworkers for the same ends. Not the old mercies repeated, but new mercies going vastly deeper than the old, — these are what men are beginning to see that the world is needing and that God is giving to the world He loves.   V. 30.

Every man is his brother's bane,
  Where sloth brings honor and labor scorn.
Of fellowship yet shall the earth be fain,
  Hasten we, hasten the happy morn.

Life is hopeless in park and slum,
  Where sloth brings honor and labor scorn.
All shall be well in the days to come,
  Hasten we, hasten the happy morn !
                    C. W. BECKETT.

BUT before I seriously undertake to make of him [the poor man] an independent, intelligent, struggling brother-man, to wake him from his torpor, to set him on his feet, to kindle in his soul that fire which keeps my own soul full of light and warmth, I must have something more than the impulse of a wise economy. This needs a sympathy which makes his life, with all its needs and miseries, my own. It demands of me to wrestle with his enemies, to undertake a fight for him which he is not yet ready to undertake himself, to sacrifice myself that I may make his true self live.

II. 343.

He stood upon the world's broad threshold ; wide
The din of battle and of slaughter rose ;
He saw God stand upon the weaker side,
That sank in seeming loss before its foes ;
Many there were who made great haste and sold
Unto the cunning enemy their swords ;
He scorned their gifts of fame, and power, and gold,
And, underneath their soft and flowery words,
Heard the cold serpent hiss ; therefore he went
And humbly joined him to the weaker part,
Fanatic named, and fool, yet well content
So he could be the nearer to God's heart,
And feels its solemn pulses sending blood
Through all the widespread veins of endless good.

JAMES RUSSELL LOWELL.

THERE are some things of the individual life which the individual cannot get save in the company of fellow-men. There are some parts of his own true life always in his brethren's keeping, for which he must go to them. That the individual may find and be his own truest and fullest self, Jesus, his Master, leads him to his fellows. The wedding guest at Cana, the Pharisee at Levi's table, the sisters with their restored brother, the brothers of the Lord in the house of the carpenter, — all, just as soon as Jesus sanctified and blessed the society in which they lived, saw coming to them as it were out of the heart of that society a selfhood which no solitary contemplation could have gained. Each of them found his Father among his brethren — reached God through the revelation of other human lives.   INFLUENCE, 97.

I tell you this for a wonder, that no man shall then be
    glad
Of his fellow's fall and mishap to snatch at the work
    he had.

Then all *mine* and *all thine* shall be *ours*, and no more
    shall any man crave
For riches that serve for nothing but to fetter a friend
    for a slave.

For all these shall be ours and all men's, nor shall any
    lack a share
Of the toil and the gain of living in the days when the
    world grows fair.

WILLIAM MORRIS.

[Simeon] said, Lord now lettest Thou Thy servant depart in peace, according to Thy word: For mine eyes have seen Thy salvation, which Thou hast prepared before the face of all people; A light to lighten the Gentiles, and the glory of Thy people Israel. — LUKE ii. 29–32.

THE waiting Jewish race — the men and women — nay, the whole world which is seen peering into the darkness, sure that some light is coming — Zacharias, Mary, Simeon, Anna, Herod, Peter, and Andrew — every man and woman of whom we read, is ready for the wonder of recognition, the wonder which comes with the fulfilment of their dreams and hopes and fears, . . . the long-imagined, long-expected, half-despaired-of manifestation of God in human life. CHRISTMAS SERMON, 7, 8.

To every Christian there come times when all the strangeness disappears from the divine humanity which stands radiant at the centre of his faith. He finds it hard to believe in himself and in his brethren perhaps; but that Christ should be and should be Christ appears the one reasonable, natural, certain thing in all the universe. In Him all broken lines unite; in Him all scattered sounds are gathered into harmony. . . . The day of our salvation has not come till every voice brings us one message; till Christ, the Light of the world, everywhere reveals to us the divine secret of our life; till everything without joins with the consciousness all alive within, and " the Spirit itself beareth witness with our spirits that we are the children of God." V. 15, 23.

When He came near, He beheld the city, and wept over it. — LUKE xix. 41.

TELL me what becomes of the hard young man, proud of his unsensitiveness, even pretending to be more unsensitive than he is, incapable of enthusiasm, incapable of tears; what becomes of him beside the knightliness of a sorrow such as that? The little child is sensitive without a thought of effort. The old man often feels the joy and pain of men as if the long years had made it his own. But in between, the young man is hardened by self-absorption; when all the time he ought — with his imagination, with his power to realize things he has not been nor seen — to go responsive through the world, answering quickly to every touch, knowing the burdened man's burden just because of the unpressed lightness of his own shoulders, feeling the sick man's pain all the more because his own flesh never knew an ache, buoyant through all with his unconquerable hope, overcoming the world with his exuberant faith, and farthest from sentimentality by the abundance and freedom of the sentiment which fills him. Be sure that there is no true escape from softness in making yourself hard. It is like freezing your arm to keep it from decay. Only by filling it with blood and giving it the true flexibility of health, so only is it to be preserved from the corruption which you fear. Be not afraid of sentiment, but only of untruth. Trust your sentiments, and so be a man.

V. 98 99.

Thou shalt worship the Lord thy God, and Him only shalt thou serve. — MATT. iv. 10.

WOE to the man who loses the faculty of worship, the faculty of honoring and loving and fearing not merely something better than himself, but something which is the absolute best, the perfect good, — his God! The life is gone out of his life when this is gone. There is a cloud upon his thought, a palsy on his action, a chill upon his love. Because you must worship, therefore you must have God.

II. 103.

Alone Lord God, in whom our trust and peace,
  Our love and our desire, glow bright with hope ;
  Lift us above this transitory scope
Of earth, these pleasures that begin and cease,
This moon which wanes, these seasons which decrease ;
  We turn to Thee ; as on an eastern slope
  Wheat feels the dawn beneath night's lingering cope,
Bending and stretching downward ere it sees.
Alone Lord God, we see not yet we know ;
By love we dwell with patience and desire,
  And living so and so desiring pray :
  Thy will be done in earth as heaven to-day ;
As yesterday it was, to-morrow so ;
Love offering love on love's self-feeding fire.

CHRISTINA ROSSETTI.

PICTURE Jesus of Nazareth set down in Rome with all the flashing splendor of imperial power all around Him ; or in Athens, with the wisdom of the philosophers on every side. Would the young Jew have cast His faith away? Too real for Him the visions that had come to Him in Nazareth ! Too real for Him the glory of His Father, which had filled His Father's house ! He would have laid fresh hold upon that truth and love which He had never so needed until now. He would have stood undazzled in the Roman glory, unpuzzled in the Grecian wisdom, because He would have known that in His heart He carried the light by which they should give light to Him. It would have been like David calmly saying in the presence of the terrors of Goliath, " The Lord that delivered me out of the paw of the lion and out of the paw of the bear, He will deliver me out of the hand of this Philistine." III. 108, 109.

How amiable are Thy tabernacles, O Lord of Hosts !
My soul longeth, yea, even fainteth for the courts of
   the Lord.

.   .   .   .

For a day in Thy courts is better than a thousand.
I had rather be a doorkeeper in the house of my God,
   than to dwell in the tents of wickedness.
For the Lord God is a sun and shield: the Lord will
   give grace and glory :
No good thing will He withhold from them that walk
   uprightly.
O Lord of Hosts, blessed is the man that trusteth
   in Thee.   Ps. LXXXIV.

Thou shalt hide them in the secret of Thy presence from the pride of man.   Thou shalt keep them secretly in a pavilion from the strife of tongues.

Ps. xxxi. 20.

This tract which the river of Time
Now flows through with us, is the plain.
Gone is the calm of its earlier shore.
Border'd by cities, and hoarse
With a thousand cries, is its stream.
And we on its breast, our minds
Are confused as the cries which we hear,
Changing and shot as the sights which we see.

And we say that repose has fled
Forever the course of the river of Time.

MATTHEW ARNOLD.

OF how much of our best society they seem to be the exact description; of how many heartless houses filled with a poor pretence of social life, David's words tell the whole story. " The pride of man and the strife of tongues," the lack of humility, the lack of love, the lack of peace ! To live in such a world, and yet to keep a soul in us at all, is very hard. We must have something under and beyond such a world to flee to to renew our life, to really recreate ourselves. That security and recreation of our life cannot come except in the source from which our life first came. We must go back to God.

I. 80.

I will hear what the Lord God may say in me.
Blest is the soul that hears its Lord's voice speaking
    within it,
And takes the word of comfort from His lips.
Blest are the ears that catch the throbbing whisper of
    the Lord,
And turn not to the buzzings of the passing world;
That listen not to voices from without,
But to the truth that teaches from within.
Blest are the eyes
That, shut to outer things,
Are busied with the inner life.
Blest are they who penetrate within,
And more and more by daily use
Strive to prepare themselves
To take the heavenly mysteries.
And blest are they who try to give their time to God,
And shake them free from all the burden of the world.
THOMAS À KEMPIS.

TO put aside everything that hinders the highest from coming to us, and then to call to us that highest which, nay, Who is always waiting to come, — fasting and prayer, — this, as the habit and tenor of a life, is noble. As an occasional effort even, if it is real and earnest, it makes the soul freer for the future. A short special communion with the unseen and eternal, prevents the soul from ever being again so completely the slave of the things of sense and time.

II. 214.

Man shall not live by bread alone, but by every word that proceedeth out of the mouth of God. — MATT. iv. 4.

EVERY word of God is both truth and duty, revelation and commandment. He who takes any new word of God completely gets both a new truth and a new duty. He, then, who lives by every word of God, is a man who is continually seeing new truth and accepting the duties that arise out of it. And it is for this, for the pleasure of seeing truth and doing its attendant duty, that he is willing to give up the pleasures of sense, and even, if need be, to give up the bodily life to which the pleasures of sense belong.
I. 273.

It is not happiness I seek,
Its name I hardly dare to speak:
It is not made for man on earth,
And Heaven alone can give it birth.

Fixed duty claiming every power,
And human love to charm each hour, —
These, these, my soul, make Blessedness ;
I ask no more, I seek no less.

And yet I know these are too much ;
My very being's life they touch,
Without them all, oh ! let me still
Find Blessedness in God's dear will.
LOUISA J. HALL.

CHRIST entered into our shame. Deep into its very heart He entered. The blackness of its darkness was around Him. But the purpose of His sacrifice was that we might be brought to Him. We have not learnt the whole if we have only felt His condescension. Not till He who has stooped to us has lifted us up to Him must we be satisfied. Not till He who hangs upon the cross beside us has said to us, " To-day thou shalt be with me in Paradise."

I. 209.

We know the way : thank God who hath showed us
    the way !
Jesus Christ our Way to beautiful Paradise,
Jesus Christ the Same for ever, the Same to-day.

CHRISTINA ROSSETTI.

" Coelum patria, Christus via," says the old motto: " Heaven the country, Christ the way." But it is true that He who is the way is also the life into which the way leads; and Christ must be country as well as path.

I. 306.

TO know first of all and deepest of all, that
that battle which goes on within us is
God's battle, is of supreme importance.   What
are our sins ?   What is your selfishness, your
untruthfulness, your cruelty ?   Is it something
which hurts and hinders you?   Indeed it is.
But beyond that it is something which usurps
a kingdom which belongs to God.   It is His
enemy.   And every movement of your conscience, every sense of usurpation and of
incongruity, is not merely the revolt of your
own outraged soul.   It is also the claim of the
true King upon His Kingdom.   It is the sound
of the monarch's trumpet summoning the rebellious castle to surrender.   Believe this, and
what a dignity enters into the moral struggle
of our life.   It is no mere restless fermentation,
the disturbed nature out of harmony with itself.
It is God, with the great moral gravitation of
universal righteousness, dragging this stray
and wayward atom back into Himself.   O deep
divine mysterious process, that goes on wherever in silent chamber or in crowded street the
humbled penitent lies prostrate in the dust, or
the resolute struggler stands wrestling with
his temptation !   IV. 276.

Do not I hate them, O Lord, that hate Thee?
And am not I grieved with those that rise up against
    Thee?
I hate them with perfect hatred ; I count them mine
    enemies.
Search me, O God, and know my heart: try me, and
    know my thoughts :
And see if there be any wicked way in me, and lead me
    in the way everlasting.   Ps. CXXXIX. 21-24.

Then the devil leaveth Him ; and, behold, angels came and ministered unto Him.— MATT. iv. 11.

JESUS had seen Satan. He had seen with what greedy and confident eyes Satan looked at that humanity of His, as if it were something that belonged to Him. Nay, in His own humanity He had felt a treacherous something, that was ready to respond to Satan and to own his mastery. Strong and victorious He came away. But was there no new solemn insight into this humanity which He had taken? Was not the Incarnation more than ever awful to the Incarnate One? He, the sinless, had gone up and looked over the edge into the deepest depths of sin. He needed the ministry of angels, and He surely came down the mountain serious and sad. And so it is with you, when you follow your Lord into that experience. It may be that you come out by His grace pure and thankful, but you come out like Him, serious and sad, for you have looked down as He looked into the possibility of sin.

I. 255, 256.

O Father, out of whose Hand none is able to pluck
    Thine own,
  Have pity on us, and be our defence against
  The hosts that rise up against us.

BOOK OF LITANIES. NEALE.

But often, in the world's most crowded streets,
But often, in the din of strife,
There rises an unspeakable desire
After the knowledge of our buried life,
A thirst to spend our fire and restless force
In tracking out our true, original course ;
A longing to inquire
Into the mystery of this heart which beats
So wild, so deep in us, — to know
Whence our thoughts come and where they go.
And many a man in his own breast then delves,
But deep enough, alas, none ever mines !

 . . . .

Yet still, from time to time, vague and forlorn,
From the soul's subterranean depths upborne
As from an infinitely distant land,
Come airs, and floating echoes, and convey
A melancholy into all our day.
MATTHEW ARNOLD.

JUST at the outset of our work, to try us
whether we are good for our work, God's
Spirit takes us into some solitude, some experience which, whether it be enacted far off in
the woods, or in the very centre of a crowded
street, makes us realize for the first time that
our deepest life is alone, is ours and no other
man's ; that we cannot live in our fathers and
our mothers ; that we must live for ourselves.
That is our wilderness, — that first realization
of our individuality.
I. 269.

WHILE it is evident that in those terrible hours (of the Temptation) the whole nature of Jesus was submitted to a fearful struggle, and that, as not the least among the elements that made up the ordeal, His intel·lectual judgments were shaken, His knowledge of truth was invaded by tumultuous doubt, His sight of His Father was obscured, — yet, at the last, and as the sum of all, the question was not one of intelligence but of will. It was a choice of obediences that made the real crisis. It was the rejection of Satan's "Fall down and worship me," and the clear acceptance of "Thou shalt serve the Lord thy God," that marked the victory. "Then the Devil leaveth Him, and behold angels came and ministered unto Him." The moment that the obedience of the life was established, the mental tumult settled into peace within it. INFLUENCE, 229.

> I worship thee, sweet will of God!
> 　And all thy ways adore,
> And every day I live I seem
> 　To love thee more and more.
>
> Thou wert the end, the blessed rule
> 　Of our Saviour's toils and tears ;
> Thou wert the passion of His Heart
> 　Those three and thirty years.

F. W. FABER.

It is written, Man shall not live by bread alone.
                              MATT. iv. 4.

WHAT a man finds in his own consciousness, he is strengthened by being able
also to recognize in the whole history of his
race.   " It is written " long ago, this which he
is doing now.   He is only tracing over with
his blood the unfaded characters which other
men have written in theirs.   It is not a mere
whim of his, this conviction that it is better to
serve God than to eat bread.   It is the cor-
porate conviction of mankind.   That is a very
mysterious support, but it is a real one.   It
plants the weak tree of your will or mine into
the rich soil of humanity.   Do not lose that
strength.   Do not so misread history that it
shall seem to you when you try to do right as
if you were the first man that ever tried it.
Put yourself with your weak little struggle
into the company of all the strugglers in all
time.   Recognize in your little fight against
your avarice, or your untruthfulness, or your
laziness, only one skirmish in that battle whose
field covers the earth, and whose clamor rises
and falls from age to age, but never wholly
dies.   See in the perpetual struggle of good
and evil that the impulse after good is eternal,
and the higher needs are always asserting
their necessity.   In their persistent assertion
read the prophecy of their final success and
take courage.   I. 277.

CHRIST is at once the inspiration of the individual and also the assertion — such as the world has never heard before — of the identity of man. . . . Here are you, seemingly insignificant, not making much of yourself, not seeming to be worthy to be made much of. Oh, if you could know two things about yourself: first, that you are a different creature from any that the world has ever seen, and second, that you are a true utterance of the same spirit of life out of which sprang Isaiah and Saint John.

V. 66, 67.

Take the least man of all mankind, as I ;
Look at his head and heart, find how and why
He differs from his fellows utterly :

   .   .   .   .

When you acknowledge that one world could do
All the diverse work, old yet ever new,
Divide us, each from other, me from you, —

Why where's the need of temple, when the walls
O' the world are that ?   What use of swells and falls
From Levites' choir, Priests' cries, and trumpet-calls ?

That one Face, far from vanish, rather grows,
Or decomposes but to recompose,
Become my universe that feels and knows !

BROWNING.

Then said Jesus, Father, forgive them ; for they know not what they do. — LUKE xxiii. 34.

CLOSE to His Father always, . . . He was hid in the secret of His Father's presence. We cannot know His peace. It must have been so absolute. There must have been such a pity in His heart when they tormented Him, when they tied Him to a column and scourged Him, when they nailed Him to the cross at last, and all the while were looking to see Him give way and tremble, and all the while the soul which they thought they were reaching and torturing was far off, beyond their reach, hid in the secret of God's presence, hid in God. It was as if men flung water at the stars and tried to put them out, and the stars shone on calmly and safely and took no notice of their persecutors, except to give them light. I. 96, 97.

May forgiveness, O Lord, we beseech Thee, proceed from the Most High. May it succour us in our misery ; may it cleanse us from our offences ; may it be granted to penitents ; may it plead for mourners ; may it bring back those who wander from the faith ; may it raise up those who are fallen into sins ; may it reconcile us to the Father ; may it confirm us with the grace of Christ ; may it conform us to the Holy Spirit.

BRIGHT'S ANCIENT COLLECTS.

Then Jesus answered and said unto her, O woman, great is thy faith : be it unto thee even as thou wilt. — MATT. xv. 28.

THIS power of weakness over strength comes to perfection in Jesus. . . . Every beggar whom He met was a king to Him. . . . When you and I are weak, Christ in a true sense owns the claim of our weakness and comes to serve us with His love. Behold, how this transfigures life! The times that make us weakest and that force our weakness most upon us, and make us most know how weak we are, those are our coronation times. The days of sickness, days of temptation, days of doubt, days of discouragement, days of bereavement and of the aching loneliness which comes when the strong voice is silent and the dear face is gone, these are the days when Christ sees most clear the crown of our need upon our foreheads, and comes to serve us with His love.

Faith is the king's knowledge of his own kingship. A weak man who has no faith in Christ is a king who does not know his own royalty. But the soul which in its need cries out and claims its need's dominion, . . . "Come to me, O Christ, for I need Thee," finds itself justified. Its bold and humble cry is honored and answered instantly; instantly by its side the answer comes: "Great is thy faith : be it unto thee even as thou wilt. What wilt thou that I should do unto thee? "

III. 175, 177, 178.

NOT only a Christ to stand outside and support with the strong hands of His forgiveness, but a Christ to come in and strengthen by the power of His incorporated life. Christ is the Staff we lean on, the Rock we stand on, the Light that leads us, the Master on whose breast we lie; but He is also the Bread of Life. He is many things outside of us, — Wisdom, Righteousness, Redemption. He is also something inside of us, Sanctification. He says, "Lean on Me, stand on Me, take hold of Me and walk." But when He takes up His deepest word it is this, — "Feed on Me; unless you feed on Me you have no life in you." He says, "Look and see how good God is; touch Me and feel God's mercy; hear Me and I will tell you how He loves you." But at the last this comes as a commandment of the deepest faith, the promise of the highest mercy, — "O taste and see that the Lord is gracious."

II, 244, 245.

Him first to love great right and reason is,
Who first to us our life and being gave,
And after, when we farèd had amiss,
Us wretches from the second death did save;
And last, the food of life, which now we have,
Even He Himself, in His dear Sacrament,
To feed our hungry souls, unto us lent.

SPENSER.

My sword shall be bathed in heaven.— Ps. xxxiv. 5.

GOD is about to smite the wickedness of the earth. His sword is in His hand. And then, as a part of the terrible announcement, there come these words: "My sword shall be bathed in heaven." What does that mean? It draws back the curtain which separates the visible world from the invisible. It reveals celestial regions in which there are also great struggles going on. It lifts up our eyes to the grander movements of the vast world of spirits. And then it declares that the sword which is to be used in fighting what seems to be the petty wars of the Hebrews and the Edomites, is the same sword which has been used in these celestial conflicts; that the means and instruments of righteousness upon the earth must be the same with the means and instruments of righteousness in the heavens. . . . In no part of His universe can God be passive. Everywhere He must be the foe of the evil and the friend of the good. Everywhere therefore throughout the great perplexed tumultuous universe, we can see the flashing of His sword. "His sword!" we say, and that must mean His nature uttering itself in His own form of force. Nothing can be in His sword which is not in His nature. And so the sword of God in heavenly regions must mean perfect thoroughness and perfect justice contending against evil and self-will, and bringing about everywhere the ultimate victory of righteousness and truth.   IV. 263, 264.

THAT every struggle of the people of God against evil in this world must be fired with eternal principles, must be instinct with thoroughness and with justice; that is the plain prosaic meaning of the word of God to Isaiah which declared, "My sword shall be bathed in heaven." . . .

So it is possible for us to deal with every sin, little or great, that we discover in our hearts. To count it God's enemy and to fight it with all His purity and strength; that is what it means for us that our sword should be bathed in heaven! Courage can only come with thoroughness. But with absolute thoroughness, courage must come. Resolve to-day that every strength of God which it is your right to invoke, because you are His child, and which prayer and consecration can bring into you from Him, shall be devoted to the overcoming of your sin, and then your sin shall certainly be overcome.   IV. 265, 279.

Was the trial sore?
Temptation sharp? Thank God a second time!
Why comes temptation but for man to meet
And master, and make crouch beneath his foot,
And so be pedestalled in triumph? Pray
"Lead us into no such temptations, Lord!"
Yea, but, O Thou whose servants are the bold,
Lead such temptations by the head and hair,
Reluctant dragons, up to who dares fight,
That so he may do battle and have praise.
                    BROWNING.

Whatsoever is born of God overcometh the world: and this is the victory that overcometh the world, even our faith. Who is he that overcometh the world, but he that believeth that Jesus is the Son of God.— I. JOHN V. 4, 5.

MAKE, then, this Incarnation the one pervading power of a man's life. Let his first feeling about this world always be, "God has been here, and so God is here still," and have you not made him strong to walk unpolluted and unscorched through the furnace of the world's most fiery corruptions? It is the low system, the constitution that is broken down and depressed in tone, that takes the contagion. . . . And a deep, living sense of God is the true vitality of a human soul which quenches the poisonous fires of corruption, as powerless to be hurt by it as the cold, calm sea is to be set on fire by the coals that you may cast burning into its bosom. Think of the day after Jesus had called John and Peter and Nathanael to be His servants. They had begun to hear His words of eternal life. They had become dimly conscious of so much above and beyond. Do you think it was as hard for them to pass unspotted by the places of temptation in Chorazin and Capernaum? They had tasted the powers of the world to come. And the true way, the only true way, to make any man who is a slave to this world, catching its corruption, free and pure, is to make him see another world, the supernatural world, the world of spiritual life above him and below him and stretching out before him into eternity, made visible by Christ's Incarnation.   I. 187

Oft have I brooded on defeat and pain,
The pathos of the stupid stumbling throng.
These I ignore to-day and only long
To pour my soul forth in one trumpet strain,
One clear, grief-shattering, triumphant song,
For all the victories of man's high endeavor,
Palm-bearing, laurelled deeds that live forever,
The splendor clothing him whose will is strong.
Hast thou beheld the deep glad eyes of one
Who has persisted and achieved?   Rejoice!
On naught diviner shines the all-seeing sun.
Salute him with free heart and choral voice,
'Midst flippant, feeble crowds of spectres wan,
The bold, significant, successful man.

EMMA LAZARUS.

ALL history bears witness that when God means to make a great man, He puts the circumstances of the world and the lives of lesser men under tribute. He does not fling His hero like an aërolite out of the sky. He bids him grow like an oak out of the earth. All earnest, pure, unselfish, faithful men who have lived their obscure lives well, have helped to make him. God has let none of them be wasted. A thousand unrecorded patriots helped to make Washington; a thousand lovers of liberty contributed to Lincoln. . . . And any man who in his small degree is living like the child of God, has a right to all the comfort of knowing that God will not let his life be lost, but will use it in the making of some great child of God, as He used centuries of Jewish lives, prophets, priests, patriots, kings, peasants, women, children, to make the human life of His Incarnate Son.   II. 133, 134.

Now there stood by the cross of Jesus His Mother.—JOHN xix. 25.

JUST as He was dying the Sufferer turned and gave His Mother to the care of His disciple. "Woman, behold thy son!" "Son, behold thy mother!" It was a pang within all the other pangs, a woe that perceptibly added to their wretchedness, when among the faces that pitied Him He saw her face who bore Him, the face into which He had looked up from His cradle. . . . The pain of any human being touched Him, but in His Mother's pain, humanity pressed itself closest to His sensibility and gave Him a special distress, proportioned to His special love.

INFLUENCE, 181, 182.

O Lord Jesus, who didst meet Thy Mother in her sorrow, and yet, because of the love Thou bearest us, wouldst not be turned aside from suffering, help us to give up all things for Thy love; going wherever Thou shalt call us, and doing whatsoever Thou wouldst have us do.

By Thy Cross and Passion, and Thy pity on Thy Mother, Let us stand with her beneath Thy Cross, and share the cup of her sorrows.

BOOK OF LITANIES. NEALE.

IT is not, if we understand it rightly, a sign of decreasing, but of increasing spirituality, that miracles have ceased. And so it is a truer discrimination that recognizes the presences of God in men, the saints that are in the world, not by the miracles they work but by the miracles they are, by the way in which they bring the grace of God to bear on the simple duties of the household and the street. The sainthoods of the fireside and of the market-place — they wear no glory round their heads; they do their duties in the strength of God ; they have their martyrdoms and win their palms, and though they get into no calendars, they leave a benediction and a force behind them on the earth when they go up to heaven.

I. 131, 132.

A SONG FOR THE LEAST OF ALL SAINTS.

Love is the key of life and death,
  Of hidden heavenly mystery ;
Of all Christ is, of all He saith,
  Love is the key.

As three times to His Saint He saith,
  He saith to me, He saith to thee,
Breathing His Grace-conferring Breath :
  " Lovest thou Me ? "

Ah, Lord, I have such feeble faith,
  Such feeble hope to comfort me :
But love it is, is strong as death,
  And I love Thee.

CHRISTINA ROSSETTI.

ONCE think it possible that God should fill a humanity with Himself, once see humanity capable of being filled with God, and can you conceive of His not doing it? Must there not be an Incarnation? Do you not instantly begin to search earth for the holy steps? Once think it possible that Christ can, and are you not sure that Christ must give Himself for our Redemption? So only, when it seems inevitable and natural, does the Christhood become our pattern. Then only does it shine on the mountain-top up toward which we can feel the low lines of our low life aspiring. The Son of God is also the Son of Man. Then in us, the sons of men, there is the key to the secret of His being and His work. Know Christ that you may know yourself. But, oh! also know yourself that you may know Christ!

V. 14, 15.

> "O Saul, it shall be
> A Face like my face that receives thee; a man like to
>   me,
> Thou shalt love and be loved by, forever! a hand like
>   this hand
> Shall throw open the gates of new life to thee! See
>   the Christ stand!"

BROWNING.

THAT is the time in life when confirmation ought to come. Not in mere childhood, when the life is still wholly under other people's influence ; not, unless it has been put off by neglect before, in those later years when manhood is an old story, and the nature is hard with long doubt and hesitation ; but it ought to come just when the new freedom is beginning to be felt, when obedience to authority is opening into personal responsibility, when the implicit faith is just asking for its soul of reason, and anticipating the changes which shall make it the peculiar faith of this peculiar life, — then it is that confirmation has its fullest meaning. It is the gathering up of all the faith and dutiful impulse of the past that it may go before the life into the untried fields.

V. 295, 296.

The shadow of the Almighty's cloud
  Calm on the tents of Israel lay,
While drooping paused twelve banners proud,
  Till He arise and lead the way.

Then to the desert breeze unrolled,
  Cheerly the waving pennons fly,
Lion or eagle — each bright fold
  A lodestar to a warrior's eye.

So should Thy champions, ere the strife,
  By holy hands o'er-shadowed kneel,
So, fearless for their charmed life,
  Bear, to the end, Thy Spirit's seal.

KEBLE.

IS there nothing that Christ as your Friend, your Lord, your Saviour, wants you to do that you are leaving undone to-day? Do you doubt one instant that with His high and deep love for your soul, He wants you to pray? — And do you pray? Do you doubt one instant that it is His will that you should honor and help and bless all these men about you who are His brethren? — And are you doing anything like that? Do you doubt one instant that His will is that you should make life serious and lofty? — And are you making it frivolous and low? Do you doubt one instant that He wants you to be pure in deed and word and thought? — And are you pure? Do you doubt one instant that His command is for you openly to own Him and declare that you are His servant before all the world? — And have you done it? These are the questions which make the whole matter clear. No, not in quiet lanes, nor in bright temple-courts as once He spoke, and not from blazing heavens as men seem sometimes to expect, — not so does Christ speak to us. And yet He speaks! I know what He, there in His glory, He here in my heart, wants me to do to-day, and I know that I am not mistaken in my knowledge. It is no guess of mine. It is His voice that tells me.

V. 356, 357.

" To-day is but a little holding, lent
  To do a mighty labor. We are one
  With heaven and the stars, when it is spent
  To serve God's aim; else, we die with the sun."

This is the will of God, even your sanctification. — I. Thess. iv. 3.

AS we stand before the font we solemnly dedicate ourselves to a struggle with the passion and inner power of sinfulness which shall know no rest until it is completely quenched and dead, until we love goodness perfectly, and hate sin perfectly, even as God does. . . . When one desires to be holy, and knowing that it is God's will as well as his that he should be, throws himself on that will of God and clings to it with eager hands, certain that it must carry him to success, for him there is no fear. He is as sure to reach the prize he seeks, as the patient stars are to be led of God around their shining orbits.

BAPTISM AND CONFIRMATION, 12, 28.

We lift to Thee our failing eyes,
Our failing wills to Thee:
O Great Lord God of Battles, rise,
Till foes and shadows flee,
And death being swallowed up of life shall cease to be.

CHRISTINA ROSSETTI.

Behold, I set before you this day a blessing, . . . if ye obey the commandments of the Lord your God. — Ex. xi. 26, 27.

THE setting of the less finite into the complete infinite nature Christ calls by various names. Sometimes it is *faith*. You must *believe* in God. Sometimes it is *affection*. You must *love* God. Always what it means is the same thing. You must *belong* to God. Then His life shall be your life. I am come to bring you to Him that so you may have life and have it more abundantly. Sometimes He seems to gather up His fullest declaration of this vital connection of man with God and call it in one mighty word, "*Obedience*." You must *obey* God and so live by Him. . . . When God says to His people, "Do This and Live," He is not making a bargain. He is declaring a necessary truth. He is pronouncing a necessity. "He who does My Will, possesses Me." For My Will is the broad avenue to the deepest chambers of My Life. There is nothing in Me that he who obeys Me may not reach according to his power. "Son, thou art ever with me and all that I have is thine." So speaks the Infinite God to the obedient child. But to disobedience the door is closed. Whatever wealth there may be is none of his. Obedience means mastery and wealth. Therefore, let us glorify obedience, which is light and life, and dread disobedience, which is darkness and death. HARVARD MONTHLY, 180.

"COMING nearer and nearer to Christ," we say; that does not mean creeping into a refuge where we can be safe. It means becoming better and better men; repeating His character more and more in ours. The only true danger is sin, and so the only true safety is holiness. What a sublime ambition! How it takes our vague, half-felt wishes and fills them with reality and strength, when the moral growth, which makes a man complete, is put before us, not abstractly, but in this picture of the dearest and noblest being that our souls can dream of, standing before us and saying to us, "Come unto me;" standing over us and praying for us, "Father, bring them where I am."

I. 313.

But, all I felt there, right or wrong,
    What is it to Thee, who curest sinning?
Am I not weak as Thou art strong?
    I have looked to Thee from the beginning,
Straight up to Thee through all the world
Which, like an idle scroll, lay furled
To nothingness on either side:
And since the time Thou wast descried,
Spite of the weak heart, so have I
Lived ever, and so fain would die,
Living and dying, Thee before!

BROWNING.

My God! my God! why hast Thou forsaken Me!
                    MATT. xxvii. 46.

THE joy of loving and the pain which only love can bring beat tumultuously together in this cry.   But underneath them both there is obedience, and the idea from which obedience proceeds.   Not for one moment does He think of coming down from the cross to find His Father.   Whether He find Him or lose Him, whether the issue of His love be the perfect joy of union or the exquisite suffering that separation brings, He must obey Him first.   Even if His doing of His Father's will seems to shut Him out of His Father's presence, there cannot be a question; the will must be done.

INFLUENCE. 178.

It were not hard to suffer by His hand,
If thou couldst see His face; but in the dark!
That is the one last trial: — be it so.
Christ was forsaken, so must thou be too;
How couldst thou suffer but in seeming, else?
Thou wilt not see the face nor feel the hand.
Only the cruel crushing of the feet,
When through the bitter night the Lord comes down
To tread the wine-press. — Not by sight, but faith,
Endure, endure, — be faithful to the end.
                    UGO BASSI'S SERMON IN THE HOSPITAL.

Whoever shall keep the whole law, and yet offend in one point, he is guilty of all. — JAMES ii. 10.

WHY? Because the consistent, habitual breakage of one point proves that the others were kept under the law of constraint, not under the law of liberty. It proves that the tendency of the nature's liberty, which breaks forth in this one place, is a bad tendency and not a good one. . . . It takes only one volcano anywhere in the earth to show that the heart of the earth is fire, and that some day it may burst through the thickest crust. . . . This is the tragedy of our single sins, dear friends. . . . Down the crack which some one transgression makes in the fair face of a smooth and blooming life, we can see waiting for God's judgment-word, the fire before which that life shall be at last consumed with fervent heat.

II. 193, 194.

I peered within, and saw a world of sin:
　Upward, and saw a world of righteousness:
Downward, and saw darkness and flame begin
　Which no man can express.

I girt me up, I gat me up to flee
　From face of darkness and devouring flame:
And fled I had, but guilt is loading me
　With dust of death and shame.

Yet still the light of righteousness beams pure,
　Beams to me from the world of far-off day : —
Lord who hast called them happy that endure,
　Lord, make me such as they.

CHRISTINA ROSSETTI.

Thou shalt love the Lord thy God with all thy heart, and with all thy soul, and with all thy mind. . . . Thou shalt love thy neighbor as thyself.

MATT. xxii. 37, 39.

THOU shalt love. The duty of loving, — there is nothing of that in the codes of abstract duty. It is impossible to exclude that from its fundamental place in the system of duty whose constant spring is in the fatherhood of God. . . . Of this quality in duty it is no Christian's place to be ashamed or afraid. None of us may melt it away or sink it out of sight. In its prominence lies the soul of the duty that we do. We may not try to make that duty cold and soulless which has its true being in the central commandment which is its living soul, — "Thou shalt love."

INFLUENCE, 61, 62.

Love is alone the worthy law of love :
  All other laws have pre-supposed a taint :
  Love is the law from kindled saint to saint,
From lamb to lamb, from tender dove to dove.
Love is the motive of all things that move
  Harmonious by free will without constraint.
  Love learns and teaches : love shall man acquaint
With all he lacks, which all his lack is love.
Because Love is the fountain, I discern
  The stream as love : for what but love should flow
    From fountain Love? not bitter from the sweet !
  I ignorant, have I laid claim to know?
    Oh teach me, Love, such knowledge as is meet
For one to know who is fain to love and learn.

CHRISTINA ROSSETTI

Unto you that fear my name shall the Sun of righteousness arise with healing in his wings.

MAL. iv. 2.

As a bird in meadows fair
  Or in lonely forest sings
Till it fills the summer air,
  And the greenwood sweetly rings,
So my heart to Thee would raise,
O my God, its song of praise
That the gloom of night is o'er,
And I see the sun once more.

If Thou, Sun of Love, arise
  All my heart with joy is stirred,
And to greet Thee upward flies,
  Gladsome as yon little bird,
Shine Thou in me clear and bright
Till I learn to praise Thee right;
Guide me in the narrow way,
Let me ne'er in darkness stray.

FROM THE GERMAN, 1580.

CHRIST, to the Christian growing older, seems to be what the sun is to the developing day, which it lightens from the morning to the evening. When the sun is in the zenith in the broad noon-day, men do their various works by his light; but they do not so often look up to him. It is the sunlight that they glory in, flooding a thousand tasks with clearness, making a million things beautiful. But as the world rolls into the evening, it is the sun itself at sunset that men gather to look at and admire and love.   II. 51, 52.

ROUTINE is a terrible master, but she is a servant whom we can hardly do without. Routine as a law is deadly. Routine as a resource in the temporary exhaustion of impulse and suggestion is often our salvation. Coleridge told the story when he sang —

> " There will come a weary day
> When, overtaxed at length,
> Both hope and love beneath
> The weight give way.
> Then with a statue's smile,
> A statue's strength,
> Patience, nothing loth,
> And uncomplaining, does
> The work of both."

But patience, while a strong power, is not quick-sighted, and works in ways and habits which have been made before.

YALE LECTURES, 93.

Then with a ripple and a radiance thro' me
  Rise and be manifest, O Morning Star!
Flow on my soul, thou Spirit, and renew me,
  Fill with Thyself, and let the rest be far.

Safe to the hidden house of thine abiding
  Carry the weak knees and the heart that faints,
Shield from the scorn and cover from the chiding,
  Give the world joy, but patience to the saints.

F. W. H. MYERS.

EVERY now and then a conscience, among the men and women who live easy, thoughtless lives, is stirred, and some one looks up anxiously, holding up some one of the pretty idlenesses in which such people spend their days and nights, and says "Is this wrong? Is it wicked to do this?" And when they get their answer, "No, certainly not wicked," then they go back and give their whole lives up to doing their innocent little piece of uselessness again. Ah, the question is not whether that is wicked, whether God will punish you for doing that. The question is whether that thing is keeping other better things away from you; whether behind its little bulk the vast privilege and dignity of duty is hid from you; whether it stands between God and your soul. If it does, then it is an offence to you, and though it be your right hand or your right eye, cut it off, pluck it out, and cast it from you. The advantage and joy will be not in its absence, for you will miss it very sorely, but in what its loss reveals, in the new life which lies beyond it, which you will see stretching out and tempting you as soon as it is gone. II. 213, 214.

We sinners beseech thee to hear us, Good Lord,
That by Thy Love the world may be crucified to us and
      we unto the world,
That we may crucify the flesh with its affections and
      lusts,
That we may daily take up our cross and follow Thee;
That we may live in Thee and die in Thee.

BOOK OF LITANIES. NEALE.

And if thou draw out thy soul to the hungry, and satisfy the afflicted soul, then shall thy light rise in obscurity, and thy darkness be as the noonday.

ISA. lviii. 10.

GO; do your duty, giving to every task the sublimest motive which you know and which you can bring to bear upon it. Get at the essence of goodness, which is not in its enthusiasms or delights, but in its heart of consecration. Sometimes the consecration may be all the more thorough and complete when the joy of consecration seems to be farthest away. And yet every consecration made in the darkness is reaching out toward the light, and in the end must come out into the light, strong in the strength which it won in its life and struggle in the dark.

V. 175.

Through love to light! Oh wonderful the way
That leads from darkness to the perfect day!
From darkness and from sorrow of the night
To morning that comes singing o'er the sea.
Through love to light! Through light, O God, to Thee,
Who art the love of love, the eternal light of light!

RICHARD WATSON GILDER.

Jesus . . . saith, I thirst. — JOHN xix. 28.

THE physical sensitiveness of Jesus no doubt helped, as no other medium could have helped, that deep, mysterious process, the development of the self-consciousness of Jesus. Why should I not believe that out of the physical difficulties which tore His hands He plucked the full flower of His knowledge of His own soul, and, wrapped up at the heart of that, His knowledge of the soul of His Father? . . . To Jesus, and to His disciples, and to all men who know the bodily life as He knew it and taught them to know it, the pain and happiness of which the human body is capable must be very noble messages.

INFLUENCE, 170, 173.

I lift mine eyes, and see
Thee, tender Lord, in pain upon the tree,
Athirst for my sake and athirst for me.

Yea, look upon Me there
Compassed with thorns and bleeding everywhere,
For thy sake bearing all and glad to bear.

CHRISTINA ROSSETTI.

FOR a few weeks let these obtrusive world-
linesses which block the door of our hearts
stand back ; and let the way be clear that He
who longs to enter in and help us may come
and meet no obstacle. This is our lenten task.
" If any man will hear My voice and open unto
Me, I will come in and sup with him," says
Jesus. To still the clatter and tumult a little
so that we may hear His voice, and to open
the door by prayer, that is the privilege and
duty of these coming weeks.

II. 215.

'Tis true, we cannot reach Christ's fortieth day ;
Yet to go part of that religious way
   Is better than to rest :
We cannot reach our Saviour's purity ;
Yet are we bid, "Be holy e'en as He."
   In both let's do our best.

Who goeth in the way which Christ hath gone,
Is much more sure to meet with Him, than one
   That travelleth by-ways.
Perhaps my God, though He be far before,
May turn, and take me by the hand, and more,
   May strengthen my decays.

Yet, Lord, instruct us to improve our fast
By starving sin, and taking such repast
   As may our faults control :
That every man may revel at his door,
Not in his parlour ; banqueting the poor,
   And among those his soul.

GEORGE HERBERT.

Within a cavern of man's trackless spirit
  Is framed an Image so intensely fair,
That the adventurous thoughts that wander near it
  Worship, and as they kneel tremble, and wear
The splendor of its Presence, and the light
  Penetrates their dreamlike frame
Till they become charged with the strength of flame.

PERCY BYSSHE SHELLEY.

YOU have your good, your spirituality, your better life; something that bears witness of God. In every man's heart there is a holy city, a Jerusalem, where, loud or muffled, in some voice from the altar or some light above the mercy-seat, the Heavenly Father bears testimony of His goodness and tempts us to Himself. It may be very dim, but there it is in all of us.

I. 45, 46.

Lighten me, good Jesus, with the bright light within,
And from my heart's cell drive away all shadows.
Bridle my many wandering thoughts;
Fight bravely for me, conquer the wild beasts —
Enticing lusts, I mean,
That in Thy strength there may be peace,
And that Thy praise may evermore resound
Within Thy holy temple —
A conscience that is pure.

.   .   .   .

Bless and sanctify my soul with blessing from above,
That it may be Thy holy dwelling place, the home of
  Thine eternal glory,
And that nothing may be found within the temple of
  Thy condescension
Offending Thy majestic gaze.

THOMAS À KEMPIS.

And Edom came out against [the children of Israel] with much people and with a strong hand. — NUM. xx. 20.

IT is there in some shape always : this good among the evil, this power of God among the forces of men, this Judah in the midst of Asia.   But always right on its border lies the hostile Edom, watchful, indefatigable, inexorable as the redoubtable old foe of the Jews. If progress falters a moment, the whole mass of obstructive ignorance is rolled upon it.   If faith leaves a loop-hole undefended, the quick eye of Atheism sees it from its watch-tower and hurls its quick strength there.   If goodness goes to sleep upon its arms, sleepless wickedness is across the valley, and the fields which it has taken months of toil to sow and ripen are swept off in a night.   Tell me, is not this the impression of the world, of human life, that you get, whether you open the history of any century or unfold your morning newspaper ?   The record of a struggling charity is crowded by the story of the prison and the court.   The world waits at the church door to catch the worshipper as he comes out.   The good work of one century relaxes a moment for a breathing spell, and the next century comes in with its licentiousness or its superstition.   Always it is the higher life pressed, watched, haunted by the lower ; always it is Judah with Edom at its gates.   No one great battle comes to settle it forever : it is an endless fight with an undying enemy.   I. 45.

YOU mean to be true; but once your truth sleeps on its guard, and the Edomite is over the valley, and the lie is right in the very midst of your well-guarded truthfulness. You love humility; but some day your humility keeps a careless feast of self-confidence, and before you know it the shout of the invader pride is in your ears. How evil crowds you. You cannot fight it out at once and have it done. You go on quietly for days and think the enemy is dead. Just when you are safest there he is again, more alive than ever. . It is the Saviour's word, " Behold, I send you forth as sheep among wolves;" only the sheep and the wolf are both within us: Judah, with Edom forever at its gate.   I. 46, 47.

Looking within myself, I note how thin
  A plank of station, chance, or prosperous fate,
Doth fence me from the clutching waves of sin; —
  In my own heart I find the worst man's mate,
  And see not dimly the smooth-hingëd gate
    That opes to those abysses
  Where ye grope darkly, — ye who never knew
  On your young hearts love's consecrating dew
    Or felt a mother's kisses,
Or home's restraining tendrils round you curled;
Ah, side by side with heart's-ease in this world
  The fatal night-shade grows and bitter rue!

JAMES RUSSELL LOWELL.

Who is this that cometh from Edom, with dyed garments from Bozrah? . . . I that speak in righteousness, mighty to save. — Isa. lxiii. 1.

IT is time for the Saviour when the world and the soul have learnt their helplessness and sin. . . . Is it possible that this one that we see coming, this one on whose step, as He moves through history, the eyes of all the ages are fastened, — is it possible that He is the conqueror of the enemy and the Deliverer of the Soul? He comes out of the enemy's direction. The whole work of the Saviour has relation to and issues from the fact of sin. If there had been no sin there would have been no Saviour. "He came not to call the righteous, but sinners to repentance." He comes from the right direction, and He has an attractive majesty of movement as He first appears. . . . The Saviour comes in the strength of righteousness. Righteousness is at the bottom of all things. Righteousness is thorough. It is the very spirit of unsparing truth. Any reform or salvation of which the power is righteousness must go down to the very root of the trouble, must extenuate and cover over nothing; must expose and convict completely, in order that it may completely heal. And this is the power of the salvation of Christ. It makes no compromise between the good and the evil, between Judah and Edom. Edom must be destroyed, not parleyed with; sin must be beaten down and not conciliated; good must thrive by the defeat and not merely by the tolerance of evil.

I. 50, 51.

THE Saviour Himself, surely He is never so dear, never wins so utter and so tender a love, as when we see what it has cost Him to save us. . . . Not merely He has conquered completely and conquered in suffering ; He has conquered *alone*.   As any one reads through the Gospels he feels how hopeless the attempt would be to tell of the loneliness of that life which Jesus lived. "I have trodden the wine-press alone, and of the people there was none with me. I looked and there was none to help. Therefore mine own arm brought salvation." He had friends, but we always feel how far off they stood from the deepest centre of His heart. He had disciples, but they never came into the inner circles of His self-knowledge. He had fellow-workers, but they only handed round the broken bread and fishes in the miracle, or ordered the guest chamber on the Passover night. They never came into the deepest work of His life. With the mysterious suffering that saved the world they had nothing to do.   I. 53, 54.

Wanderers in far countrie
O think of Him who came, forgot,
To His own, and they received Him not —
Jesus of Galilee.

O all ye who have trod
The wine-press of affliction, lay
Your hearts before His heart this day —
Behold the Christ of God.
DINAH MULOCH CRAIK.

I have trodden the wine-press; I will tread them in mine anger and trample them in my fury, and their blood shall be sprinkled upon my garments, and I will stain all my raiment. — Isa. lxiii. 3.

BEHOLD, it is no holiday monarch coming with a bloodless triumph. It has been no pageant of a day, this strife with sin. The robes have trailed in the blood. . . . The power of God had struggled with the enemy and subdued him only in the agony of strife. My friends, far be it from me to undertake to read all the deep mystery that is in this picture. Only this I know is the burden and soul of it all, this truth, — that sin is a horrible, strong, positive thing, and that not even divinity grapples with him and subdues him except in strife and pain. . . . This symbol of the blood bears this great truth, which has been the power of salvation to millions of hearts, and which must make this conqueror the Saviour of your heart too, the truth that only in self-sacrifice and suffering could even God conquer sin. Sin is never so dreadful as when we see the Saviour with that blood upon His garments. . . . The Lord Himself conquers sin. He brings out victory in His open hand. From His hand we take it by the power of prayer, and to Him alone we render thanks here and forever.

l. 52, 53, 54.

Once o'er this painful earth a man did move,
The Man of griefs, because the Man of Love.

The wine of Love can be obtained of none,
Save Him who trod the wine-press all alone.
R. C. TRENCH.

THIS conqueror who comes, comes strong,
—"travelling in the greatness of His
strength." He has not left His might behind
Him in the struggle. He is all ready, with the
same strength with which He conquered, to
enter in and rule and educate the nation He
has saved. And so the Saviour has not done
all when He has forgiven you. By the same
strength of love and patience which saved you
upon Calvary, He will come in, if you will let
Him, and train your saved life into perfectness
of grace and glory. He has conquered sin, so
that you need not be its servant any longer.
Now let Him conquer you by His great love,
and so let His victory be complete.   I. 55. 56.

Surely He cometh, and a thousand voices
    Shout to the saints and to the deaf are dumb ;
Surely He cometh, and the earth rejoices
    Glad in His coming who hath sworn, I come.

This hath He done and shall we not adore Him ?
    This shall He do and can we still despair ?
Come let us quickly fling ourselves before Him,
    Cast at His feet the burden of our care,

Flash from our eyes the glow of our thanksgiving,
    Glad and regretful, confident and calm,
Then thro' all life and what is after living
    Thrill to the tireless music of a psalm.

F. W. H. MYERS.

WHEN we think how imperfectly Christ has been welcomed and adopted here — how only to the outside of our life He has penetrated, then there opens before us a glorious vision of what the city might be in which He should be totally received, where He should be wholly King.

III. 48.

The earth is the Lord's, the nations are His children,
Yea, though their birthright they know not, or deny ;
Rending asunder what God hath willed united.
O come, Son of Mary,
Jesu, our Redeemer,
O come, King triumphant, and reign on earth !

Even by the meek, who pray for His appearing,
Even by the strong, who gird them to the fight,
The kingdoms of this world shall be made our Christ's
dominion.
O come, Son of Mary,
Jesu, our Redeemer,
O come, King triumphant, and reign on earth !

Then rise Lord, we pray Thee, and heal the nations'
sickness !
Rise Thou, for Whom amid the night we wait !
Our eyes are dim with vigils, our hearts with hope are
aching.
O come, Son of Mary,
Jesu, our Redeemer,
O come, King triumphant, and reign on earth !

SELWYN IMAGE.

Behold, we go up to Jerusalem, and all things that are written concerning the Son of man shall be accomplished. — LUKE xviii. 30.

THINK how the life of Jesus gets its glory and beauty from the way in which it is always, from the very first, tending on to the thing which it was at last to reach. That tendency began at His birth, and it never ceased until He was hanging on the cross outside the city gate. Then He had come to Jerusalem and it was finished. The angels sang about Jerusalem when the shepherds heard them. The boy's thoughts were full of Jerusalem as He worked in the carpenter's shop. Egypt, where they carried the babe to get Him out of danger, was on the way to Jerusalem, where He was finally to be killed. The visit to the temple when He was twelve years old, was a nearer glimpse of the Jerusalem to which He did not then really come, though His feet trod its streets, but which He then accepted as the only sufficient issue of His life. He was baptized in consecration to the life-long journey to Jerusalem. " For this cause was I born. For this cause came I into the world." " My time is not yet come." Those words, and words like those, dropped here and there, along His path, are like footprints in the road He walked, all pointing to Jerusalem. At last He came there. . . . The most intense, persistent purpose that the world had ever seen, had reached its completion. He had come to the Jerusalem of His intention, and mankind was saved.   IV. 318.

IN all of Christ's associations the same inevitable mingling of the sad and glad appears. There was a little family at Bethany in which He often made His home, and the last time He left the hospitable door He carried out with Him two memories, — the memory of how the eyes of Mary had looked up into His face, eager with the desire to understand all His sacred truth, and the memory of how the same eyes had streamed with tears beside her brother's tomb. The same voices of the populace at Jerusalem which cried "Hosanna!" cried "Crucify him!" before the week was done. One day He saw a poor widow in the Temple give a true charity; but the same sensitiveness of soul which made Him find pleasure in her simple act laid Him open to the distress which only such a soul could feel at the ostentatious hypocrisy of the Pharisees.

INFLUENCE, 189, 190.

Think you to escape
What mortal man can never be without?
What saint upon the earth has ever lived apart from
     cross and care?
Why, even Jesus Christ our Lord was not even for
     one hour free from His passion's pain.
"Christ," says He, "needs must suffer,
Rising from the dead,
And enter thus upon His glory."
And how do *you* ask for another road
Than this — the Royal Pathway of the Holy Cross?

THOMAS À KEMPIS.

JESUS had a disciple whom He saw slipping more and more away from Him, who He saw would some day betray Him with the worst ingratitude. And yet I think that every man whose sad and anxious office it has ever been to try to lift a soul which in spite of all his struggles has been always sinking deeper and deeper into the depths, will bear me witness that in the patience and wisdom and faithfulness which his Master lavished upon Judas Iscariot for years there must have been a pathetic pleasure, peculiar and subtle because of the growing hopelessness of results which compelled each effort to find its satisfaction in its own essential nature. . . . And both in Peter and in Judas . . . the truth appears that it was not for the joy or for the sorrow that their society would bring that Jesus sought them. Peter and Judas alike He sought because they were the sons of God; the pain or pleasure they would give Him came afterwards and as an accident.

INFLUENCE, 189.

A beneficent power, if we obey it, blesses and helps us; but the same power, if we disobey it, curses and ruins us. That law runs everywhere. . . . Was not Judas cursed by the same friendship with Jesus that perfected John?

IV. 302, 305.

Judas, dost thou betray Me with a kiss?
Canst thou find hell about My lips? and miss
Of life, just at the gates of life and bliss?
Was ever grief like Mine?

GEORGE HERBERT.

THE great Christian sacrament, which embodies this idea of which we have been treating, the idea of the feeding of the soul upon the flesh of Christ, is all filled full of memories of the agony in which the flesh was offered. What does this mean ? Does it not mean this, — that however man longs for his God; however man sees that in the incarnate Christ there is the God he needs and whom his nature was made to receive; it is only when man sees that Divine Being suffering for him, only when he stands by the cross and beholds the love in the agony, that his hungry nature is able to take the food it needs, that is so freely offered ? The flesh must be broken before we can take it. This is what Christ says, and the histories of thousands of souls have borne their witness to it, that it is the suffering Saviour, the Saviour in His suffering, that saves the soul.   II. 250.

Would I suffer for him that I love? So wilt Thou - - so
    wilt Thou !
So shall crown Thee the topmost, ineffablest, uttermost
    Crown —
And Thy love fill infinitude wholly, nor leave up nor
    down
One spot for the creature to stand in ! It is by no breath,
Turn of eye, wave of hand, that Salvation joins issue
    with death !
As thy Love is discovered almighty, almighty be proved
Thy power, that exists with and for it, of Being beloved !
                                        BROWNING.

OUR Lord's death . . . was the gathering up of the mighty love of God in all its mass behind the barrier that separated the Father's soul from the child's soul, until the barrier gave way, and the confined and hampered love poured in and flooded the hungry soul of " whosoever believeth." It was not done without a struggle. The agony, the strong cryings and tears, the blood and insult of Gethsemane and Calvary, are everlasting pictures of what it cost. But it was done. I hear the breaking and tearing of the obstacle of sin, and the rush of great love set free to find the soul, when with the thin voice of the dying Conqueror that cry of victory, that " It is finished " was spoken so loud that it has pierced through history and rung round the world. It was the deepest and most original and spiritual nature of God, that " love," which " God is " breaking through every encumbrance, and declaring itself supreme. This is the triumph of the Christhood.

OXFORD REVIEW.

Thou Who wast Centre of the whole earth on Calvary
Reign over north and south, east and west.

CHRISTINA ROSSETTI.

*These things have I spoken unto you, that in Me
ye might have peace. In the world ye shall have
tribulation ; but be of good cheer ; I have overcome the world.* — JOHN xvi. 33.

IT is as if Jesus walked under a cloud, and
yet felt always that in the very substance
of cloud there was suffused and softened light.
The cloud had light in its darkness, and darkness in its light ; and so the explanation of it
all was clear. A sunlight through the cloud
He felt, and behind the sunlight there must be
a sun. Behind the bitter circumstances lay a
law, the blessed law of obedience, which was
fellowship with God ; and behind the law a
truth, which was God Himself.

Under that same cloud of circumstances we
must walk ; but if there is behind it for us,
too, that law and that truth which really made
the life of Jesus, — the law of obedience and
the truth of sonship, — then for us too, light
shall come through the cloud, and mingling
with its darkness, make that new condition in
which it is best for a man's soul to live, that
sweet and strong condition in which both joy
and sorrow may have place, but which is
greater than either of them, — the condition
which He called peace.   INFLUENCE, 204, 205.

There is no calm like that when storm is done ;
  There is no pleasure keen as pain's release :
  There is no joy that lies so deep as peace,
No peace so deep as that by struggle won.
HELEN GRAY CONE.

Behold I am alive for evermore. — REV. I. 18.

THIS new life, — the life that has conquered death by tasting it, which has enriched itself with a before unknown sympathy with men whose lives are forever tending towards, and at last all going down into the darkness of the grave, — this life stretches on and out forever. It is to know no ending. So long as there are men living and dying, so long above them and around them there shall be the Christ, the God-man, who liveth, and was dead, and is alive for evermore.   I. 215.

> . . . ay, that Life and Death
> Of which I wrote "it was" — to me, it is ;
> — Is, here and now : I apprehend naught else.
> Is not God now i' the world His power first made?
> Is not His love at issue still with sin,
> Closed with and cast and conquered, crucified
> Visibly when a wrong is done on earth?
> Love, wrong, and pain, what see I else around?
> Yea, and the Resurrection and Uprise
> To the right hand of the throne — what is it beside,
> When such truth, breaking bounds, o'erfloods my soul,
> And, as I saw the sin and death, even so
> See I the need yet transiency of both,
> The good and glory consummated thence?

BROWNING.

AS you sit thinking of man's fragmentariness, his certainty of death, his doubt about a future, let this voice come to you, a voice clear with personality, and sweet and strong with love: "I am He that liveth, and was dead; and am alive for evermore." "He that liveth!" And at once your fragment of life falls into its place in the eternity of life that is bridged by His being. "He that was dead!" And at once death changes from the terrible end of life into a most mysterious but no longer terrible experience of life. "He that is alive for evermore!" And not merely there is a future beyond the grave, but it is inhabited by One who speaks to us, who went there by the way that we must go, who sees us and can help us as we make our way along, and will receive us when we come there.

I. 216.

EMMAUSWARD.

Lord Christ, if Thou art with us and these eyes
Are holden, while we go sadly and say
"We hoped it had been He, and now to-day
Is the third day, and hope within us dies,"
Bear with us, oh our Master, Thou art wise
And knowest our foolishness ; we do not pray
"Declare Thyself, since weary grows the way
And faith's new burden hard upon us lies."
Nay, choose Thy time ; but ah ! Whoe'er Thou art
Leave us not ; where have we heard any voice
Like Thine? Our hearts burn in us as we go ;
Stay with us ; break our bread ; so, for our part
Ere darkness falls haply we may rejoice,
Haply when day has been far spent may know.
EDWARD DOWDEN.

Peace I leave with you. — JOHN xiv. 27.

IF we are really Christ's, then back into the very bosom of His Father where Christ is hid, there He will carry us.   We too shall look out and be as calm and as independent as He is.   The needs of men shall touch us just as keenly as they touch Him, but the sneers and strifes of men shall pass us by as they pass by Him and leave no mark on His unruffled life. . . . For us, just as for Him, this will not mean a cold and selfish separation from our brethren.   We shall be infinitely closer to their real life when we separate ourself from their outside strifes and superficial pride, and know and love them truly by knowing and loving them in God.

This is the power and progress of true Christianity.   It leads us into, it abounds in peace.   It is a brave, vigorous peace, full of life, full of interest and work.   It is a peace that means thoroughness, that refuses to waste its force and time in little superficial tumults which come to nothing, while there is so much real work to be done, so much real help to be given, and such a real life to be lived with God.   That peace, His peace, may Jesus give to us all.   I. 97.

Grant us Thy peace, that like a deepening river
   Swells ever outward to a sea of praise.
O Thou, of peace the only Lord and Giver,
   Grant us Thy peace, O Saviour, all our days !
                              ELIZA SCUDDER.

We see Jesus, who was made a little lower than the angels for the suffering of death, crowned with glory and honor; that He by the grace of God, should taste death for every man.

Forasmuch then as the children are partakers of flesh and blood, He also Himself likewise took part of the same; that through death He might destroy him who had the power of death, that is, the devil; and deliver them who through fear of death were all their lifetime subject to bondage.

HEB. ii. 9, 14, 15.

AS Christ drew near to death, He Himself trembled. It was an experience of all His creation, but He had never felt it. To His humanity, His assumed flesh, it seemed terrible. Gethsemane bears witness how terrible it seemed. But He passed into it for love of us. And as He came out from it He declared its nature. " It is an experience of life, not an end of life. Life goes on through it and comes out unharmed. Look at me. I am He that liveth, and was dead! "

I. 214, 215.

By Thy joy when Thy blessed Humanity was glorified by God the Father in Thy Resurrection,
Good Lord deliver us.

By Thy joy, when the Love which on the Cross filled Thee with intolerable anguish, in the Resurrection filled Thee with incomparable honour and Glory,
Good Lord deliver us.
BOOK OF LITANIES. NEALE.

And if I go and prepare a place for you, I will come again and receive you unto Myself; that where I am, there ye may be also. — JOHN xiv. 3.

I AM sure that in the Bible something is promised, some close, perpetual association of the souls of Christ's redeemed to Him, which, over and above the likeness which is to come between their souls and His, shall correspond in some celestial way to that close, visible, tangible propinquity with which they sat by one another at the table in the upper chamber. The " seeing His face," the " walking with Him in white," in heaven, are not wholly figures. What they mean those know to-day who through the lapsing years have gone from us one by one to be with Christ.

Take me away, and in the lowest deep
    There let me be,
And there in hope the lone night-watches keep,
    Told out for me.
There, motionless and happy in my pain,
    Lone, not forlorn, —
There will I sing my sad perpetual strain
    Until the morn.
There will I sing, and soothe my stricken breast,
    Which ne'er can cease
To throb and pine and languish, till possest
    Of its Sole Peace.
There will I sing my absent Lord and Love :
    Take me away,
That sooner I may rise, and go above,
And see Him in the truth of everlasting day.

JOHN HENRY NEWMAN.

As the Father knoweth Me, even so know I the Father. — JOHN X. 15.

"THE Father knoweth me." That means, "God has a will for every act of mine." What then can "I know the Father," mean, except "In every act of mine I do the Father's will." Obedience becomes the organ and utterance, nay becomes the substance and reality of knowledge on the side of him who is aware that in this more special sense God knows him. I think of Jesus on that day when He called Lazarus back from the dead to life. He travels all the way from Galilee to Bethany. At last He stands beside the tomb. His soul is full of sympathy. The dreadfulness of death oppresses Him. Then He becomes aware of a will of God. . . . Behold! He lifts His head. His face shines like the sun! The gloom is gone! He stretches out His hand! He opens His lips with the cry of life! "Lazarus, come forth!" "And he that was dead came forth, bound hand and foot with grave clothes!"

God's will and Christ's obedience! Here then there is the perfect mutualness, the absolute understanding and harmony of the Father and the Son. If it were not the morning of the miracle at Bethany, but the awful morning of the cross, it would be still the same. "Father, into Thy hands I commend My spirit." There, in those words of completed obedience, the mutual knowledge of Father and Son is perfect, and being blends with being; the veil and barrier of the human flesh no longer hangs between.

IV. 290, 291.

THERE is a class of passages in the Bible which to me seem mysteriously beauti-ful, and which appear to rest the peace of the human soul upon the mere fact of the existence of the larger life of God. Such is that verse of the forty-sixth Psalm, "Be still, and know that I am God." "Thou shalt know that I, the Lord, am," is the noble promise that comes again and again, full of reassurance. And when God's people, tram-pled, bruised, broken, trodden in the dust in Egypt, asked by Moses for the name of the God who had promised them His deliverance, it was a mere assertion of the awful and supreme existence that was given in reply: "I AM hath sent me." It is because God is, that man is bidden to be at peace.   I. 103, 104.

It fortifies my soul to know
That, though I perish, Truth is so:
That, howsoe'er I stray and range,
Whate'er I do, Thou dost not change.
I steadier step when I recall
That, if I slip, Thou dost not fall.

ARTHUR HUGH CLOUGH.

JUST as the children's lives set themselves into the life of their father which seems to them really eternal; just as the leaves coming and going, growing and dropping, find their reason and consistency in the long, unchanging life of the tree on which they grow; so our lives find their place in this long, unchanging life of Christ, and lose the vexation of their own ever-shifting pasts and futures in the perpetual present of His being. It is the thought of an eternal God that really gives consistency to the fragmentary lives of men, the fragmentary history of the world. A Christ that liveth redeems and rescues into His eternity the broken, temporary lives and works of His disciples.

I. 213.

Hearken! Hearken!
God speaketh in thy soul,
Saying, O thou that movest
With feeble steps across this earth of mine,
To break beside the fount thy golden bowl,
And spill its purple wine,
Look up to heaven and see how like a scroll
My right hand hath thy immortality
In an eternal grasping.

ELIZABETH BARRETT BROWNING.

The tasks, the joys of earth the same in heaven will be;
Only the little brook has widened to a sea.

R. C. TRENCH.

LET this be the glory that gathers around your daily experiences, my Christian friends. Poor, weak, homely, commonplace as they may be, they are preparing you for something far greater and more perfect than themselves. Be true in them, learn them down to their depths and they shall open heaven to you some day. The powers and affection which are training in your family, your business, and your church are to find their eternal occupation along the streets of gold. "Well done, good and faithful servant, thou hast been faithful over a few things. I will make thee ruler over many things. Enter thou into the glory of thy Lord." And so the long life of heaven shall be bound to the short life of earth forever.

V. 304, 305.

Courage in all the worlds is the same courage. Truth before the throne of God is the same thing as when neighbor talks with neighbor on the street. Mercy will grow tenderer and finer, but will be the old blessed balm of life in the fields of eternity that it was in your workshop and your home. Unselfishness will expand and richen till it enfolds the life like sunshine, but it will be the same self-denial, opening into a richer self-indulgence, which it was when it first stole in with one thin sunbeam on the startled soul. There is no new world of virtues in any heaven or in any heavenly experience of life.

V. 13.

DROP the old remnants of a past life into
the ever-fruitful soil, and all the possibilities of new life open.   The spring-time
finds last summer's roots still remaining in the
ground, and quickens them to life again, and
multiplies them into a richer summer still.   In-
genious Nature finds a germ wherever it is
dropped; but without the germ she will do
nothing.   Mere spontaneity she disowns and
disproves more and more.   Think what a place
the world would be to live in if this were not
so, if nature were a wizard, fitful and whim-
sical, doing her wonders in no sequel or connection with each other, with her pets and
favorites, instead of being, as she is, a mother
with her great, wise, reasonable laws of the
house which press alike on all her children,
which no one of the children thinks of seeing
changed or violated.   That is what makes the
world such a good home for man to dwell in,
his school-room and his home at once.

II. 131, 132.

April cold with dropping rain,
Willows and lilacs brings again
The whistle of returning birds,
And trumpet-lowing of the herds;
The scarlet maple-keys betray
What potent blood hath modest May;
What fiery force the earth renews,
The wealth of forms, the flush of hues;
What Joy in rosy waves outpoured,
Flows from the heart of Love, the Lord.

EMERSON.

Choose you this day whom ye will serve.
*The Lord our God will we serve and His voice
will we obey.* — JOSH. xxiv. 15, 24.

THERE is a noble economy of the deepest
life. There is a watchful reserve which
keeps guard over the powers of profound anxiety and devoted work, and refuses to give
them away to any first applicant who comes
and asks. Wealth rolls up to the door and
says, "Give me your great anxiety;" and
you look up and answer, "No, not for you;
here is a little half-indifferent desire which is
all that you deserve." Popularity comes and
says, "Work with all your might for me;"
and you reply, "No; you are not of consequence enough for that. Here is a small
fragment of energy which you may have, if
you want it; but that is all." Even knowledge comes and says, "Give your whole soul
to me;" and you must answer once more,
"No; great, good, beautiful as you are, you
are not worthy of a man's whole soul." . . .
But then at last comes One greater than them
all, — God comes with His supreme demand
for goodness and for character, and then you
open the doors of your whole nature and bid
your holiest and profoundest devotion to come
trooping forth. Now you rejoice that you kept
something which you would not give to any
lesser lord.   V. 248. 249

IF we can live in Christ and have His life in us, shall not the spiritual balance and proportion which were His become ours too? If He were really our Master and our Saviour, could it be that we could get so eager and excited over little things? If we were His, could we possibly be wretched over the losing of a little money which we do not need, or be exalted at the sound of a little praise which we know that we only half deserve and that the praisers only half intend? A moment's disappointment, a moment's gratification, and then the ocean would be calm again and quite forgetful of the ripple which disturbed its bosom.

V. 251.

He who loves Jesus and loves truth,
The man of really inner life,
From unchecked passions free,
Can turn himself with ease to God,
And lift himself above himself in thought,
And rest in peace, enjoying Him.
　　The man who tastes life as it really is,
Not as men talk of it,
Not as men value it,
He is the true philosopher,
Taught of God, and not of men.
The man who learns to walk the inward road,
Weighing outward life as little,
Asking for no set places, wanting no fixed times
To pray his holy prayers,
He soon collects his thoughts,
Because he never dissipates his life
Upon the outward world.

THOMAS À KEMPIS.

The joy of the Lord is your strength.
NEH. viii. 10.

THE denial, the trial, the scourging, the crucifixion, follow fast.   Yet even in the midst of their horror there is room for some momentary gleams of joy.   The wavering of Pilate; the cries of a few sympathetic voices among the hooting mobs as He passed through the street; the group of friends at the foot of the cross; and then that great joy which must have fallen into His spirit when from the other cross there came a cry of faith and hope; at last the utter satisfaction which fills His soul as He exclaims, " It is finished," —all of these come in to show that the very agony of agonies was charged with the divine capacity of joy.

INFLUENCE, 204.

In the Cross is safety,
In the Cross is life,
In the Cross protection from our foes,
In the Cross is sweetness
Poured on us from above;
In the Cross is spiritual joy,
In the Cross the sum of virtues;
In the Cross is holiness in perfect beauty.

THOMAS À KEMPIS.

*The sower soweth the word . . . and these are
they which are sown on good ground ; such as hear
the word, and receive it, and bring forth fruit,
some thirty fold, some sixty, and some an hundred.*

MARK iv. 14, 20.

IF one gives me a diamond to carry across
the sea, I may estimate its value and
know just how much poorer I shall be and the
world will be if I let it drop into the water
and it sinks to the bottom. But if one gives
me a seed of some new fruit to bring to
this new land, I look at it with awe. It is
mysteriously valuable. I cannot tell what
preciousness is in it. Harvests on harvests,
food for whole generations, are shut up in its
little bulk. There always must be a difference as to the essential value set on truth,
between him who thinks that truth is final
and him who thinks that truth is germinal,
between him who thinks it a diamond and him
who thinks it a seed. . . . In the name of all
you hope to know, cling close to what you
know already. . . . It is not good for any
man to let the vastness of unknown truth
make him disparage the little that he knows.
It is good for him to count his little precious
because it is of the same kind with, and may
introduce him to, the greater after which he
aspires.

II. 139.

THE devils of discontent, despair, selfishness, sensuality, how they are scattered before that voice, really heard, of the risen and everlasting Christ! He stands before the door of His tomb and speaks, and these dark forms that have enchained the souls and fettered the activities of men fall on their faces, like the Roman soldiers, who in the gray dawn of the morning saw Him come forth from the tomb of the Arimathean, and trembled with fright, and knew that their day was over, and that the prisoner they thought was dead was indeed too strong for them to keep.   I. 216, 217.

Good, to forgive
   Best, to forget!
   Living, we fret,
Dying we live.
Fretless and free,
   Soul, clap thy pinion!
   Earth have dominion
Body, o'er thee!

Wander at will,
   Day after day, —
   Wander away,
Wandering still.
Soul that canst soar!
   Body may slumber:
   Body shall cumber
Soul-flight no more.

Waft of soul's wing!
   What lies above?
   Sunshine and Love,
Sky-blue and Spring!
Body hides where?
   Ferns of all feather,
   Mosses and heather,
Yours be the care!

BROWNING.

THE whole position of duty is elevated by the thought, the knowledge of immortality. Duty is a vast power, and needs a vast world to work in. . . . Duty is the one thing on earth that is so vital that it can go through death and come to glory. Duty is the one seed that has such life in it that it can lie as long as God will in the mummy hand of death, and yet be ready any moment to start into new growth in the new soil where He shall set it.

I. 223, 224.

Stern Daughter of the Voice of God!
O Duty! if that name thou love
Who art a light to guide, a rod
To check the erring, and reprove;
Thou, who art victory and law
When empty terrors overawe;
From vain temptations dost set free;
And calm'st the weary strife of frail humanity!

Stern Lawgiver! yet thou dost wear
The Godhead's most benignant grace;
Nor know we anything so fair
As is the smile upon thy face:
Flowers laugh before thee on their beds
And fragrance in thy footing treads;
Thou dost preserve the Stars from wrong;
And the most ancient Heavens, through Thee, are
    fresh and strong.

WORDSWORTH.

I will lift up mine eyes unto the hills, from whence cometh my help. — Ps. cxxi. 1.

THE fear of pain, the fear of disgrace, the fear of discomfort, and the shame that comes with the loftiest companionship, — we may have to appeal to them all for support in the hours, which come so often in our lives, when we are very weak. But, after all, the appeal to these helpers is not the final cry of the soul. They are like the bits of wood that the drowning sailor clutches when he must have something at the instant or he perishes. They are not the solid shore on which at last he drops his tired feet and knows that he is safe. Or rather, perhaps, the man who trusts them is like a dweller in some valley down which a freshet pours, who drives the stakes of his imperilled tent deeper into the ground; not like one who leaves the valley altogether and escapes to the mountain where the freshet never comes. . . . Not until a man has laid hold "behind and above everything else" upon the absolute assurance that the right is right and that the God of righteousness will give His strength to any feeblest will in all His universe which tries to do the right in simple unquestioning consecration; not until he has thus appealed to duty and to the dear God of whose voice she is the " stern daughter ;" not till then has he summoned to his aid the final perfect help; only then has he really looked up to the hills.

II. 275. 276.

God dwelleth in a light far out of human ken —
Become thyself that light and thou shalt see Him then.
ANGELUS SILESIUS.

IT is a blessed thing that in all times, and never more richly than in the Reformation days, there have always been other men to whom religion has not presented itself as a system of doctrine, but as an elemental life in which the soul of man came into very direct and close communion with the soul of God. It is the mystics of every age who have done most to blend the love of truth and the love of man within the love of God, and so to keep alive or to restore a healthy tolerance. Indeed, the mystic spirit has been almost like a deep and quiet pool in which tolerance, when it has been growing old and weak, has been again and again sent back to bathe itself and to renew its youth and vigor. The German mystics of the fourteenth century made ready for the great enfranchisement of the fifteenth. The English Platonists, who had the mystic spirit very strongly, became almost the re-creators of tolerance in the English Church. The mysticism of to-day gives great hope for the earnest freedom of the future.

TOLERANCE, 35, 36.

THE little lives which do in little ways that which the life of Jesus does completely the noble characters of which we think we have the right to say that they are the lights of human history, . . . they reveal and they inspire. . . . They faintly catch the feeble reflection of His life who is the true Light of the World, the real illumination and inspiration of humanity.   V. 5, 6.

" Faces, faces, faces of the streaming marching surge,
    Streaming on the weary road, toward the awful
        steep,
    Whence your glow and glory, as ye set to that sharp
        verge,
    Faces lit as sunlit stars, shining as ye sweep? "

    .   .   .   .

Lo, the Light ! (they answer) *O the pure, the pulsing
    Light,
Beating like a heart of life, like a heart of love,
Soaring, searching, filling all the breadth and depth and
    height,
Welling, whelming with its peace worlds below, above !*

" O my soul, how art thou to that living Splendor blind,
    Sick with thy desire to see even as these men see ! —
    Yet to look upon them is to know that God hath
        shined :
    Faces lit as sunlit stars, be all my light to me ! "
                                    HELEN GRAY CONE.

HERE is the power of true self-sacrifice; here is the secret which takes out of it all the bitterness and brutality. Always it is the giving up of a symbol that you may have the reality. In the great sacrifice of all, Christ lays down His life, but it is that He may take it again. Do you think that Christ did not care for life and all that makes life beautiful to us? Surely He did, but He cared more for that which they represent, — the living purely, the doing of His Father's will, and the serving of His brethren. That was why He was able to do without the things which seem to be absolutely essential to our lives; because He was so much more full than we are of the beauty and glory of the life with God.

1. 290, 291.

Could we but crush that ever-craving lust
For bliss, which kills all bliss, and live our life,
Our barren unit life, to find again
A thousand lives in those for whom we die!
So were we men and women, and should hold
Our rightful rank in God's great universe,
Wherein, in heaven and earth, by will or nature,
Naught lives for self.

CHARLES KINGSLEY.

THE onward reach, the struggle to an apprehended purpose, the straight clear
line right from His own self-knowledge to His
work, was perfect in the Lord. "For this
cause was I born," He cried. His life pierced
like an arrow through the cloud of aimless
lives, never for a moment losing its direction,
hurrying on with a haste and assurance which
were divine. . . . We revel in the making
of specialists. Perhaps we overdo it, but no
thinking man dreams of saying that the thing
itself is wrong. This movement of a man's
whole life along some clearly apprehended line
of self-development and self-accomplishment,
this reaching of a life out forward to its own
best attainment, no man can live as a man
ought to live without it. The men who have
no purpose are good for nothing. They lie in
the world like mere pulpy masses, giving it no
strength or interest or character.   II.

Cleave thou the waves that weltering to and fro
  Surge multitudinous. The eternal Powers
  Of sun, moon, stars, the air, the hurrying hours,
The wingèd winds, the still dissolving show
Of clouds in calm or storm, forever flow
  Above thee; while the abysmal sea devours
  The untold dead insatiate, where it lowers
O'er glooms unfathom'd, limitless, below.

No longer on the golden-fretted sands,
  Where many a shallow tide abortive chafes,
Mayst thou delay; life onward sweeping blends
  With far-off heaven: the dauntless one who braves
The perilous flood with calm unswerving hands,
  The elements sustain: cleave thou the waves.
                              MATHILDE BLIND.

LET us stand in the country he has saved and which is to be his grave and monument, and say of Abraham Lincoln what he said of the soldiers who had died at Gettysburg. He stood there with their graves before him, and these are the words he said:

"We cannot dedicate, we cannot consecrate, we cannot hallow this ground. The brave men who struggled here have consecrated it far beyond our power to add or detract. The world will little note, nor long remember what we say here, but it can never forget what they did here. It is for us, the living, rather to be dedicated to the unfinished work which they who fought here have thus far so nobly advanced. It is rather for us to be here dedicated to the great task remaining before us, that from these honored dead we take increased devotion to that cause for which they gave the last full measure of devotion ; that we here highly resolve that these dead shall not have died in vain ; and this nation, under God, shall have a new birth of freedom, and that government of the people, by the people, and for the people shall not perish from the earth."

May God make us worthy of the memory of Abraham Lincoln.　　　SERMON ON ABRAHAM LINCOLN.

IT seems to me that this sight of the super-
ficialness of our own judgments of others,
the way in which we have often pronounced
solemn-sounding verdicts which really meant
nothing, and uttered cheap ridicule which we
should have despised the man if he had minded,
gives us very often a startling sense of what a
superficial thing this criticism is that comes to
us from our brethren of which we make so
much and to which we are always trimming
our action.

> O Lord of bliss,
>   Remember this:
> How man's mind is like the moon;
> Is variable,
> Frail and unstable,
> At morning, night, and noon.
> Though he, unkind,
> Have not in mind
> What Ye for him have done,
> Yet have compassion,
> For our salvation
> Forsake not man so soon.
> A while him spare,
> He shall prepare
> Himself to You anon;
> With heart and mind,
> Loving and kind,
> To serve but You alone!

1530.

THE great impression of the life of Jesus, as it seems to me, must always be of the subordinate importance of those things in which only the æsthetic nature finds its pleasure. There is no condemnation of them in that wise deep life. But the fact always must remain that the wisest deepest life that was ever lived left them on one side, was satisfied without them. And His religion, while it has developed and delighted in their culture, has always kept two strong habits with reference to art which showed that in it was still the spirit of its Master. It has always been restless under the sway of any art that did not breathe with spiritual and moral purpose. Never has Christian art reached the pure æstheticism of the classics. And in its more earnest moods, in its reformations, in its puritanisms, it has always stood ready to sacrifice the choicest works of artistic beauty for the restoration or preservation of the simple majesty of righteousness, the purity of truth, or the glory of God.

INFLUENCE, 200, 201.

If Greece must be
A wreck, yet shall its fragments reassemble,
And build themselves again impregnably
In a diviner clime,
To Amphionic music, on some Cape sublime,
Which frowns above the idle foam of Time.

SHELLEY.

UNDER one fatherhood the whole world becomes sacred. The old distinctions of useful and useless knowledge will not hold. The responsibility of each man for the working of his intellect must be acknowledged. The sin of mental carelessness or wilfulness must take its place among the sins against which men struggle and for which they repent. The application of moral standards to history, to art, and to pure letters must be learned and taught. The isolation of the artistic impulse from all moral judgments and purposes must be restrained and remedied. The whole thought of art must be enlarged and mellowed till it develops a relation to the spiritual and moral natures as well as to the senses of mankind. It will lose, perhaps, the purity and simplicity which has belonged to the idea of art in classic and unchristian times, but it will become more and more a part of the general culture of human life. That is the change which has come between the Venus of Milo and the Moses of Michael Angelo; between the Iliad and Paradise Lost; between the Idyls of Theocritus and the best modern novel. Mere simplicity of method and effect has given place to harmony of method and effect, littleness to largeness, fastidiousness to sympathy, and the Christian world has really learned more and more to believe what the Christian poet sang, that

> He who feels contempt
> For any living thing, hath faculties
> That he hath never used : and Thought with him
> Is in its infancy.

INFLUENCE, 267, 268.

Paul said, I would to God that not only thou, but also all that hear me this day, were both almost and altogether such as I am, except these bonds.

ACTS xxvi. 29.

THIS must always be the first joy of any really good life, its first joy and its first anxiety at once, — the desire that others should enter into it. Indeed here is the test of a man's life. Can you say, " I wish you were like me " ? Can you take your purposes and standards of living, and quietly, deliberately wish for all those who are dearest to you that they should be their purposes and standards too ? If you are a true Christian you can. If you are trying to serve Christ, however imperfect be your service, still you can say to your child, your friend, " I wish that you were with me where I am, on this good road of serving Christ, though far beyond me in it." . . . It is not good for a man to be living any life which he would not desire to see made perfect and universal through the world. Paul says, " Be what I am ; " but Dives cries out of the fire where he lies, " Oh, send and warn my seven brethren lest they come where I am ! " . . . Oh, test your lives thus ! Do not consent to be anything which you would not ask the soul that is dearest to you to be. Be nothing which you would not wish all the world to be !

I. 304, 305.

DEATH did not close Christ's being, but it was only an experience which that being underwent. That spiritual existence which had been going on forever, on which the short existences of men had been strung into consistency, now came and submitted itself to that which men had always been submitting to. And lo! instead of being what men had feared it was, what men had hardly dared to hope that it was not, the putting out of life, it was seen to be only the changing of the circumstances of life without any real power over the real principle of life; any more power than the cloud has over the sun that it obscures. . . . That was the wonder of Christ's death.

I. 214.

I lift mine eyes to see : earth vanisheth.
  I lift up wistful eyes and bow my knee :
Trembling, bowed down, and face to face with Death,
  I lift mine eyes to see.

  Lo, what I see is Death that shadows me :
Yet, while I, seeing, draw a shuddering breath,
  Death like a mist grows rare perceptibly.

Beyond the darkness, light, beyond the scathe
  Healing, beyond the Cross, a palm-branch tree,
Beyond Death Life, on evidence of faith :
  I lift mine eyes to see.

CHRISTINA ROSSETTI.

WHAT shall we make of some man rich in attainments and in generous desires, well educated, well behaved, who has trained himself to be a light and help to other men, and who, now that his training is complete, stands in the midst of his fellow-men completely dark and helpless? . . . These men are unlighted candles; they are the spirit of man, elaborated, cultivated, finished to its very finest, but lacking the last touch of God. As dark as a row of silver lamps, all chased and wrought with wondrous skill, all filled with rarest oil, but all untouched with fire, — so dark in this world is a long row of cultivated men, set up along the corridors of some age of history, around the halls of some wise university, or in the pulpits of some stately church, to whom there has come no fire of devotion, who stand in awe and reverence before no wisdom greater than their own.   II. 9, 10.

The world's philosophers and they that taste the flesh
     fail in Thy philosophy.
There is many a vanity;
There men find death.

   .   .   .   .

Wide, wide apart the savour of Creator and created,
As of eternity and time,
A candle and the uncreated beam.

O blaze that shines forever,
High above all the fires of the earth,
Lighten in flashes from above,
Finding a way into the secret chambers of my heart.
Make pure,
Make glad,
Make clear, make quick my spirit and its powers.
                              THOMAS À KEMPIS.

TO him (who believes in immortality) death is a jar, a break, a deep mysterious change, but not the end of life. . . . See how free it makes him. How it breaks his tyrannies! He can undertake works of self-culture, or the development of truth, far, far too vast for the earthly life of any Methuselah to finish, and yet smile calmly and work on when men tell him that he will die before his work is done. Die! Shall not the sculptor sleep a hundred times before the statue he begins to-day is finished, and wake a hundred times more ready for his work, bringing with a hundred new mornings to his work the strength and the visions that have come to him in his slumber ?

I. 221.

> That low man seeks a little thing to do,
>   Sees it and does it :
> This high man, with a great thing to pursue,
>   Dies ere he knows it.
> That low man goes on adding one to one,
>   His hundred's soon hit :
> This high man, aiming at a million,
>   Misses an unit.
> That, has the world here — should he need the next,
>   Let the world mind him !
> This, throws himself on God, and unperplext,
>   Seeking, shall find Him.
>
> ROBERT BROWNING.

I will bring the third part through the fire, and will refine them as silver is refined, and will try them as gold is tried; they shall call on My Name, and I will hear them: I will say, It is My people: and they shall say, The Lord is my God. — ZECH. xiii. 9.

HE has had little experience of God who has not often felt how sometimes, with a question still unanswered, a deep doubt in the soul unsolved, the Father will fold about His doubting child a sense of Himself so deep, so true, so self-witnessing, that the child is content to carry his unanswered question because of the unanswerable assurance of His Father which he has received.

I 10.

We are led to believe a lie
When we see *with* not *through* the eye,
Which was born in a night to perish in a night
When the soul slept in beams of light.
God appears and God is light
To those poor souls who dwell in night:
But doth a human form display
To those who dwell in realms of day.

WILLIAM BLAKE.

Great is our Lord, and of great power: His understanding is infinite. — Ps. cxlvii. 5.

When Thy word goeth forth, it giveth light and understanding. — Ps. cxix. 2.

THERE are some men whose minds are wholly sceptical of Christian truth, who yet allow themselves a sort of religion on the weaker side. They let their emotions be religious, while they keep their minds in the hard clear air of disbelief; the heart may worship, while the brain denies. I will not stop to ask the meaning of this last strange condition, interesting as the study might be made. I only want you all to feel how thoroughly Christianity is bound to reject indignantly this whole treatment of itself. Just think how the great masters of religion would receive it! Think of David and his cry — "Thy testimonies are wonderful. I have more understanding than my teachers, for Thy testimonies are my study." Think of Paul — "O the depth of the riches both of the wisdom and knowledge of God." Think of Augustine, Luther, Calvin, Milton, Edwards, and a hundred more, the men whose minds have found their loftiest inspiration in religion, how would they have received this quiet and contemptuous relegation of the most stupendous subjects of human thought to the region of silly sentiment? They were men who loved the Lord their God with all their minds.

III. 38, 39.

I WOULD present true sainthood to you as the strong chain of God's presence in humanity running down through all history, and making of it a unity, giving it a large and massive strength able to bear great things and to do great things too. This unity which the line of sainthood gives to history is the great point that shows its strength.   I. 122.

Thy saints, O Lord, who now rejoice with Thee, high
    in the kingdom of the sky,
Waited the coming of Thy glory all their lives, trust-
    fully, very patiently.
That they believed in, I believe in too ;
That they hoped for, I hope too ;
Whither they came,
Thither I trust that through thy grace I shall come too.
Till then I walk in faith, strengthened by the pattern
    set by them.

Rejoice, ye humble,
And exult, ye poor ;
God's kingdom yours,
If ye but walk in truth.

THOMAS À KEMPIS.

WE have full tolerance for the Buddhist and the Mohammedan ; less for the Quaker and the Congregationalist ; least of all for the man of our own Church, but of another "school of thought" from ours.

———

So far from earnest personal conviction and generous tolerance being incompatible with one another, the two are necessary each to each. "It is the natural feeling of all of us," said Frederick Maurice in one of those utterances of his which at first sound like paradoxes, and by and by seem to be axioms, — "it is the natural feeling of all of us that charity is founded upon the *uncertainty* of truth. I believe it is founded on the *certainty* of truth."

TOLERANCE, 27, 9.

To veer, how vain ! On, onward strain,
  Brave barks ! In light, in darkness too,
Through winds and tides one compass guides —
  To that, and your own selves, be true.

But O blithe breeze ! and O great seas,
  Though ne'er, that earliest parting past,
On your wide plain they join again,
  Together lead them home at last.

One port, methought, alike they sought,
  One purpose hold where'er they fare, —
O bounding breeze, O rushing seas !
  At last, at last, unite them there.

ARTHUR HUGH CLOUGH.

If we be dead with Him, we shall also live with Him : if we suffer, we shall also reign with Him.

II. TIM. ii. 11, 12.

CHRIST was humiliated into our condition that we might be exalted unto His. Christ was crucified with man that man might rejoice in being crucified with Christ. Both the depth to which He went to seek man and the height up to which He would carry man, were set forth in the cross. Alas for him who, . . . looking at the crucifixion, does not see both of these, does not learn at once how low his Saviour went to find him, and how high he may go if he will make his Saviour's life his own!

i. 195.

O mine enemy,
Rejoice not over me !
   Jesus waiteth to be gracious :
   I will yet arise,
Mounting free and far
Past sun and star,
   To a house prepared and spacious
   In the skies.

Lord, for Thine own sake
Kindle my heart and break ;
   Make mine anguish efficacious
   Wedded to Thine own :
Be not Thy dear pain,
Thy love in vain,
   Thou who waitest to be gracious
   On Thy Throne.

CHRISTINA ROSSETTI

I built my soul a lordly pleasure-house,
    Wherein at ease for aye to dwell.
I said, " O Soul, make merry and carouse,
    Dear soul, for all is well."

        .   .   .   .

Full oft the riddle of the painful earth
    Flashed through her as she sat alone,
Yet not the less held she her solemn mirth,
    And intellectual throne.

And so she throve and prospered : so three years
    She prospered : on the fourth she fell,
Like Herod, when the shout was in his ears,
    Struck through with pangs of hell.

                                        TENNYSON.

IT seems to me a wonderful thing that the supremely rich human nature of Jesus never for an instant turned with self-indulgence in on its own richness, or was beguiled by that besetting danger of all opulent souls, the wish, in the deepest sense, just to enjoy himself. How fascinating that desire is. How it keeps many and many of the most abundant natures in the world from usefulness. Just to handle over and over their hidden treasures, and with a spiritual miserliness to think their thought for the pure joy of thinking, and turn emotion into the soft atmosphere of a life of gardened selfishness. Not one instant of that in Jesus. All the vast richness of His human nature only meant for Him more power to utter God to man.   II. 16.

THE NEW BIRTH.

'Tis a new life ; — thoughts move not as they did,
With slow uncertain steps across my mind ;
In thronging haste fast pressing on they bid
The portals open to the viewless wind,
That comes not save when in the dust is laid
The crown of pride that gilds each mortal brow,
And from before man's vision melting fade
The heavens and earth ; — their walls are falling now.
Fast crowding on, each thought asks utterance strong ;
Storm-lifted waves swift rushing to the shore,
On from the sea they send their shouts along,
Back through the cave-worn rocks their thunders roar ;
And I, a child of God, by Christ made free,
Start from death's slumbers to eternity.

JONES VERY.

WHEN a man, strong in the conviction of immortality, really counts himself a stranger and a pilgrim among the multitudes who know no home, no world but this, then he is free among them ; free from the worldly tyrannies that bind them ; free from their temptations to be cowardly and mean. The wall of death, beyond which they never look, is to him only a mountain that can be crossed, from whose top he shall see eternity, where he belongs. . . . What is there in scorn or criticism, that dies the day it is born, that can terrify, however it may pain, the man who is to live forever ? He is free. He has entered into the glorious liberty of the children of God.

I. 222, 223.

We do not present our supplications before Thee for our righteousness, but for Thy great mercies. O Lord, hear ; O Lord, forgive ; O Lord, hearken and do. — DAN. ix. 18, 19.

EVERY true prayer has its background and its foreground.   The foreground of prayer is the intense, immediate desire for a certain blessing which seems to be absolutely necessary for the soul to have ; the background of prayer is the quiet, earnest desire that the will of God, whatever it may be, should be done.   What a picture is the perfect prayer of Jesus in Gethsemane !   In front burns the strong desire to escape death and to live ; but, behind, there stands, calm and strong, the craving of the whole life for the doing of the will of God. . . . Leave out the foreground — let there be no expression of the wish of him who prays — and there is left a pure submission which is almost fatalism.   Leave out the background — let there be no acceptance of the will of God — and the prayer is only an expression of self-will, a petulant claiming of the uncorrected choice of him who prays.   Only when the two, foreground and background, are there together, — the special desire resting on the universal submission, the universal submission opening into the special desire, — only then is the picture perfect and the prayer complete !   V. 120, 121.

WHEN the sun rose this morning it found this great sleeping world and woke it. It bade it be itself. It quickened every slow and sluggish faculty. It called to the dull streams, and said, "Be quick;" to the dull birds and bade them sing; to the dull fields and bade them grow; to the dull men and bade them talk and think and work. It flashed electric invitation to the whole mass of sleeping power which really was the world, and summoned it to action. It did not make the world. It did not sweep a dead world off and set a live world in its place. It did not start another set of processes unlike those which had been sluggishly moving in the darkness. It poured strength into the essential processes which belonged to the very nature of the earth which it illuminated. It glorified, intensified, fulfilled the earth.

V. 3, 4.

Through wood and stream and field and hill and ocean,
  A quickening life from the earth has burst,
As it has ever done, with change and motion,
  From the great morning of the world when first
God dawned on chaos; in its stream immersed,
  The lamps of heaven flash with a softer light;
All baser things pant with life's sacred thirst;
  Diffuse themselves; and spend in love's delight,
The beauty and the joy of their renewèd might.

SHELLEY.

I HEAR men praying everywhere for more faith, but when I listen to them carefully and get at the real heart of their prayers, very often it is not more faith at all that they are wanting, but a change from faith to sight. . . . Faith says not, "I see that it is good for me, and so God must have sent it," but " God sent it, and so it must be good for me." Faith walking in the dark with God only prays Him to clasp its hand more closely, does not even ask Him for the lifting of the darkness so that the man may find the way himself.

V. 351, 352.

Oh that the soul might be at rest;
   Might yield her quest,
With the sole thought of God possessed !

That she might close her wearied eyes
   And blindfold-wise
Walk on as under shining skies ;

As seeing Him who is unseen ;
   And wait serene
Though twofold night should intervene !

O touch of God, O miracle
   That none may tell !
Her eyes are closed, and all is well.

Though twofold night doth round her press
   She knows no less
He will not leave her comfortless.

The desolate Cry on Calvary's height,
   Its mid-day night,
Her pledges are of coming light.

HARRIET MCEWEN KIMBALL.

When He ascended up on high, He led captivity captive, and gave gifts unto men. — EPH. iv. 8.

O sing praises, sing praises unto our God.   Alleluia.
O sing praises, sing praises unto our King.   Alleluia.

CHRIST was not primarily the Deed-Doer or the Word-Sayer.   He was the Life-Giver.   He made men live.   Wherever He went He brought vitality.   Both in the days of His Incarnation and in the long years of His power which have followed since He vanished from men's sight, His work has been to create the conditions in which all sorts of men should *live*.

HARVARD MONTHLY.

Thrice for us the Word Incarnate high on holy hills
        was set,
Once on Tabor, once on Calvary, and again on Olivet;
Once to shine and once to suffer, and once more as
        King of kings,
With a merry noise ascending borne by Cherubs on
        their wings,
Till the glad Angelic voices hail the wardens of the
        Gate,
" Lift ye up the doors, ye princes, for the Victor comes
        in state."

And the guards celestial answer from within to that
        strange cry,
" Who is He the mighty Victor Who claims entrance
        to the sky?"
Back from His triumphant legions comes reply in
        joyous swell,
" It is He, the King of Glory, Who hath vanquished
        death and hell:
Lord of Hosts and strong in battle, Who upon this
        holy tide,
Leads captivity in fetters, and hath trampled Satan's
        pride."

R. F. LITTLEDALE.

The light of the body is the eye; if, therefore, thine eye be single, thy whole body shall be full of light. — MATT. vi. 22.

I LOOK at Jesus on the cross. I see Him there convicting sin by the sight of its terrific consequence. I see Him also drawing men's souls up, away from the earth and from themselves, up to God, by that amazing sign of how God loved them. And when I turn from looking at the Sufferer and look into the faces of those men and women to whom His suffering has brought its power, I see how, in the struggle against sin under the power of the love of God, to which the cross has summoned them, they are knowing God; how, in St. Paul's great words, "the God of our Lord Jesus Christ, the Father of Glory, is giving unto them the spirit of wisdom and revelation in the knowledge of Him, the eyes of their understanding being enlightened."

II. 89, 90.

O Light of Souls,
Let us not walk in darkness.

By the Love whereby Thou didst cause the blind to see:
Enlighten our minds with the Spirit of truth.

BOOK OF LITANIES. NEALE.

December days were brief and chill,
  The winds of March were wild and drear,
And nearing and receding still,
  Spring never would, we thought, be here.
The leaves that burst, the suns that shine,
  Had, not the less, their certain date : —
And thou, O human heart of mine,
  Be still, refrain thyself and wait.
                        ARTHUR HUGH CLOUGH.

IT will be good for us to see how widely prevalent the principle is which comes to its consummation in the giving of Himself by Christ to men. Everywhere faith, or the capacity of receiving, has a power to claim and command the thing which it needs. Nature would furnish us many an exhibition of the principle. You plant a healthy seed into the ground. The seed's health consists simply in this, that it has the power of true relations to the soil you plant it in. And how these spring-days bear us witness that the soil acknowledges this power : no sooner does it feel the seed than it replies ; it unlocks all its treasures of force ; the little hungry black kernel is its master. "O seed, great is thy faith!" the ground seems to say ; "be it unto thee even as thou wilt ;" and so the miracle of growth begins.
                                III. 163.

Little Lamb, who lost thee? —
  I, myself, none other. —
Little Lamb, who found thee? —
  Jesus, Shepherd, Brother.
Ah, Lord, what I cost Thee !
  Canst Thou still desire? —
Still mine arms surround Thee,
  Still I lift Thee higher,
  Draw Thee nigher.

CHRISTINA ROSSETTI.

Father, I will that they also, whom thou hast given me, be with me where I am.

JOHN xvii. 24.

IT certainly would make it harder for us to do wrong this coming week, easier to do what is right, harder to be selfish, easier to be Christ-like, if this week we could constantly hear Christ praying for us that we might be with Him where He is.   That prayer would draw us to Him, into His life, into His character, and make this week a foretaste of that eternity whose promised glory is that there we are to be " forever with the Lord."

I. 314.

He giveth to all life, and breath, and all things.

ACTS xvii. 25.

WHEN the spring comes, the oak-tree with its thousands upon thousands of leaves blossoms all over. The great heart of the oak-tree remembers every remotest tip of every farthest branch, and sends to each the message and the power of new life. And yet we do not think of the heart of the oak-tree as if it were burdened with such multitudinous remembrance. It is simply the thrill of the common life translated into these million forms. . . . Somewhat in that way it seems to me that we may think of God's remembrance of His million children. . . . That patient sufferer, that toilsome worker, are far-off leaves on the great tree of His life; far-off, and yet as near to the beating of His heart as any leaf on all the tree. He remembers them as the heart remembers the finger-tips to which it sends the blood. . . . If any doubt about Him, issuing from them, stops up the channel so that He cannot get to them, He waits behind the hindrance, behind the doubt, and tries to get it away, and feels the withering of the unbelieving, unfed leaf as if a true part of Himself were dying. And when the obstacle gives way, and the doubt is broken and the path is once more open, it is almost with a shout which we can hear that the life-blood leaps to its work again.   III. 172, 173, 174.

The graves were opened; and many bodies of the saints which slept, arose, and came out of the graves after His resurrection, and went into the holy city, and appeared unto many.

MATT. xxvii. 52, 53.

IF the city of our heart is holy with the presence of a living Christ, then the dear dead will come to us and we shall know they are not dead but living, and bless Him who has been their Redeemer, and rejoice in the work that they are doing for Him in His perfect world, and press on joyously towards our own redemption, not fearing even the grave, since by its side stands He whom we know and love, who has the keys of death and hell.

I. 227.

Dear dead ! they have become
  Like guardian angels to us ;
And distant heaven like home,
  Through them begins to woo us ;
Love that was earthly wings
  Its flight to holier places ;
The dead are sacred things
  That multiply our graces.

They whom we loved on earth
  Attract us now to heaven ;
Who shared our grief and mirth
  Back to us now are given.
They move with noiseless foot
  Gravely and sweetly round us,
And their soft touch hath cut
  Full many a chain that bound us.

F. W. FABER.

Curse ye Meroz, saith the angel of the Lord, Curse ye bitterly the inhabitants thereof; because they came not to the help of the Lord, to the help of the Lord against the mighty. — JUDGES V. 23.

THE curse of Meroz is the curse of uselessness; and these are the sources out of which it comes — cowardice and false humility and indolence. They are the stones piled upon the sepulchres of vigor and energy and work for God, whose crushing weight cannot be computed. Who shall roll us away those stones? Nothing can do it but the power of Christ. The manhood that is touched by Him rises into life. . . . To be working with God, however humbly; to have part of that service which suns and stars, which angels and archangels, which strong and patient and holy men and women in all times have done; to be, in some small corner of the field, stout and brave and at last triumphant in our fight with lust and cruelty and falsehood, with want or woe or ignorance, with unbelief and scorn, with any of the enemies of God . . . what a change it is when a poor, selfish, cowardly, fastidious, idle human creature comes to this! Blessed is he that cometh to the help of the Lord, to the help of the Lord against the mighty. There is no curse for him. No wounds that he can receive while he is fighting on that side can harm him. To fight there is itself to conquer, even though the victory comes through pain and death, as it came to Him under whom we fight, the Captain of our Salvation, Jesus Christ.

II. 303, 304.

THERE is a wonderful power in sympathy to open and display the hidden richness of a man's own seemingly narrow life. . . . The holiest soul, pitying the brother-soul which has fallen into vilest vice, gains, while it keeps its own purity unsoiled, something of the sight of that other side of God, the side where justice and forgiveness blend in the opal mystery of grace, which it would seem as if only the soul that looked up out of the depths of guilt could see.

II. 120, 121.

Not wrath, dear Lord, Thy mercy seals.
  Our own unrighteous hands
Hold back Thy shining chariot-wheels,
  And rob the wistful lands.

For none shall walk in perfect white
  Till every soul be clean ;
So close for sorrow and delight
  These human spirits lean.

But thou go forth and do thy deed,
  In forest and in town,
Nor sigh for ease, while pain and need
  Are plucking at thy gown.

And thus, when bitter turneth sweet,
  And every heart is blest,
Perchance to thee God's hand shall mete
  His unimagined rest.

KATHERINE LEE BATES

When He the Spirit of truth is come, He will guide you into all truth . . . He shall glorify Me: for He shall receive of mine, and shall show it unto you. — JOHN xvi. 13, 14.

THIS absorption of every struggle between the good and the evil that is going on in the world into the one great struggle of the life and death of Jesus Christ . . . follows necessarily from any such full idea as we Christians hold of what Jesus Christ is and of what brought Him to this world. If He be really the Son of God, bringing in an utterly new way the power of God to bear on human life; if He be the natural creator-king of humanity, come for the salvation of humanity; then it would seem to follow that the work of salvation must be His and His alone; and if we see the process of salvation, the struggle of the good against the evil, going on all over the world, we shall be ready still to feel that it is all under His auspices and guidance. . . .

Once accept what is the central truth of operative Christianity, the power of an ever-present unseen Spirit, always manifesting Christ and making Him influential, and then it is not hard to see that, men being the same, open to the same influence everywhere, they may be and they are turned to the one same goodness by the power of the one same spirit of Christ.

I. 40, 42.

THE power of the Holy Spirit!—an everlasting spiritual presence among men.
What but that is the thing we want? That
is what the old oracles were dreaming of, what
the modern spiritualists to-night are fumbling
after. The power of the Holy Ghost by which
every man who is in doubt may know what is
right, every man whose soul is sick may be
made spiritually whole, every weak man may
be made a strong man,—that is God's one
sufficient answer to the endless appeal of man's
spiritual life; that is God's one great response
to the unconscious need of spiritual guidance,
which He hears crying out of the deep heart
of every man.   II. 106, 107.

   Wilt Thou not visit me?
The plant beside me feels Thy gentle dew,
   And every blade of grass I see
From Thy deep earth its quickening moisture drew.

   Come, for I need Thy love,
More than the flower the dew or grass the rain;
   Come, gently as Thy holy dove;
And let me in Thy sight rejoice to live again.

   Yes, Thou wilt visit me:
Nor plant nor tree Thine eye delights so well,
   As, when from sin set free,
My spirit loves with Thine in peace to dwell.
                          JONES VERY.

THAT is a noble time, a bewildering and exalting time in any of our. lives, when into everything that we are doing enters the Spirit of God, and thenceforth moving ever up toward the God to whom it belongs, that Spirit, dwelling in our life, carries our life up with it ; not separating our life from the earth, but making every part of it, while it still keeps its hold on earth, soar up and have to do with heaven ; so completing life in its height, by making it divine.

II. 123.

O God the Holy Ghost Who art Light unto Thine
    elect,
  Evermore enlighten us.
Thou Who art Fire of Love
  Evermore enkindle us.
Thou who art Lord and Giver of Life,
  Evermore live in us.
Thou Who art Holiness,
  Evermore sanctify us.
Thou Who bestowest Sevenfold Grace,
  Evermore replenish us.
As the Wind is Thy symbol,
  So forward our goings.
As the Dove,
  So launch us heavenwards.
As Water,
  So purify our spirits.
As a Cloud,
  So abate our temptations.
As Dew,
  So revive our languor.
As Fire,
  So purge out our dross.

CHRISTINA ROSSETTI.

The Spirit of the Lord is upon me;
Because the Lord hath anointed me to preach
good tidings unto the meek;
He hath sent me to bind up the broken-hearted,
To proclaim liberty to the captives, and the
opening of the prison to them that are bound.

ISA. lxi. 1.

BOTH in belief and in duty, this is the work of the Holy Spirit; to make belief profound by showing us the hearts of the things that we believe in; and to make duty delightful by setting us to doing it for Christ. O, in this world of shallow believers and weary, dreary workers, how we need that Holy Spirit! Remember, we may go our way, ignoring all the time the very forces that we need to help us do our work. The forces still may help us. The Holy Spirit may help us, will surely help us, just as far as He can, even if we do not know His name or ever call upon Him. But there is so much more that He might do for us if we would only open our hearts and ask Him to come into them. II. 230.

Let Thy mercy, O Lord, be upon us, and the brightness of Thy Spirit illumine our inward souls; that He may kindle our cold hearts and light up our dark minds, Who abideth evermore with Thee in glory.
ANCIENT COLLECTS. BRIGHT.

I will pour out my Spirit upon all flesh; and your sons and your daughters shall prophesy, your old men shall dream dreams, your young men shall see visions; and also upon the servants and upon the handmaids in those days will I pour out my Spirit, — the spirit of wisdom and understanding, the spirit of counsel and might, the spirit of knowledge and of the fear of the Lord.
JOEL ii. 28, 29. ISA. xi. 2.

THE intellectual life of Christendom tends to democracy. Less and less will it consent to be the privilege of the selected few. . . . It is impossible to keep the bounds of mental life shut against any man when the source of all men's knowledge is in God, who is the Father of us all, and when the faculty of knowledge is closely connected with the faculty of moral obedience, which is the right and duty of mankind. Instantly this began when Christianity was once a living fact. Peter stepped out of the chamber of the Pentecost and spoke to the great multitude in words which assumed in them the power of understanding, of judging, of deciding questions which up to that time had been the sacred possession of the scribes and doctors. There was nothing like that speech before that day. The germs of the modern sermon, the modern lecture, and the modern school were in it. Thenceforth men's intellects might differ, but the intellectual chance was open to every man. To the dullest child belonged the right to learn all that he could learn, all that was in him to learn, of his Father. INFLUENCE, 269, 270.

OH, my dear friends, do not let your religion satisfy itself with anything less than God. Insist on having your soul get at Him and hear His voice. Never, because of the mystery, the awe, perhaps the perplexity and doubt which come with the great experiences, let yourself take refuge in the superficial things of faith. It is better to be lost on the ocean than to be tied to the shore. It is better to be overwhelmed with the greatness of hearing the awful voice of God than to become satisfied with the piping of mechanical ceremonies or the lullabies of traditional creeds. Therefore seek great experiences of the soul, and never turn your back on them when God sends them, as He surely will.

V. 78, 79.

I am borne out to Thee upon the wave,
   And the land lessens ; cry nor speech I hear,
Nought but the leaping waters and the brave
   Pure winds commingling. O the joy, the fear !

Alone with Thee ; sky's rim and ocean's rim
   Touch, overhead the clear immensity
Is merely God ; no eyes of seraphim
   Gaze in . . . O God, Thou also art the sea !

EDWARD DOWDEN

LET the life be filled with the spirit of the springtime. Let the voice in its heart always keep saying to it, " You are to go on filling yourself with vitality and joy, day after day, month after month, and then cometh the end, then cometh the end ; " and then it is not a cessation of life, but fuller life which the heart expects. The end which comes to the promise of springtime shall be the luxuriance of summer !

V. 364.

Under gentle types, my Spring
Masks the might of Nature's king,
An energy that searches thorough
From Chaos to the dawning morrow ;
Into all our human plight,
The soul's pilgrimage and flight ;
In city or in solitude,
Step by step, lifts bad to good,
Without halting, without rest,
Lifting Better up to Best ;
Planting seeds of knowledge pure,
Through earth to ripen, through heaven endure.

EMERSON.

Death ! since thy darksome mist
Encircled the all-glorious head of Christ
    Thou now dost shine
    A halo all divine.

Anna E Hamilton.

THE crucifixion of Jesus has been illumi‑ nated by the resurrection, the ascension, and the Pentecost. . . . Behind its shame and pain it has opened a heart of love and glory, and St. Paul, summing up his life in its best privileges and holiest purposes, says, "I am crucified with Christ." . . . As Christ, by his self-sacrifice, entered into the company of man, so there is a self-surrender by which man enters into the company of Christ. He came down to us, and tasted on our cross the misery of sin. We may go up to His cross, and taste, with Him, the glory and peace of perfect obedience and communion with God.

I. 203.

O Love, Who once in time wast slain,
    Pierced through and through with bitter woe :
O Love, Who wrestling thus didst gain
    That we eternal joy might know
O Love, I give myself to Thee,
    Thine ever, only Thine to be.

J. Scheffler. Tr. by C. Winkworth.

REVELATION is not the unveiling of God,
but a changing of the veil that covers
Him; not the dissipation of mystery, but the
transformation of the mystery of darkness
into the mystery of light.   To the Pagan, God
is mysterious because He is hidden in clouds,
mysterious like the storm.   To the Christian,
God is mysterious because He is radiant with
infinite truth, mysterious like the sun.   II. 311.

My sight, becoming purified,
Was entering more and more into the ray
Of the High Light which of itself is true.

.   .   .   .

O grace abundant, by which I presumed
To fix my sight upon the Light Eternal,
So that the seeing I consumed therein !
I saw that in its depth far down is lying
Bound up with love together in one volume,
What through the universe in leaves is scattered;
Substance, and accident, and their operations,
All interfused together in such wise
That what I speak of is one simple light.

.   .   .   .

O how all speech is feeble and falls short
Of my conceit, and this to what I saw
Is such, 'tis not enough to call it little !
O Light Eterne, sole in thyself that dwellest,
Sole knowest thyself, and, known unto thyself
And knowing, lovest and smilest on thyself !

DANTE

I AM sure that the divine nature is three persons, but one God; but how much more than that I cannot know. That deep law which runs through all life, by which the higher any nature is, the more manifold and simple at once, the more full of complexity and unity at once, it grows, is easily accepted as applicable to the highest of all natures, — God. In the manifoldness of His being these three personal existences, Creator, Redeemer, Sanctifier, easily make themselves known to the human life. I tell the story of them, and that is my doctrine of the Trinity. But let me not say that that is all. To other worlds of other needs, and so of other understandings (for our needs are always the avenues for our intelligence), other sides of the personal force of the divine life must have issued. It is not for us to catalogue and inventory Deity; only in humble gratitude and reverence to bear our witness of the manifestation of God to us for our salvation. And so our doctrine of the Trinity is our account of what we know of God.

I. 230.

The holy Church throughout all the world doth
 acknowledge Thee ;
The Father : of an infinite Majesty ;
Thine adorable, true and only Son ;
Also the Holy Ghost : the Comforter.

*Who coverest Thyself with light as with a gar-
ment.*— Ps. civ. 2.

NOT as the answer to a riddle, which leaves
all things clear, but as the deeper sight
of God, prolific with a thousand novel questions which were never known before, clothed
in a wonder which only in that larger light dis-
played itself, offering new worlds for faith and
reverence to wander in,— so must the New
Testament revelation, the truth of Father, Son,
and Spirit, one perfect God, offer itself to man.

II. 314.

If it be so, as we believe it is, that in the
constitution of humanity we have the fairest
written analogue and picture of the Divine
existence, then shall we not say that the
human Christ gave us, in the value which He
set on human relationships, in His social
thought of man, an insight into the essential-
ness and value of that social thought of God
which we call the doctrine of the Trinity?
May it not be that only by multiplicity and
interior self-relationship can Divinity have the
completest self-consciousness and energy?
Surely, the reverent and thoughtful eye must
see some such meaning when Jesus Himself
makes the eternal companionship of the life of
Deity the pattern and picture of the best
society of the souls of earth, and breathes out
to His Father these deep and wondrous words,
"As thou Father art in Me and I in Thee, that
they all may be one in Us."   INFLUENCE, 85.

THE divinity of the Father needs assertion first of all. Let men once feel it, and then nature and their own hearts will come in with their sweet and solemn confirmations of it. But nature and the human heart do not teach it of themselves. The truest teaching of it must come from souls that are always going in and out before the divine Fatherhood themselves. By the sight of such souls others must come to seek the satisfaction that comes only from a divine end of life, — must come to crave access to the Father. So we believe and so we tempt other men to believe in God the Father.

I. 236.

All the earth doth worship Thee: the Father everlasting.

We praise Thee, we bless Thee, we worship Thee, we glorify Thee, we give thanks to Thee for Thy great glory, O Lord God, heavenly King, God the Father Almighty.

MY friend says God sends Christ into the world and therefore Christ is not God. I cannot see it so. It seems to me just otherwise. God sends Christ just because Christ is God. He sends Himself. His sending is a coming. . . . He [our Master] is the Son of God. Think of it. Does not "Son" mean just this which the church's faith, with the best words that it could find, has labored to express, "Two persons and one substance." That is the Father and the Child. Separate personality but one nature. Unity and distinctness both, but the unity as true a fact as the distinctness. Nay, the unity the fact which made the essence of His mission, the fact which made Him the true, fit, only perfect messenger of God and Saviour of the world.

I. 239.

Thou art the King of Glory: O Christ. Thou art the everlasting Son of the Father.

O Lord, the only-begotten Son, Jesus Christ; O Lord God, Lamb of God, Son of the Father, that takest away the sins of the world, have mercy upon us.

REMEMBER, the Holy Spirit is God, and God is love. And no man ever asks God to come into his heart and holds his heart open to God, without God's entering. Children, pray the dear God, the blessed Holy Spirit, to come and live in your heart and show you Jesus, and make you love to do what is right for His sake. Old men, aspire to taste already here what is to be the life and joy of your eternity. Men and women in the thick of life, do not go helpless when there is such help at hand; do not go on by yourselves, struggling for truth and toiling at your work, when the Holy Spirit is waiting to show you Christ, and to give you in Him the profoundness of faith and the delightfulness of duty.

II. 230, 231.

Come, Holy Ghost, our souls inspire,
And lighten with celestial fire.
Thou the anointing Spirit art,
Who dost Thy seven-fold gifts impart.
Thy blessed unction from above,
Is comfort, life, and fire of love.
Enable with perpetual light
The dulness of our blinded sight.
Anoint and cheer our soilèd face
With the abundance of Thy grace.
Keep far our foes, give peace at home;
Where Thou art guide, no ill can come.
Teach us to know the Father, Son,
And Thee, of Both, to be but One;
That, through the ages all along,
This may be our endless song:
    Praise to Thy eternal merit,
    Father, Son, and Holy Spirit.

Through Him we both have access by one Spirit unto the Father. — EPH. ii. 18.

IF it be not to the Father, the Son's redemption is in vain. If it be not through the Son, the Father waits and the Spirit moves for naught. If it be not by the Spirit, the Father's heart stands open and the method of grace is perfect, but the unmoved soul stands inactive and unsaved. The Scripture revelation comes to tell us that end, method, and power, all are perfect, and each must thus be worthy of the rest. The three are one. Each is eternal, and yet as the old creed cries, " There are not three Eternals, but one Eternal." Each is God, and yet "there are not three Gods, but one God," — not three salvations, but one salvation, with its equal end and method and power, and so by the Trinity in Unity the soul is saved.

I. 233.

Glory be to the Father, and to the Son, and to the Holy Ghost;

As it was in the beginning, is now, and ever shall be: world without end. Amen.

THE partialness which we see in man, and which lets us easily divide our fellow-men into classes and label them the men of intellect or the men of action, passes away as we mount to any thought of God which is at all worthy of Him. What God knows is one and the same with the love with which He loves and the resolve with which He wills. You cannot draw a fence through the great ocean of infinity. Mythology dreams of its many gods with many functions. The moment that one God stands forth above all gods, the many things which the partial deities do lose themselves in the one perfect thing which the one only Deity is. And all wisdom unites with all power and all love no less in the guiding of a little child along the slippery path which leads to manhood, than in the vast conduct of the destinies of the colossal man who lives through all the generations of the race.

INFLUENCE, 221.

I saw the Power ; I see the Love, once weak,
Resume the Power; and in this word, " I see,"
Lo, there is recognized the Spirit of both
That, moving o'er the spirit of man, unblinds
His eye, and bids him look.

BROWNING.

I believe in God the Father Almighty, Maker of heaven and earth :
And in Jesus Christ his only Son our Lord :
I believe in the Holy Ghost.

SOMETIMES, when vitality grows feeble, when disappointments and, shall I not say still more, success makes the whole business of existence seem tawdry, or not worth the pains it costs — when the morning brings no stimulus and the evening no satisfaction — . . . in all that ebbing and flagging of the tide of life, do you know what it is to find strength and healthiness, again, in believing in God, in believing in the Trinity? Does that sound strange ? What ! shall belief in a doctrine quicken the feeble pulse and fill again the empty channels of a worn and weary life ? But, unless it can do this, what is the use of your belief ? Nay, shall we not have such faith in our great doctrine that we shall confidently say that if it does not do that for a man, the man who says that he believes it does not truly believe it. David said "My heart and my flesh fail, but God is the strength of my heart and my portion for-ever." And how much more we know of God than David knew ? All that the life of Jesus told, all that the Christian centuries have told — the eternally Living One, the great I Am, who is both Creator and Father ; the Son, in whom was life, which was the light of the world : the Spirit, who is the Lord and Giver of life — not many gods, but one God — not many partial springs, but one great sea of life heard behind all.　　OxFORD REVIEW.

NOTHING can really haunt us except what we have the beginning of, the native capacity for, however hindered, in ourselves. The highest angel does not tempt us because he is of another race from us ; but God is our continual incitement because we are His children. So the ideal life is in our blood, and never will be still. We feel the thing we ought to be beating beneath the thing we are. Every time we see a man who has attained our human idea a little more fully than we have, it wakens our languid blood and fills us with new longings. When we see Christ, it is as if a new live plant out of the southern soil were brought suddenly in among its poor stunted, transplanted brethren, and, blossoming in their sight, interpreted to each of them the restlessness and discontent which was in each of their poor hearts. . . . And when we die and go to God, it is as if at last the poor shrub were plucked up out of its exile and taken back and set where it belonged, in the rich soil, under the warm sun, where the patience which it had learned in its long waiting should make all the deeper and richer the flower into which its experience was set free to find its utterance.   I. 35. 36.

See, love, afar, the heavenly man
  The Will of God would make,
The thing I must be when I can
  Love now, for faith's dear sake.
                    GEORGE MACDONALD

Hail, holy Light, offspring of Heaven first-born !
. . . . before the sun,
Before the Heavens thou wert, and at the voice
Of God, as with a mantle did'st invest
The rising world of waters dark and deep,
Won from the void and formless infinite.

MILTON.

WITH the mystery of darkness we are familiar. Of the mystery of light we have not thought, perhaps, so much. . . . Supposing that . . something really rich and profound, were brought out of the darkness into a sudden flood of sunlight, would it grow less or more mysterious ? Suppose it is a jewel, and instead of having to strain your eyes to make out the outline of its shape, you can look now deep into its heart; see depth opening beyond depth, until it looks as if there were no end to the chambers of splendor that are shut up in that little stone ; see flake after flake of luminous color floating up out of the unseen fountain which lies somewhere in the jewel's heart. Is the jewel less or more mysterious than it was when your sight had to struggle to see whether it was a topaz or an emerald? Suppose it is a landscape. One hour all its features are vague and dim in twilight ; hill, field, and stream in almost indistinguishable confusion. Six hours later the whole is glowing in the noonday sun, the streams burning with silvery light, the colors of the fresh spring hillsides striking far away upon the senses, filling them with delight and wonder. Everything is thrilling and bursting with manifest life. Has not the mystery increased with the ascending sun?

II. 307, 308.

IT was to the American nature, long kept by God in His own intentions, till His time should come, at last emerging into sight and power, and bound up and embodied in this best and most American of all Americans, Abraham Lincoln, to whom we and those poor frightened slaves at last might look up together and love to call him, with one voice, our Father. . . .

The American nature, the American truths, of which our President was the anointed and supreme embodiment, have been embodied in multitudes of heroes who marched unknown and fell unnoticed in our ranks. For them, just as for him, character decreed a life and a death.

SERMON ON ABRAHAM LINCOLN.

Blow, trumpets, all your exultations blow !
For never shall their aureoled presence lack :
I see them muster in a gleaming row,
With ever youthful brows that nobler show ;
We find in our dull road their shining track ;
    In every nobler mood
We feel the orient of their spirit glow,
Part of our life's unalterable good,
Of all our saintlier aspiration ;
    They come transfigured back,
Secure from change in their high-hearted ways,
Beautiful evermore, and with the rays
Of morn on their white Shields of Expectation.

JAMES RUSSELL LOWELL.

Phillips Brooks ordained Priest, 1860.

THIS seems to me to be the ever-increasing joy of the minister's life, if one may venture for once to speak of his own work. A man becomes a minister because God says, "Go speak in the temple the words of this life." He begins the service of his fellow-men in pure obedience to God's command, but the joy and ever-richening delight of the minister's work is in finding how deep this human soul to which his Lord has sent him really is. The nature to which he ministers, as he meets its exhibitions here and there, is always amazing him with its spiritual capacity, is always proving itself capable and worthy of so much better and higher ministry than he can give it. So the minister of the Gospel finds his own humility and the delightfulness of his work ever increasing together.

I. 349.

THE WORK OF PHILLIPS BROOKS.

Yet each will have one anguish — his own soul
Which perishes of cold.

MATTHEW ARNOLD

We know this anguish.   By the closèd door
Of their own lives men listen for the slow
And fluttering breath of souls by doubt laid low,
Which freeze in darkness, now they hope no more.
The door of thy great life stood wide, and o'er
The threshold leaned thy eager soul, aglow
With that warm hope the apostles used to know.
With that strong faith the prophets preached of yore.
O glorious soul !   How many lips shall bless
That faithfulness, that wealth of hopefulness
That like God's sun persisted in its cheer !
Forged at such heat thy swift word struck the ear
To pierce men's souls — which, finding day still shine,
Rose and unbarred their lives to life divine.

HANNAH PARKER KIMBALL.

THE rich atmosphere and rich earth surround the stone just as they surround the rose. They are as free to one as to the other. But the rose grows red and soft and fragrant, and the stone lies cold and hard and gray. The same rich humanity, the same culture, the same beauty lies about two men, as free to one as to the other, and one grows harder and more brutal and more insensible day by day, and the other grows kindlier, truer, and more sensitive.   MSS.

"God's spirit falls on me as dewdrops on a rose
    If I but like a rose my heart to Him unclose."

" In all eternity no tone can be so sweet
    As where man's heart with God in unison doth beat."

" Whate'er thou lovest, man, that too become thou must.
    God if thou lovest God ; dust if thou lovest dust."

" Immeasurable is the Highest ; who but knows it ?
    And yet a human heart can perfectly enclose It."

EVERY healthy growth creates the conditions of new growth, makes new growth possible. The illustrations are numberless everywhere. Every ray of sunlight that gives ripeness to an apple makes the apple opener to more sunlight, which shall ripen it still more. . . . Every summer is also a spring-time. Indeed we may make this a test of growth. Every ray of sun which does not open the ground to new sunlight, is not feeding it but baking it. This is the true test of growing force. It opens the beautiful reactions between itself and the growing thing, and creates an openness for yet more of itself.   II. 41, 42.

> The twig sprouteth,
> The moth outeth,
> The plant springeth,
> The bird singeth :
> Tho' little we sing to-day,
> Yet are we better than they ;
> Tho' growing with scarce a showing,
> Yet, please God, we are growing.
>
> The twig teacheth,
> The moth preacheth,
> The plant vaunteth,
> The bird chanteth,
> God's mercy overflowing
> Merciful past man's knowing.
> Please God to keep us growing
> Till the awful day of mowing.

CHRISTINA ROSSETTI.

Christ in you, the hope of glory.—COL. i. 27.

GREAT is the work that Christ does for us. Greater, deeper still, because without it all the other would be purposeless and useless, is the work that Christ does in us. How wonderful it is. The world glows with the assurance of redemption. Heaven opens, and there the saints and elders are prostrate before the throne. The whole spiritual universe trembles with the new spiritual life which has come to it out of the marvellous death. In the midst of it all lies one soul, dead and incapable of action, though intensely alive with desire for a share in all this glorious vitality. . . . The world about it is strong with the promise and temptation of holy things. The soul itself is weak with its own unholiness. Then comes the better, perfect, completing promise of a change of soul. The Christ who has done all this offers to do one thing more, to make the dead soul alive and able to enjoy and use it all. He will come into us, not merely stand without us. He will come in and be Himself the power which lays hold of His own invitations. We may feed on Him. Nay, let us take His own strong word and say, "He that eateth Me, the same shall live by Me." That is the inner life, Christ in the soul rising up and laying hold of the infinite possibilities which redemption has prepared.

II. 245, 246.

*If any man offend not in word, the same is a
perfect man, and able also to bridle the whole body.*

JAMES iii. 2.

BE profoundly honest. Never dare to say,
. . . through ardent excitement or con-
formity to what you know you are expected to
say, one word which at the moment when you
say it, you do not believe. It would cut down
the range of what you say, perhaps, but it
would endow every word that was left with
the force of ten.   PREACHING, 107.

But why are we so glad to talk and take our turns to
    prattle,
When so rarely we get back to the stronghold of our
    silence
With an unwounded conscience?
Our talk is often empty, often vain.
This comfort from without
Is no small enemy to that from God which speaks to
    us within.
So we must watch and pray,
For fear our days go idly by.
If you may talk and it be best for you,
Talk and build up the soul;
But evil habit, and carelessness about our prattle,
Make us neglect the doorway of our mouth.
Yet holy communing about the things of God leads us
    no little way along the spiritual road,
And most of all when man meets man
Like to himself in heart and mind, like to himself — in
    God.

THOMAS À KEMPIS.

MY dear friends, never let the seeming worthlessness of sympathy make you keep back that sympathy of which, when men are suffering around you, your heart is full. Go and give it without asking yourself whether it is worth the while to give it. It is too sacred a thing for you to tell what it is worth. God, from whom it comes, sends it through you to His needy child. Do not ever let any low skepticism make you distrust it, but speak out what God has put it in your heart to speak to any sufferer. The sympathy of God for man has just this same difficulty about it, if we try to analyze it. We cannot say that He has done anything for us. We cannot tell even of any thought that He has put into our minds. Merely He has been near us. He has known that we were in trouble and He has been sorry for us.

I. 108, 109.

For I, a man, with men am linked,
And not a brute with brutes ; no gain
That I experience must remain
Unshared ; but should my best endeavor
To share it, fail—subsisteth ever
God's care above, and I exult
That God by God's own ways occult
May—doth I will believe—bring back
All wanderers to a single track

BROWNING.

See that thou make all things according to the pattern shewed to thee in the mount. — HEB. viii. 5.

FOR man to accept the pattern of his living absolutely from any other being besides God in all the universe would be for him to sacrifice his self and to lose his originality. But for man to find and simply reproduce the picture of his life which is in God is for him not to sacrifice but to find his self. For the man is in God. The ideal, the possible perfection of everything that he can do or be, is there in God; and to be original for any man is not to start aside with headlong recklessness and do what neither brother-man nor God dreamed of our doing; but it is to do with filial loyalty the act which, because God is God, a being such as we are ought to do under the circumstances, in the conditions in which we stand. Because no other being ever was or ever will be just the same as you, and because precisely the same conditions never before have been and never will be grouped about any other mortal life as are grouped around yours, therefore for you to do and be what you, with your own nature in your own circumstances, ought in the judgment of the perfect mind to do and be, that is originality for you.

III 12, 13.

IS not Christ the mountain up into which the believer goes, and in which he finds the divine idea of himself? As a mountain seems to be the meeting-place of earth and heaven, the place where the bending skies meet the aspiring planet, the place where the sunshine and the cloud keep closest company with the granite and the grass: so Christ is the meeting-place of divinity and humanity; He is at once the condescension of divinity and the exaltation of humanity; and man wanting to know God's idea of man, any man wanting to know God's idea of him, must go up into Christ, and he will find it there.

III. 16.

There littleness was not; the least of things
Seemed infinite; and there his spirit shaped
Her prospects, nor did he believe, — he *saw*.
What wonder if his being thus became
Sublime and comprehensive! Low desires,
Low thoughts, had there no place; yet was his heart
Lowly; for he was meek in gratitude,
Oft as he called those ecstasies to mind,
And whence they flowed; and from them he acquired
Wisdom, which works through patience; thence he
    learned
In oft recurring hours of sober thought
To look on Nature with a humble heart,
Self-questioned where it did not understand,
And with a superstitious eye of love.

WORDSWORTH.

And He laid His right hand upon me, saying unto me, Fear not; I am the first and the last: I am He that liveth, and was dead; and, behold I am alive for evermore, Amen. — REV. i. 17, 18.

"I AM He that liveth, and was dead." We do not begin to know how wonderful that is. Remember the eternally living, the very life of all lives. And yet into that life of lives death has come, — as an episode, an incident. I do not speak now of the immense provocation, the immense love that brought so strange a thing as the submission to death on the part of the Ever-living One. I speak only of this, that when death came to Him it was seen to be not the end of life, but only an event in life.

I. 214.

"Thou knowest not now ; for here we see but darkly
    The outlines of His Grace ;
The rest is learned in Heaven's eternal glory,
    And face to face.

"Then thou shalt know ; that passionless hereafter
    Shall solve all mystery :
Dream not that life can hold the tide of wonder
    In store for thee."

THE disciples began as fishermen who could not do without their nets and boats and houses and fishing friends and sports and gains and gossipings. Jesus carried them up till they were crying, "Lord, show us the Father, and it sufficeth us." That wonderful change — how wonderful it was we forget, because the story is so familiar — He brought about by showing them His salvation. When, living with Him, they saw the glory of forgiveness and regeneration, saw the new life that opened before those who really knew His grace, everything changed to them. It was not so important how they fared, what food they ate, what they wore, how many fish they caught. "All these things do the nations of the earth seek after." To them the questions shifted. The tests of life swept higher up. Were they indeed His? Had they caught His spirit? Were they living His life? Had they part in His eternity? And so when you and I really desire the salvation of Christ, He will do for us all that He did for them. Our tests of life, too, shall sweep up. I. 297, 298.

How inexhaustibly the spirit grows!
One object she seemed 'erewhile born to reach
With her whole energies, and die content,
So like a wall at the world's end it stood,
With naught beyond to live for — is it reached?
Already are new undreamed energies
Out-growing under, and extending further
To a new object; — there's another world!

BROWNING.

JESUS spends the night in prayer and med-
itation. Out of this solitude, out of this
mysterious communion with His Father, in
which He has, as it were, refilled Himself with
the assurance that the human is son to the
Divine, He comes when morning breaks, and
gathering His disciples around Him, He speaks
to them, and the multitude who have thronged
about Him, the Sermon on the Mount. . . .

Neander calls the Sermon on the Mount " the
Magna Charta of the kingdom of God." It is
a fine phrase, and in one sense it is completely
true. But really the idea of God which fills the
great discourse is not the idea of king, but the
idea of father. . . . What gives it its great,
everlasting value, is the passing over of kingship into fatherhood ; or, if you please to put it
so, the opening and deepening of kingship till it
reveals the fatherhood which lies folded at the
heart of it.   Influence, 25, 26, 27,

Thou Who wast Centre of all Heights on the Mount of
    Beatitudes
Grant us to sit with Thee in heavenly places.
                        Christina Rossetti.

WHAT do you know about the uses of the Lord, of this great work which the Lord has to do; what do you know of it that gives you the right to say that your power is little? God may have some most critical use to put you to as soon as you declare yourself His servant. Men judge by the size of things; God judges by their fitness. . . . Fitness is more than size. You can see something of your size; but you can see almost nothing of your fitness until you understand all the wonderful manifold work that God has to do. It is a most wanton presumption and pride for any man to dare to be sure that there is not some very important and critical place which just he and no one else is made to fill. It is almost as presumptuous to think you can do nothing as to think you can do everything. The latter folly supposes that God exhausted Himself when He made you; but the former supposes that God made a hopeless blunder when he made you, which it is quite as impious for you to think. II. 298, 299.

Lord, teach me how to do Thy will,
And to walk worthily and humbly before Thee.
Thou art my wisdom; Thou dost really know me,
Thou knewest me before the world was made, or ever
    I was born in it.
THOMAS À KEMPIS.

I saw the dead, small and great, stand before God. — REV. xx. 12.

TAKE these three ideas, and I think that we can see something of what it must have been for souls to stand, as John the Evangelist in his great vision saw them standing before God. They had gone up above all the small and temporary standards, and laid their lives close upon the one perfect and eternal standard by which men must be judged. No longer did it matter to them whether they were rich or poor, whether men praised them, or abused them, or pitied them. The one question about themselves, into which all other questions gathered and were lost, was whether they were good, whether they were obedient to God.

And then, along with this, there had come to them a true and cordial meeting with their brethren. No child of their Father was too lofty or too low for them to be truly his brethren, when they stood, small and great, together before God.

And yet, again, in presence of the Infinite, they had comprehended their immortality. They had seen how, within that life to which their lives belonged, there was room for a growth · which might go on to all eternity.

No wonder that as St. John looked upon that vision it filled all his soul with joy.   IV. 70, 71.

REMEMBER that there is an atheism which still repeats the creed. There is a belief in God which does not bring Him, nay, rather say which does not let Him come, into close contact with our daily life. The very reverence with which we honor God may make us shut Him out from the hard tasks and puzzling problems with which we have to do. Many of us who call ourselves theists are like the savages who, in the desire to honor the wonderful sundial which had been given them, built a roof over it. Break down the roof; let God in on your life.

II. 160.

> The thought of God, the thought of Thee,
>   Who liest in my heart,
> And yet beyond imagined space
>   Outstretched and present art, —
>
> The thought of God is like the tree
>   Beneath whose shade I lie,
> And watch the fleets of snowy clouds
>   Sail o'er the silent sky.
>
> 'Tis like that soft invading light,
>   Which in all darkness shines,
> The thread that through life's sombre web
>   In golden pattern twines.
>
> The wild flower on the mossy ground
>   Scarce bends its pliant form,
> When overhead the autumnal wood
>   Is thundering like a storm.
>
> So is it with our humbled souls
>   Down in the thought of God,
> Scarce conscious in their sober peace
>   Of the wild storms abroad.

F. W. FABER.

Enter into thy closet, and when thou hast shut thy door, pray to thy Father which is in secret.

MATT. ii. 6.

> I need not leave the jostling world,
>   Or wait till daily tasks are o'er,
> To fold my palms in secret prayer
>   Within the close-shut closet door.
>
> There is a viewless cloistered room
>   As high as heaven, as fair as day,
> Where, though my feet may join the throng,
>   My soul can enter in and pray.
>
> No human step approaching breaks
>   The blissful silence of the place ;
> No shadow steals across the light
>   That falls from my Redeemer's face.
>
> One hearkening even cannot know
>   When I have crossed the threshold o'er;
> For He alone who hears my prayer
>   Has heard the shutting of the door.

HARRIET McEWEN KIMBALL.

JESUS never did a deed, He never thought a thought, that He did not carry it back with His soul before it took its final shape and get His Father's judgment on it.　He lifted His eyes at any instant and talked through the open sky, and on the winds came back to Him the answer. He talked with Pilate and with Peter, with Herod and with John ; and yet His talk with them was silence ;　it did not begin to make His life, to be His life, compared with that perpetual communion with His Father which made the fundamental consciousness as it made the unbroken habit of His life.

V. 83.

When the burnt offering began, the song of the Lord began with the trumpets.

II. Chron. xxix. 27.

An offering of a free heart will I give Thee, and praise Thy name, O Lord. — Ps. liv. 6.

NOT in a gloomy silence, as if the people were doing a hard duty which they would not do if they could help it, did the smoke of their offering ascend to God; but with a burst of jubilant music and with a song of triumphant joy, which rang down through the crowded courts, the host of the Jews claimed for themselves anew their place in the obedience of God. The act of sacrifice was done amid a chorus of delight.

II. 22.

Nothing more grateful can I offer Him,
Than wholly to give up my heart to God, joining it
    closely unto His.
Then all my inward self shall leap for joy,
When my soul shall wholly be at one with God.
Then shall He say to me,
" Wilt thou be with Me?
I will be with thee."
And I shall answer,
" O Lord, bow down and stay with me,
And I shall love to be with Thee ;
This is the end of my desire,
A heart made one with Thee."

THOMAS À KEMPIS.

No chastening for the present seemeth to be joyous, but grievous: nevertheless afterward it yieldeth the peaceable fruit of righteousness unto them which are exercised thereby. — HEB. xii. 11.

WHEN a man conquers his adversaries and his difficulties, it is not as if he never had encountered them. Their power, still kept, is in all his future life. They are not only events in his past history, they are elements in all his present character. His victory is colored with the hard struggle that won it. His sea of glass is always mingled with fire, just as this peaceful crust of the earth on which we live, with its wheat fields, and vineyards, and orchards, and flower-beds, is full still of the power of the convulsion that wrought it into its present shape, of the floods and volcanoes and glaciers which have rent it, or drowned it, or tortured it. Just as the whole fruitful earth, deep in its heart, is still mingled with the ever-burning fire that is working out its chemical fitness for its work, just so the life that has been overturned and overturned by the strong hand of God, filled with the deep revolutionary forces of suffering, purified by the strong fires of temptation, keeps its long discipline forever, roots in that discipline the deepest growths of the most sunny and luxuriant spiritual life that it is ever able to attain.

IV. 113.

THE NEW COLOSSUS.

[The Bartholdi Statue of Liberty.]

Not like the brazen giant of Greek fame,
With conquering limbs astride, from land to land ;
Here at our sea-washed, sunset gates shall stand
A mighty woman with a torch, whose flame
Is the imprisoned lightning, and her name
Mother of Exiles. From her beacon-hand
Glows world-wide welcome ; her mild eyes command
The air-bridged harbor that twin cities frame.
"Keep, ancient lands, your storied pomp!" cries she
With silent lips. "Give me your tired, your poor,
Your huddled masses yearning to breathe free,
The wretched refuse of your teeming shore.
Send these, the homeless, tempest-tossed to me,
I lift my lamp beside the golden door!"

EMMA LAZARUS.

MY patriotism lives and flutters as a sentiment unless I know that the land I love is really making, by its constant life, a contribution to the righteousness and progress of the world. When I know that, then I set my patriotic impulse free to act. My land becomes to me merely the special spot where I am placed to labor for the universal spiritual benefit of man. Then the old Psalmist's words become real to me ; and as I live my life of citizen or public officer, as I take my office or cast my vote or pay my tax, I say with David, "Because of the house of the Lord our God, I will seek to do thee good." Such was the perpetual, self-limited character of the love of Jesus for His native land.

INFLUENCE, 133

YOU remember, perhaps, in Tennyson's "Enoch Arden" how, when Enoch has made his resolution and deliberately determined that he will not claim the home to which he has a right, and has settled down to his solitary life, these lines describe his condition :

> " He was not all unhappy. His resolve
> Upbore him, and firm faith, and evermore
> Prayer from a living source within the will,
> And beating up thro' all the bitter world,
> Like fountains of sweet water in the sea,
> Kept him a living soul."

What are such words as these but an echo of the strong words of Jesus, which declared that if a man lost his life for the highest purposes, " for my sake and the gospel's," he should find it. Indeed there are various half-mystic words of Christ which explain and illuminate this truth, of which our own experience bears witness, that when a man voluntarily surrenders that which is legitimately his for some sublimer claim, he does not really lose it; its spiritual essence, its precious soul, remains with him, and is still his. . . . Shall we not think that Christ spoke all His deep words out of His own experience ? He himself had known what it was to gain the life He lost, to have the thing that He surrendered. When He gave up the home of the foxes and the birds, it was to find a home all the more deeply in His Father's love.

III. 238-240.

Finally, brethren, whatsoever things are true, whatsoever things are honest, whatsoever things are just, whatsoever things are pure, whatsoever things are lovely, whatsoever things are of good report; if there be any virtue and if there be any praise, think on these things. — PHIL. iv. 8.

SOME people seem to be here in the world just on their guard all the while, always so afraid of doing wrong that they never do anything really right. They do not add to the world's moral force; as the man, who, by constant watchfulness over his own health, just keeps himself from dying, contributes nothing to the world's vitality. All merely negative purity has something of the taint of the impurity that it resists. The effort not to be frivolous is frivolous itself. The effort not to be selfish is very apt to be only another form of selfishness.

I. 183, 184.

Is it then true that none of us can keep himself unspotted from the world unless his life be full of reverence for God and trust in Christ and tender pity for his fellow-men? What is that but to say, that " Except a man be born again he cannot enter into the kingdom of God " ? Oh, what poor makeshifts all our laws and decencies and proprieties appear beside the live power of the new manhood of grace. Oh, how hard and hopeless seems the prudent, watchful, timid man, who is trying to save himself by constant self-denials, beside the new freeman of the Lord Jesus Christ, full of the high ambitions and sure hopes of the heavenly life.

I. 191.

PUT your hand in Christ's, that as He leads you other men, who have turned away from Him, may look and see you walking with Him, learn to love Him through your love. I do not believe any man ever yet genuinely, humbly, thoroughly gave himself to Christ without some other finding Christ through him. I wish it might tempt some of your souls to the higher life. I hope it may. At least I am sure that it may add a new sweetness and nobleness to the consecration which some young heart is making of itself to-day, if it can hear, down the new path on which it is entering, not merely the great triumphant chant of personal salvation, " unto Him that loved us and washed us from our sins be glory and dominion ; " but also the calmer, deeper thanksgiving for usefulness, " Blessed be the God of comfort, who comforteth us that we may be able to comfort them that are in tribulation."

I. 16, 17.

If there be some weaker one,
Give me strength to help him on ;
If a blinder soul there be,
Let me guide him nearer Thee.
Make my mortal dreams come true
With the work I fain would do ;
Clothe with life the weak intent,
Let me be the thing I meant ;
Let me find in thy employ
Peace that dearer is than joy ;
Out of self to love be led
And to heaven acclimated,
Until all things sweet and good
Seem my natural habitude.   WHITTIER

THINK what the study of nature might become, if, keeping every accurate and careful method of investigation of the way in which the universe is governed and arranged, it yet was always hearing, always rejoicing to hear, behind all methods and governments and machineries, the sacred movement of the personal will and nature which is the soul of all. Whether we call such hearing science or poetry, it matters not. If we call it poetry, we are only asserting the poetic issue of all science. If we call it science, we are only declaring that poetry is not fiction but the completest truth. The two unite in religion, which, when it has its full chance to do all its work, shall bring poetry and science together in the presence of a recognized God, whom the student then shall not shrink from, but delight to know, and find in Him the illumination and the harmony of all his knowledge.

V. 79, 80.

But we, fraile wights ! whose sight cannot sustaine
The sun's bright beames when he on us doth shyne,
But that their points rebutted back againe
Are duld, how can we see with feeble eyne
The glory of that Majestie Divine
In sight of whom both Sun and Moone are dark
Comparèd to His least resplendent sparke.
The meanes, therefore, which unto us is lent
Him to behold, is on his workes to looke
Which He hath made in beauty excellent
And in the same as in a brasen book
To reade enregistred in every nooke
His goodnesse, which his beautie doth declare,
For all that's good is beautiful and fair.

SPENSER.

THE unconscious needs of the world are all appeals and cries to God. He does not wait to hear the voice of conscious want. The mere vacancy is a begging after fulness; the mere poverty is a supplication for wealth; the mere darkness cries for light. Think then a moment of God's infinite view of the capacities of His universe, and consider what a great cry must be forever going up into His ears to which His soul longs and endeavors to respond. . . . "He first loved us!" Our hope is in the ear which God has for simple need; so that mere emptiness cries out to Him for filling, mere poverty for wealth.

II. 95, 96.

If there had anywhere appeared in space
  Another place of refuge, where to flee,
Our hearts had taken refuge in that place,
  And not with Thee.

For we against creation's bars had beat
  Like prisoned eagles, through great worlds had sought
Though but a foot of ground to plant our feet,
  Where Thou wert not.

And only when we found in earth and air,
  In heaven or hell that such might nowhere be —
That we could not flee from Thee anywhere,
  We fled to Thee.

R. C. TRENCH.

*God, who at sundry times and in diverse man-
ners spake in time past unto the fathers by the
prophets, hath in these last days spoken to us by
His Son.*—HEB. i. 1, 2.

NO one can read the Gospel of St. John and
then turn to what is left us of the life
of Socrates, without being struck and almost
startled with the suggested comparison between
the account of Christ's last talk with His disciples before His crucifixion, which is given in five
chapters of that Gospel, and the beautiful story
of what Socrates said to Simmias and Cebes
and his other friends in the prison at Athens
just before he drank the hemlock,—the story
which Plato has written for us in the Phædo.
And nowhere could the essential difference as
well as the likeness of the two great teachers
become more apparent. . . . I can almost dream
what Socrates would say to any man who said
there was no difference between Jesus and him.
But how shall we state the difference? One is
divine and human; the other is human only.
One is Redeemer; the other is philosopher.
One is inspired, and the other questions. One
reveals, and the other argues. These statements, doubtless, are all true. And in them all
there is wrapped up this, which is the truth of
all the influence of Jesus over men's minds,
that where Socrates brings an argument to meet
an objection, Jesus always brings a nature to
meet a nature,—a whole being which the truth
has filled with strength, to meet another whole
being which error has filled with feebleness.

INFLUENCE, 235, 245.

[Ye] are built upon the foundation of the apostles and prophets, Jesus Christ Himself being the chief corner-stone; in whom all the building fitly framed together groweth up into an holy temple in the Lord.

EPH. ii. 20, 21.

THERE are the multitudes who go in and out, who count the church as theirs, who gather from her thought, knowledge, the comfort of good company, the sense of safety; and then there are others who think they truly, as the light phrase so deeply means, "belong to the church." They are given to it, and no compulsion could separate them from it. They are part of its structure. They are its pillars. Here and hereafter they can never go out of it. Life would mean nothing to them outside the church of Christ.

II. 68, 69.

Behold, O Lord, how thy faithful Jerusalem rejoices in the triumph of the Cross and the power of the Saviour; grant, therefore, that those who love her may abide in her peace, and those who depart from her may one day come back to her embrace; that when all sorrows are taken away, we may be refreshed with the joys of an eternal resurrection, and be made partakers of her peace, through Thy mercy, O our God, Who art blessed, and dost live, and govern all things, world without end.

ANCIENT COLLECTS, BRIGHT.

THERE is some duty which God has made
ready for you to do to-morrow; nay, to-
day! He has built it like a house for you to
occupy. You have not to build it. He has
built it, and He will lead you up to its door
and set you with your feet upon its threshold.
Will you go in and occupy it? Will you do
the duty which He has made ready? Perhaps
it is the great comprehensive duty of the consecration of yourself to Him. Perhaps it is
some special task. Whatever it is, may He
who anticipated your love by His own in giving you the task, now help you to fulfil His
love with yours by doing it. Amen.   v. 56.

If to-day you are not ready,
Will you be to-morrow?
And to-morrow is a day you must not count on;
How do you know that you will have the morrow for
    your own?

    .   .   .   .

Lord,
  All is Thine
In heaven and earth.
I long to give myself to Thee, a free-will offering,
And be forever Thine.
Lord, in my simple heart I give myself to-day to be
    Thy servant ever,
To listen unto Thee, and be a sacrifice of everlasting
    praise.
                         THOMAS À KEMPIS.

When to the sessions of sweet silent thought
I summon up remembrance of things past,
I sigh the lack of many a thing I sought,
And with old woes new wail my dear time's waste:
Then can I drown an eye, unused to flow,
For precious friends hid in death's dateless night,
And weep afresh love's long since cancell'd woe,
And moan the expense of many a vanish'd sight:
Then can I grieve at grievances foregone,
And heavily from woe to woe tell o'er
The sad account of fore-bemoaned moan,
Which I new pay as if not paid before.
　　But if the while I think on thee, dear friend,
　　All losses are restored and sorrows end.

SHAKESPEARE.

SURELY there is no more beautiful sight to see in all this world, — full as it is of beautiful adjustments and mutual ministrations, — than the growth of two friends' natures who, as they grow old together, are always fathoming, with newer needs, deeper depths of each other's life, and opening richer veins of one another's helpfulness. And this best culture of personal friendship is taken up and made, in its infinite completion, the gospel method of the progressive saving of the soul by Christ.

II. 54.

How many loaves have ye? — MATT. xv. 34.

IT is the completeness of the nature of Jesus, the way in which it is all one, and works and lives as one, that makes Him often so very different from us. Our lives are disjointed. One part of us works at a time. It is hard for us to be brave and prudent together ; hard for us to be liberal and just at the same time. . . .

Now in this miracle of Jesus which I have recalled to you there is a meeting of generosity and frugality which is striking and suggestive. These two things do meet indeed with us. We try to be generous and frugal at the same time, but the result in us is mean. We try to give and yet to save. We try to satisfy the instinct which makes us want to aid our brethren, and at the same time not to disappoint the instinct which makes us want to save and spare the things we have. But the result in us is mean. When Christ unites generosity and frugality the result in Him is noble. We feel His pity and care for the poor people a great deal more when we see Him take the wretched little stock of food which they possessed into His hands and make that the basis of His bounty, than if with an easy sweep of His hand He had bid the skies open and rain manna and quails once more upon the hungry host. His generosity is emphasized for us by its frugal methods, and His frugality is dignified by its generous purpose.　　　II. 128, 129.

A MAN comes up to our life, and looking round upon the crowd of our fellow-men, he says, "See, I will strike the life of this brother of ours and you shall hear how true it rings." He does strike it, and it does seem to them to ring true, and they shout their applause; but we whose life is struck feel running all through us at the stroke the sense of hollowness. Our soul sinks as we hear the praises. They start desire but they reveal weakness. No true man is ever so humble and so afraid of himself as when other men are praising him most loudly.

1. 254.

Or what if Heaven for once its searching light
   Lent to some partial eye, disclosing all
The rude bad thoughts that in our bosom's night
   Wander at large, nor heed Love's gentle thrall?

  .   .   .   .

Thou know'st our bitterness — our joys are Thine;
   No stranger Thou to all our wanderings wild:
Nor could we bear to think how every line
   Of us, Thy darkened likeness and defiled,

Stands in full sunshine of Thy piercing eye,
   But that Thou call'st us Brethren: sweet repose
Is in that word! the Lord who dwells on high
   Knows all, yet loves us better than He knows.

JOHN KEBLE.

THIS church of all the saints is a great power in the world. Every true servant of God must belong with this mighty service of God; must get his strength through it, and contribute his strength into it. Ever from out the past, from the old saints who lived in other times, from Enoch, David, Paul, and John, Augustine, Jerome, Luther, Leighton, there comes down the power of God to us. Because they were full of it, we, by association with them, grow fuller of it than we could be by ourselves. . . . Our faith mounts up with their exultant prayers. Our weak devotion, tired and drooping, rests against the strong pillars of their certain trust. Their quick sight teaches our half-opened eyes the way to look toward the light that shall unseal them wholly.

I. 123.

I think of the saints I have known, and lift up mine
    eyes
To the far away home of beautiful Paradise,
Where the song of saints gives voice to an undividing
    sea
On whose plain their feet stand firm while they keep
    their jubilee.
As the sound of waters their voice, as the sound of thun-
    derings,
While they all at once rejoice, while all sing and while
    each one sings;
Where more saints flock in, and more, and yet more,
    and again yet more,
And not one turns back to depart thro' the open en-
    trance door.
O sights of our lovely earth, O sound of our earthly
    sea,
Speak to me of Paradise, of all blessed saints to me;
Or keep silence touching them, and speak to my heart
    alone
Of the Saint of saints, the King of kings, the Lamb on
    the Throne.

CHRISTINA ROSSETTI.

THE child [Jesus] clasped His tiny arms about
His mother's neck, or laid His little hand
into the strong hand of Joseph, as they walked
on the long road to Egypt, with the same simple desire to utter love and to find love which is
the first sign of Life akin to their own that millions of parents' hearts have leaped to recognize
in their first-born. Nay, he but little understands
the dignity and unity of all God's vast creation
who is offended or distressed when he is told that
in the Lord of Life these primal affections were of
the same sort with those which make the beauty
of the life of the beings which are less than man.
Even the dog, the bird, the lion, know these
first instincts of companionship which found their
consummate exhibition upon earth when the Son
of Mary clung to a human mother with a human
love.

INFLUENCE, 79, 80.

. . . Whate'er be the fate that has hurt us or joyed,
Whatever the face that is turned to us out of the void ;
Be it cursing or blessing ; or night, or the light of the
    sun ;
Be it ill, be it good ; be it life, be it death, it is One ; —

One thought, and one law, and one awful and infinite
    power ;
In atom and world ; in the bursting of fruit and of
    flower ;
The laughter of children, and the roar of the lion un-
    tamed ;
And the stars in their courses — one name that can
    never be named.

RICHARD WATSON GILDER.

Phillips Brooks ordained Deacon, 1859.

He preached Christ . . . that He is the Son of God. — ACTS xx. 20.

ONLY he who consents to enlarge his own conception of the possibilities of faith with God's can calmly watch the everlasting growth of revelation, see the old open into the new, and yet know that the truth of Christ is the truth of eternity, and that when the soul of God claimed the soul of man in the Incarnation, it took possession of it forever ; and so Christian faith can never die. There have been no nobler servants of God and of humanity than they whose special mission it has been to teach this truth to men. . . .

To discriminate between the eternal substance of Christianity and its temporary forms, to bid men see how often forms had perished and the substance still survived, to make men know the danger of imperfect and false tests of faith, to encourage them to be not merely resigned but glad as they beheld the one faith ever casting its old forms away, and by its undying vitality creating for itself new — this was the noble work which Dean Stanley did for multitudes of grateful souls all over Christendom. He led countless hearts out of the surprise and fear of their own day into the unsurprised and fearless peace of faith in God. Thus it was that he opened wide the great gates of the Divine Life, and made the way more clear for the children to their Father.

III. 81, 82.

LOVING obedience, loving obedience is the only atmosphere in which the vision of the general purpose and the faithfulness in special work grow in their true proportion and relation to each other. The distant hills with the glory on their summits, and the close meadow where the grass waits for the scythe, — they meet completely in the broad kingdom of a loved and obeyed Lord. And who is Lord but Christ ? And where but in the soul of him who finds in Christ the worthy revealer of the life's purpose and the sufficient master of every deed shall the great ideals of life and the petty details of life come harmoniously together ? Obey Him, love Him, and nothing is too great, nothing is too little ; for love knows no struggle of great or little. No impulse is too splendid for the simplest task ; no task is too simple for the most splendid impulse.

V. 119, 120.

> I love thy men and women, Lord,
>   The children round thy door ;
> Calm thoughts that inward strength afford —
>   Thy will, O Lord, is more.
>
> But when thy will my life shall hold,
>   Thine to the very core,
> The world which that same will did mould,
>   I shall love ten times more.

GEORGE MACDONALD.

WHILE the union of duty and joy is natural it is not essential and unbreakable.
The plant ought to come to flower, but if the
plant fails of its flower it is still a plant.   The
duty should open into joy, but it may fail of
joy and still be duty.   If the joy is not there,
still hold the duty, and be sure that you have
the real thing while you are holding that.   Be
all the more dutiful, though it be in the dark.
Do righteousness and forget happiness, and so
it is most likely that happiness will come.

I. 29.

Do only Thou, in that dim shrine,
Unknown or known, remain, divine;
There, or if not, at least in eyes
That scan the fact that round them lies,
The hand to sway, the judgment guide,
In sight and sense, Thyself divide:
Be Thou but there, — in soul and heart,
I will not ask to feel Thou art.

ARTHUR HUGH CLOUGH.

Land of the willful gospel, thou worst and thou best;
Tall Adam of lands, new-made of the dust of the West;
Thou wroughtest alone in the Garden of God, unblest
Till He fashioned lithe Freedom to lie for thine Eve on
    thy breast.

.   .   .   .

Knowledge of Good and of Ill, O Land, she hath given
    thee;
Perilous godhoods of choosing have rent thee and riven
    thee;
Will's high adoring to Ill's low exploring hath driven
    thee—
Freedom, thy Wife, hath uplifted thy life and clean
    shriven thee.

SIDNEY LANIER.

ON my country's birthday . . . I may ask
    you for your prayer in her behalf.   That
on the manifold and wondrous chance which
God is giving her,—on her freedom (for she is
free, since the old stain of slavery was washed
out in blood); on her unconstrained religious
life; on her passion for education, and her
eager search for truth; on her jealous care for
the poor man's rights and opportunities; on
her countless quiet homes where the future
generations of her men are growing; on her
manufactures and her commerce; on her wide
gates open to the east and to the west; on her
strange meetings of the races out of which a
new race is slowly being born; on her vast
enterprise and her illimitable hopefulness,—
on all these materials and machineries of manhood, on all that the life of my country must
mean for humanity, I may ask you to pray
that the blessing of God the Father of man,
and Christ the Son of man, may rest forever.

II. 21.

I am not come to destroy, but to fulfil.

MATT. v. 17.

TEAR your sins away.   Starve your tumultuous passions.   Resist temptations.   Aye, if you will, punish yourself with stripes for your iniquities.   Cry out to yourself and to your brethren, with every voice that you can raise, "Cease to do evil;" but all the time, down below, as the deepest cry of your life, let there be this other, "Learn to do well."   If you can indeed grow vigorously brave and true and pure, then cowardice and falsehood and licentiousness must perish in you.   O wondrous silent slaughter of our enemies!   O wondrous casting out of fear as love grows perfect!   O death to sin, which comes by the new birth to righteousness!   O destruction, which is but the utterance of fulfilment on the other side!   O everlasting assurance, that evil has of right no place in the world: and that if good would only lift itself up to its completeness, it might claim the whole world and all of manhood for itself !

IV. 218, 219.

Into the woods my Master went,
Clean forspent, forspent.
Into the woods my Master came,
Forspent with love and shame.
But the olives they were not blind to Him,
The little gray leaves were kind to Him :
The thorn-tree had a mind to Him
When into the woods He came.

Out of the woods my Master went,
And He was well content.
Out of the woods my Master came,
Content with death and shame.
When Death and Shame would woo Him last,
From under the trees they drew Him last :
'Twas on a tree they slew Him — last
When out of the woods He came.

Sidney Lanier.

IN the garden of Gethsemane reason seemed to totter on her throne. For the last time the desperate hands had to cling to the truth in instant fear. But there, too, it is not by the direct conviction of the reason; it is by the adjustment of the whole life in obedience — to which, no doubt, the reason gave its assent, but which was a transaction far beyond the reason's limits — that the trembling reason finds composure. When He said, " Thy will be done," all the obscurity began to scatter, and those words which He said four days later, after He had risen, to His disciples, " Ought not Christ to have suffered these things ? " . . . words full of the peace of satisfied intelligence, — began to take shape upon His lips. Influence, 230.

SOME of you may remember how our New England poets' poet sings to the farmer over whose fields he has been wandering :

> " One harvest from thy field
>   Homeward brought the oxen strong ;
> A second crop thine acres yield,
>   Which I gather in a song."

This is what makes the everlasting interest of nature ; her capacity of endless association with man, from whom all real interest in the world must radiate, and to whom it always must return.   As Emerson sings again of those whom he had loved, and who made the landscape in the midst of which he had loved them for ever dear :

> " They took this valley for their toy,
>   They played with it in every mood :
> A cell for prayer, a hall for joy --
>   They treated nature as they would.

> " They coloured the horizon round ;
>   Stars flamed and faded as they bade ;
> All echoes hearkened for their sound, —
>   They made the woodlands glad or mad."

" They treated nature as they would."   So all men, all races, treat nature according to their wills, whether their wills be the deep utterances of their characters or only the light and fickle impulses of self-indulgence.   And what they are to nature, nature is to them — to one man the siren, who fascinates him to drunkenness and death ; to another, the wise friend, who teaches him all lessons of self-restraint and sobriety and patient hope and work.   III. 270, 272.

Years of the modern! years of the unperform'd!
Your horizon rises, I see it parting away for more au-
    gust dramas,
I see not America only, not only Liberty's nation, but
    other nations preparing,
I see tremendous entrances and exits, new combina-
    tions, the solidarity of races,
I see that force advancing with irresistible power on
    the world's stage.

.   .   .   .

Your dreams, O years, how they penetrate through me!
    (I know not whether I sleep or wake:)
The perform'd America and Europe grow dim, retiring
    in shadow behind me,
The unperform'd, more gigantic than ever, advance,
    advance upon me.

WALT WHITMAN.

WE must never lose out of our sight the vision, never lose out of our ears the music
of the real Church and the real world struggling each into perfection for itself, and so both
into unity and identity with one another.

Very interesting have been in history the
pulsations, the brightening and fading, the coming and going of this great truth of the Church
and the world ideally identical. That truth is
always present in the words of Jesus. . . .
The ideal Church, which was the real Church
in his eyes, knew no limit but humanity. . . .
The relation of the Church to the active world,
the conflict and the possible harmony between
them, the message of the Church to the world,
the turning of the world into the Church, these
are the problems and the visions which are
more and more occupying the minds of thoughtful vision-seeing men.

IV. 52, 53, 54.

"OBEYING Christ," we say; and what is Christ? I think over all that I know of Him, and this is what He is: first, He is the utterance of the eternal righteousness, the setting forth before men of that supreme nature in which there is the source and pattern of all goodness, — God; second, He is a man of clear, sharp, definite character, who lived a life in Palestine which still shines with a distinctness that no other human life can rival; third, by His spirit He is a perpetual presence, a constant standard and inspiration in the heart of every man who loves and trusts Him. All those things come up to me when I say "Christ." And now can such a Christ speak to me? . . .

There is some act that you are questioning, about to-morrow or to-day. If Jesus were at hand, you would go out and ask Him, "Is it Thy will that I should do it, oh, my Lord?" Can you not ask Him now? Is the act right? Would He do it? Will it help your soul? . . . And if the answer to them all is "yes!" then it is just as truly His command that you should do that act as if His gracious figure stood before your sight and His finger visibly pointed to the task.   V. 355, 356.

And the Christ who came of old to His own
    As truly comes to them now,
Where the faithful before His altar throne
    With hearts believing bow, —
EMMANUEL, then and now.

                        HARIET MCEWEN KIMBALL.

NOT merely to make men love you and honor you, but to know how to be loved and honored without losing yourself and growing weak, — that is the problem of many of the sweetest, richest, most attractive lives. . . .

If the much-beloved man can look up and demand the love of God ; if, catching sight of that, he can crave it and covet it infinitely above all other love ; if, laying hold of its great freedom, he can make it his, and know that he loves God, and know that God loves him, — then he is free.   Then let him come back and take into a glowing heart the warmest admiration and affection of his brethren ; let him walk the earth with hosts of friends, the heaven that he carries in his heart preserves him.   They cannot make him conceited, for he who lives with God must be humble.   They cannot drown his selfhood, for the God he loves and serves is always laying upon him his own personal duties, and bringing the soul before its own judgment-seat every day.

V. 154.

To pass through life beloved as few are loved,
To prove the joys of earth as few have proved,
And still to keep the soul's white robe unstained,
Such is the victory thou hast gained.

.   .   .   .

And Love, that guards where wintry tempests beat,
To thee was shelter from the summer heat.
What need for grief to blight or cares annoy
The heart whose God was her exceeding joy?

ELIZA SCUDDER.

THE same light which showed you the heaven that you were made for has always showed you the rock that you were chained to; as the same word of Jesus which showed the young nobleman the treasures in heaven brought back before his mind the treasures on earth from which he could not tear himself away. This makes the sacredness and awfulness of life when we come to know it, that we are never so near our highest as when we are most sensible of the danger of our lowest, and the danger of the lowest is never so real to us as when the splendor of the highest stands wide open.

I. 344.

O Lord, how wonderful in depth and height,
But most in man, how wonderful Thou art!
With what a love, what soft persuasive might
Victorious o'er the stubborn fleshly heart,
Thy tale complete of saints Thou dost provide,
To fill the thrones which angels lost through pride!

.   .   .   .

O what a shifting parti-colored scene
Of hope and fear, of triumph and dismay,
Of recklessness and penitence, has been
The history of that dreary, lifelong fray!
And O the grace to nerve him and to lead,
How patient, prompt, and lavish at his need!

JOHN HENRY NEWMAN.

Aaron said, Thou knowest the people, that they are set on mischief. For they said unto me, Make us gods, which shall go before us. . . . And I said unto them, Whosoever hath any gold, let them break it off. So they gave it me: then I cast it into the fire and there came out this calf.

Ex. xxxii. 22, 23, 24.

THE father says of his profligate son whom he has never done one wise or vigorous thing to make a noble and pure-minded man: "I cannot tell how it has come. It has not been my fault. I put him into the world and this came out." The father whose faith has been mean and selfish says the same of his boy who is a sceptic. Everywhere there is this cowardly casting off of responsibilities upon the dead circumstances around us. It is a very hard treatment of the poor, dumb, helpless world which cannot answer to defend itself. It takes us as we give ourselves to it. It is our minister fulfilling our commissions for us upon our own souls. If we say to it, "Make us noble," it does make us noble. If we say to it, "Make us mean," it does make us mean. And then we take the nobility and say, "Behold, how noble I have made myself." And we take the meanness and say, "See how mean the world has made me."

III. 48. 49.

ALL the separation from sin, all the self-sacrifice by which alone you could preserve your own purity and help your brethren, has been in you the renewal, the echo, of that terrible giving of Himself for truth and man which Christ accomplished. But if, as you have sacrificed yourself in any way, there has come into you the rich divine assurance of God's love, the deep and peaceful joy in obeying God, and far bright hopes for your humanity, broken but glorious prospects of what an obedience, perfect where yours is stumbling, complete where yours is partial, shall some day make this world to be ; if all this has come to you upon your cross, as it came to the Lord on His, then the glory as well as the grief of the crucifixion is renewed in you, and the satisfaction as well as the pain of your new life is uttered when you say, in soft and solemn words, " I, too, am crucified with Christ."

I. 207.

But if, impatient, thou let slip thy cross,
Thou wilt not find it in this world again,
Nor in another ; here, and here alone
Is given thee to *suffer* for God's sake.
In other worlds we shall more perfectly
Serve Him and love Him, praise Him, work for Him,
Grow near and nearer Him with all delight ;
But then we shall not any more be called
To suffer, which is our appointment here.

  .   .   .   .

And while we suffer, let us set our souls
To suffer perfectly : since this alone,
The suffering, which is this world's special grace,
May here be perfected and left behind.

UGO BASSI'S SERMON IN THE HOSPITAL.

Plainness and clearness without shadow of stain !
Clearness divine !
Ye heavens, whose pure dark regions have no sign
Of languor, though so calm, and though so great
Are yet untroubled and unpassionate !
Who, though so noble, share in the world's toil,
And, though so task'd, keep free from dust and soil !
I will not say that your mild deeps retain
A tinge, it may be, of their silent pain
Who have long'd deeply once, and long'd in vain ;
But I will rather say that you remain
A world above man's head, to let him see
How boundless might his soul's horizons be,
How vast, yet of what clear transparency !
How it were good to live there, and breathe free !
How fair a lot to fill
Is left to each man still !

Matthew Arnold.

WE have all taken a sorrow or a perplexity out into the noontide or the midnight and felt its morbid bitterness drawn out of it, and a great peace descend and fill it from the depth of the majesty under whose arch we stood. . . . The sweet and solemn influence which comes to you out of the noontide or the midnight sky does not take away your pain, but it takes out of it its bitterness. It lifts it to a higher peace. It says, "Be still and wait." It gives the reason power and leave and time to work. It gathers the partial into the embrace of the universal.

V. 235.

IT is not as the present possessor of all truth that (the church) invites men to her household. She must not claim that. Men will discover that her claim is false if she does. But it is as the possessor of truth out of which God will call, nay is forever calling new truth, that she summons men not merely to a present which she offers, but to a future in which she believes. The church is progressive by her very essence. The church is man occupied by Christ. And since Christ cannot at once occupy man completely, and cannot be satisfied until He has occupied man completely, the church must make progress. If she ceases to advance she dies. Only in all her progress she believes in the continuity and economy of God. She looks for the truth which she is to know to come out of the truth which she knows already ; and she is sure that no duty done or light attained in any most obscure corner of her life is wasted, but helps to the perfect duty and the perfect light that are to be. That is why in her is the true home for the man who most hopes and prays for the progress of mankind.

II. 137.

Past and Future are the wings
On whose support harmoniously conjoined
Moves the great spirit of human knowledge.
WORDSWORTH.

WHO of us has not bowed his will to some supreme law, accepted some obedience as the atmosphere in which his life must live, and found at once that his mind's darkness turned to light, and that many a hard question found its answer? Who has not sometimes seemed to see it all as clear as daylight, that not by the sharpening of the intellect to supernatural acuteness, but by the submission of the nature to its true authority, man was at last to conquer truth; that not by agonizing struggles over contradictory evidence, but by the harmony with Him in whom the answers to all our doubts are folded, a harmony with Him brought by obedience to Him, our doubts must be enlightened? INFLUENCE, 231.

O Thou who makest both light and darkness,
Thine is also the light invisible, the revelation of God
     to our souls.
God is the Eternal, who shows us light; bind the sacri-
     fice of our hearts, with the cords of good-will.
If we have lost Thee, O Lord, show Thyself to us again!
     let us seek Thee chiefly in well-doing.
O Thou that alone makest all contradictions clear, in
     Thy light let us see light.
Illuminate our minds with practice of humility, and
     confirm them with growth of faith.
Make our thoughts the lively echoes of Thy command-
     ments; and take our hearts for Thy kingdom.
BOOK OF LITANIES. ROWLAND WILLIAMS.

MAN is made so that some sense of criticalness is necessary to the most vigorous
and best life always.   Let me feel that nothing but this moment depends upon this moment's action, and I am very apt to let this
moment act pretty much as it will.   Let me
see the spirits of the moments yet unborn
standing and watching it anxiously and I must
watch it also for their sakes.   I. 327, 328.

Daughters of Time, the hypocritic Days,
Muffled and dumb like barefoot dervishes,
And marching single in an endless file,
Bring diadems and fagots in their hands.
To each they offer gifts after his will,
Bread, kingdoms, stars, and sky that holds them all.
I, in my pleachéd garden, watched the pomp,
Forgot my morning wishes, hastily
Took a few herbs and apples, and the Day
Turned and departed silent.   I, too late,
Under her solemn fillet saw the scorn.

EMERSON.

TO open the eyes and find a Christ beside us, — not to go long journeys to discover a Christ with whom before we have had nothing to do, — this is the Christian conversion. . . . How did the Saviour first prove Himself to you? Was it not by the past which suddenly or gradually became full of Him, so that you recognized that He had been busy on you when you did not know it, that He had been leading you when you thought you had been wandering, so that you saw your past thoughts grow luminous as His inspirations, your past dreams as the contagions of His presence and the prophecies of His touch? Was not this His answer when you called Him? Not, "I am coming," away off in the distance, but "Here I am," spoken right out of the very soul and centre of your life.

V. 212.

Thou Life within my life, than self more near!
Thou veilèd Presence infinitely clear!
From all illusive shows of sense I flee,
To find my centre and my rest in Thee.

Take part with me against these doubts that rise
And seek to throne Thee far in distant skies!
Take part with me against this self that dares
Assume the burden of these sins and cares!

How shall I call Thee who art always here,
How shall I praise Thee who art still most dear,
What may I give Thee save what Thou hast given,
And whom but Thee have I in earth or heaven?

ELIZA SCUDDER.

And the ransomed of the Lord shall return,
And come to Zion with songs and everlasting joy
  upon their heads :
They shall obtain joy and gladness, — and sorrow
  and sighing shall flee away. — Ps. xxxv. 10.

JOY and pain, so far from being inconsistent with and contradictory to one another, are, in some true sense, each other's compliments, and neither alone, but both together, make the true sum of human life. There is a conceivable world where pure, unclouded joy can come, just as there are countries where the mountains are very lofty and all nature is on so grand a scale that it can bear a pure, unclouded sky, and in its unveiled splendor, perfectly satisfy the eye. But there are other lands whose inferior grandeur needs for its perfect beauty the effects of mist and cloud that give its lower mountains the mystery and poetry which they could not have in themselves. So one may compare the Swiss and the Scotch landscapes. And something of the same sort is true about this world and marks its inferiority, proves that it is not yet the perfect state of being. It needs the pain of life to emphasize its joy. Its joy is not high or perfect enough to do without the emphasis of pain.

II. 30.

ONCE in the hours while He hung there, a cry of desolation, abandonment, and disgrace, burst from the Sufferer's lips. "My God! My God! why hast thou forsaken me?" He cries, making His own the words of an old psalm of woe. When I read what men have written to explain the meaning of Jesus in that cry, I always feel anew how much deeper than our comprehension went his identification with humanity when He plunged into the darkness of its sin. "He was made flesh!" Into what mysterious contact with the sinfulness to which the flesh of man had given itself that being made flesh brought him, I know no man has ever fathomed. . . . Christ, who, in His love, had gone down to the deepest and most terrible depths of humanity, even to being crucified between two thieves, seemed for a moment to have lost himself, and cried out to the Father, with whom He was eternally and inseparably one, "Oh, why hast Thou forsaken Me?" If the cry bewilders as we try to comprehend the deity to which it appeals, it may at least reveal to us something of the depth out of which it ascends.

I. 198, 199, 200.

He who did most shall bear most: the strongest shall
    stand the most weak.
'Tis the weakness in strength that I cry for: my flesh
    that I seek
In the Godhead. I seek and I find it.

BROWNING.

W E cannot attain to all abundance in this one short life which is our only one, but if we can come to God and be His servants, the knowledge of how to be things which we shall never be may enter into us. In poverty we may have the blessing of riches; in enforced ignorance the blessing of knowledge; in loneliness the blessing of friendship; and in suspense and doubt the blessing of peace and rest.

V. 157.

I wept, I prayed
A solemn prayer, conceived in agony,
Blessed with response instant, miraculous;
For in that hour my spirit was at one
With Him who knows and satisfies her needs;
The supplication and the blessing sprang
From the same source, inspired divinely both.
I prayed for light, self-knowledge, guidance, truth,
And these like heavenly manna were rained down
To feed my hungered soul.

.   .   .   .

Here was the lofty truth revealed, that each
Must feel himself in all, must know where'er
The great soul acts or suffers or enjoys,
His proper soul in kinship there is bound,
Then my life-purpose dawned upon my mind,
Encouraging as morning.

EMMA LAZARUS.

Whosoever hath, to him shall be given, and he shall have more abundance. — MATT. xiii. 12.

THIS has been always true, that the new idea has always been born of the old, that when men have advanced to higher truth it has been from the basis of the truth which they have held already. It has been not by flinging their net out into the heavens in hopes to catch a star, but by digging deeper into the substance of the earth on which they stood, and finding there a root. And that is what we have to look for in the future. You and I cling to the old historic statements of our faith. We hold fast by the old historic Church as it appears to-day. What is our feeling as we hold fast there? . . . We stand expecting change and progress, new truth, new light. But we stand here in the historic Church, in the historic truth, because we believe that the new truth must come out of this old truth, the perfect truth out of this partial truth, some day. We keep close to the seven loaves because we believe that when the multitude is fed it will be with an abundance blessed by God out of this, which, however meagre, is still real.

II. 136.

NOT by mere moods, not by how I feel to-day or how I felt yesterday, may I know whether I am indeed living the life of God, but only by knowing that God is using me to help others. No mood is so bright that it can do without that warrant. No mood is so dark that, if it has that, it need despair. It is good for us to think no grace or blessing truly ours till we are aware that God has blessed some one else with it through us.

I. 18

We cannot kindle when we will
   The fire which in the heart resides,
The spirit bloweth and is still,
In mystery our soul abides :
   But tasks in hours of insight will'd
   Can be through hours of gloom fulfill'd.

With aching hands and bleeding feet
   We dig and heap, lay stone on stone ;
We bear the burden and the heat
Of the long day and wish 'twere done.
   Not till the hours of light return
   All we have built do we discern.

MATTHEW ARNOLD.

*Glorify God in your body, and in your spirit,
which are God's. — I. Cor. vi. 20.*

THERE is no true care for the body which
forgets the soul.   There is no true care
for the soul which is not mindful of the body.
The pressure of psychology on physiology, the
wise and learned, also the unwise and ignorant, methods of reaching physical conditions
through the change of mental states which are
so prominent in the medical practice of to-day,
bear witness to the first fact.   All the kind of
teaching which a few years ago went by the
name of muscular Christianity gives testimony
to the second.

. . . The duty of physical health and the
duty of spiritual purity and loftiness are not
two duties ; they are two parts of one duty, —
which is the living of the completest life which
it is possible for man to live.   And the two
parts minister to one another.   Be good that
you may be well ; be well that you may be
good.   Both of those two injunctions are reasonable, and both are binding on us all.

V. 229, 230.

As the bird wings and sings
Let us cry : all good things
Are ours, nor soul helps flesh more now than flesh
helps soul.

BROWNING.

TO how many a saint the day and place where he first heard God's voice will be earth's one sacred memory, even long after earth's life is over. Do you think that Moses will not speak of the bush, and Samuel of the little temple-chamber, and Peter and John of their boats on the still lake, and Paul of the Damascus road, and Matthew of his tax-table, and the poor woman of the wayside well, when they are met above? Only the last day shall tell how much of earth is hallowed ground. . . . It is indeed a goodly spirit that treasures its past miracles, that goes down the gracious avenues of life to find the bushes out of which it first heard God's voice.

II 55, 56.

Magnificent
The morning rose, in memorable pomp,
Glorious as e'er I had beheld, — in front,
The sea lay laughing at a distance; near,
The solid mountains shone, bright as the clouds,
Grain-tinctured, drenched in empyrean light;
And in the meadows and the lower grounds
Was all the sweetness of a common dawn, —
Dews, vapors, and the melody of birds,
And laborers going forth to till the fields.
Ah! need I say, dear Friend! that to the brim
My heart was full? I made no vows, but vows
Were made for me; bond unknown to me
Was given, that I should be, else sinning greatly,
A dedicated Spirit. On I walked
In thankful blessedness, which yet survives.

WORDSWORTH.

WHEN Christ showed us God, then man had only to stand at his highest and look up to the Infinite above him to see how small he was. And, always, the true way to be humble is not to stoop till you are smaller than yourself, but to stand at your real height against some higher nature that shall show you what the real smallness of your greatest greatness is. The first is the unreal humility that always goes about depreciating human nature; the second is the genuine humility that always stands in love and adoration, glorifying God.

I. 340, 341.

I have gone the whole round of Creation: I saw and I
    spoke!
I, a work of God's hand for that purpose, received in
    my brain
And pronounced on the rest of His handwork — returned
    Him again
His creation's approval or censure: I spoke as I saw.
I report, as a man may of God's work — all's love yet
    all's law!

   .   .   .   .

And thus looking within and around me, I ever renew
(With that stoop of the soul which in bending upraises
    it too)
The submission of Man's nothing-perfect to God's All-
    Complete,
As by each new obeisance in spirit, I climb to His feet!

BROWNING.

*O wretched man that I am! who shall deliver
me from the body of this death? I thank God
through Jesus Christ our Lord. The law of the
Spirit of life in Christ Jesus hath made me free
from the law of sin and death.*

ROM. vii. 24, 25 ; viii. 2.

I HAVE no patience with the foolish talk which
would make sin nothing but imperfection,
and would preach that man needs nothing but
to have his deficiencies supplied, to have his
native goodness educated and brought out, in
order to be all that God would have him be.
The horrible incompetency of that doctrine
must be manifest enough to any man who knows
his own heart, or who listens to the tumult of
wickedness which rises up from all the dark
places of the earth.   Sin is a dreadful, positive,
malignant thing.   What the world in its worse
part needs is, not to be developed, but to be destroyed.   Any other talk about it is shallow and
mischievous folly.   The only question is about
the best method and means of destruction.   Let
the sharp surgeon's knife do its terrible work.
Let it cut deep and separate as well and thoroughly as it can, the false from the true, the
corrupt from the uncorrupt : it never can dissect
away the very principle of corruption which is
in the substance of the blood itself.   Nothing
but a new reinforcement of health can accomplish that.

IV. 217, 218.

THE power of mere activity is often over-
rated. It is not what the best men do,
but what they are, that constitutes their truest
benefaction to their fellow-men. The things that
men do get their chief value, after all, from the
way in which they are able to show the existence of character which can comfort and help
mankind. . . . It seems to me that there is reassurance here for many of us who seem to
have no chance for active usefulness. We can
do nothing for our fellow-men. But still it is
good to know that we can be something for
them ; to know (and this we may know surely)
that no man or woman of the humblest sort
can really be strong, gentle, pure, and good,
without the world being better for it, without
somebody being helped and comforted by the
very existence of that goodness.   I. 105.

Our destiny, our being's heart and home,
Is with infinitude, and only there ;
With hope it is, hope that can never die,
Effort, and expectation, and desire,
And something evermore about to be.
Under such banners militant the soul
Seeks for no trophies, struggles for no spoils
That may attest her prowess, blest in thoughts
That are their own perfection and reward,
Strong in herself and in beatitude
That hides her, like the mighty flood of Nile
Poured from his fount of Abyssinian clouds
To fertilize the whole Egyptian plain.
WORDSWORTH.

And He said, Whereunto shall we liken the kingdom of God? or with what comparison shall we compare it?

It is like a grain of mustard seed, which when it is sown in the earth, is less than all the seeds that be in the earth:

*But when it is sown, it groweth up, and becometh greater than all herbs, and shooteth out great branches; so that the fowls of the air may lodge under the shadow of it.—*MARK iv. 30–32.

OH, wondrous tree, whose seed came surely from the hand of God, whose growth has never passed out of His watchful care, which He has set here in this rich, wayward, tumultuous soil of human life, how hast thou wrestled for existence with this bounteous yet reluctant ground, how hast thou sent thy roots into the pierced heart of man's affections! Through what dark stormy nights hast thou struggled with the winds, and grown strong in wrestling! How hast thou drawn up into thyself what is eternal and spiritual in man and made it claim its kinship to divinity! Oh, wondrous tree! oh, Christian faith! oh, Christian Church! so small, so strong! what would the world be without thee? What wouldst thou be without the world? Grow on till in thy life the perfect union of the earth and heaven, of God and man, shall be complete!

V. 278.

THERE is as yet no culture, no method of progress known to men, that is so rich and complete as that which is ministered by a truly great friendship. No natural appetite, no artificial taste, no rivalry of competition, no contagion of social activity, calls out such a large, healthy, symmetrical working of a human nature, as the constant, half-unconscious power of a friend's presence whom we thoroughly respect and love. In a true friendship there is emulation without its jealousy; there is imitation without its servility. When one friend teaches another by his present life, there is none of that divorce of truth from feeling, and of feeling from truth, which in so many of the world's teachings makes truth hard, and feeling weak; but truth is taught, and feeling is inspired, by the same action of one nature on the other, and they keep each other true and warm.

II. 54.

My careful heart was free again,
O friend, my bosom said,
Through thee alone the sky is arched,
Through thee the rose is red;
All things through thee take nobler form,
And look beyond the earth,
The mill-round of our fate appears
A sun-path in thy worth.
Me too thy nobleness has taught
To master my despair;
The fountains of my hidden life
Are through thy friendship fair.

EMERSON.

"HE who does not lose his reason in certain things," says Lessing, "has none to lose." But the reason is lost, not by any palsy or death that falls on it, but by the vehement life of will and affections, among which the life of the reason takes its true place as but one member of the perfect whole.

There is a noble passage of Wordsworth which tells this same story, and shows how under the greatest influences of nature the same rich blending of the life takes place. He is describing the consecrating effects of early dawn :

" What soul was his when from the naked top
  Of some bold headland he beheld the sun
  Rise up and bathe the world in light. He looked —
  Ocean and earth, the solid frame of earth
  And ocean's liquid mass, beneath him lay
  In gladness and deep joy. The clouds were touched
  And in their silent faces did he read
  Unutterable love. Sound needed not
  Nor any voice of joy ; his spirit drank
  The spectacle ; sensation, soul, and form
  All melted into him. They swallowed up
  His animal being ; in them did he live
  And by them did he live. They were his life.
  In such access of mind, in such high hour
  Of visitation from the Living God,
  Thought was not ; in enjoyment it expired.
  No thanks he breathed, he proffered no request ;
  Rapt into still communion that transcends
  The imperfect offices of prayer and praise,
  His mind was a thanksgiving to the Power
  That made him ; it was blessedness and love ! "

INFLUENCE, 225, 230.

*The mountains shall bring peace to the people,
and the little hills, by righteousness.* — Ps. lxxii. 3.

CHRIST set men close to God, to their true selves, to the souls of their brethren, to the immensity of duty ; and He said to them there, what there they understood, " Be humble ! "

It was as if He took a proud, fretful man out of the worrying life of the selfish city and set him among the solemn mountains, and the mountains brought to him the blessed peace of humility and the sense of his own insignificance.

I. 351.

RETURN TO THE HILLS.

Ah ! with boldness of lovers who wed
  I make haste to your feet,
And as constant as lovers who die,
  My surrender repeat ;
And I take as the right of my love,
  And I keep as its sign,
An ineffable joy in each sense
  And new strength as from wine,
A seal for all purpose and hope,
  And a pledge of full light,
Like a pillar of cloud for my day,
  And of fire for my night.

HELEN HUNT JACKSON.

Him that overcometh will I make a pillar in the temple of my God: and he shall go no more out.
REV. iii. 12.

SLOWLY, through all the universe, that temple of God is being built. Wherever, in any world, a soul, by free-willed obedience, catches the fire of God's likeness, it is set into the growing walls, a living stone . . . . In what strange quarries and stone-yards the stones for that celestial wall are being hewn ! Out of the hillsides of humiliated pride ; deep in the darkness of crushed despair ; in the fretting and dusty atmosphere of little cares ; in the hard, cruel contacts that man has with man ; wherever souls are being tried and ripened, in whatever commonplace and homely ways ; — there God is hewing out the pillars for His temple. O, if the stone can only have some vision of the temple of which it is to lie a part forever, what patience must fill it as it feels the blows of the hammer, and knows that success for it is simply to let itself be wrought into what shape the Master wills. II. 71, 72.

Whereas on earth
Temples and palaces are formed of parts
Costly and rare, but all material,
So in the world of spirits nought is found,
To mould withal and form into a whole,
But what is immaterial ; and thus
The smallest portions of this edifice,
Cornice, or frieze, or balustrade, or stair,
The very pavement is made up of life —
Of holy, blessed, and immortal beings,
Who hymn their Maker's praise continually.

JOHN HENRY NEWMAN.

Thou art a gentle and most loving Lamb,
Wounded to give us balm;
And still, wherever sin doth reign,
Thou day by day art slain.
When will man cease to give Thee pain?
ANNA E. HAMILTON.

WE come to the profoundest knowledge and the profoundest hatred of sin when we come to this, that it crucified the Son of God with wicked men, it made Jesus the sharer of our human woe. Sin did this. Whose sin? What sin? Then it is that the terrible identity of sin comes out. Here in the presence of God's suffering and dying Son the oneness of God's family is clear. All that we have ever done that has helped to make the world a different place from that holy ground on which the Holy God might have walked in perfect sympathy with His obedient children, all our wilfulness, all our disobedience, all our untruth, all our passion, all our lust, all our selfishness, all our wickednesses which we call little wickednesses at home or in the street, they all take their place in, they all declare their oneness with, that sin which brought Christ to the cross.
I. 201, 202.

Lord, if Thy wounds have filled the world with peace,
What shall Thy joy do, when all sin shall cease,
And the new earth shall yield her full increase!
CAROLINE M. NOEL

I will see you again, and your heart shall rejoice, and your joy no man taketh from you.

JOHN xvi. 22.

IT was a special joy, the inmost, the most secret and sacred of all joys which their Master promised.   Not for those disciples more than for other men was nature to be changed, or their relations with their fellow-men to be robbed of the power of painfulness. . . . Still, just as before Christ gave them His promise, their reverence was shocked, their love was wounded, their trust was betrayed, their motives were misjudged by fellow-men.   But behind all this His words revealed to them a self out of men's power, something which no fellow-man could touch. . . . There is nothing at all of self-sufficiency in what is promised.   It is not that these men are to develop some interior strength, or to drift into some region of calm indifference where the influences of their fellow-men shall not touch them any longer.   It is that they are to come to a new life with Him.   The new joy which is to enter into them, which they are to enter into, is to be distinctly a joy of relationship and not of self-containment, a joy which is to escape the invasion of the men who disturb all other joys by being held in the hand of a stronger being out of which no earthly power shall be able to pluck it away.   III. 229, 294.

How can this man give us His flesh to eat?
JOHN vi. 52.

HOW can He? Certainly He can if you will go to Him and pray to Him and love Him and obey Him and receive Him. And what a strength comes of that holy feeding! Where is the task that terrifies the man who lives by Christ? Where is the discouragement over which he will not walk to go to the right which he must reach? You may starve him, but he has this inner food. You may darken his life, but he has this inner light. You may make war about him, but he has this peace within. You may turn the world into a hell, but he carries his inner heaven safely through its fiercest fires. He is like Christ Himself. He has meat to eat that we know not of, and in the strength of it he overcomes at last and is conqueror through his Lord.   II. 251, 252.

'Twas August, and the fierce sun overhead
Smote on the squalid streets of Bethnal Green,
And the pale weaver, through his windows seen
In Spitalfields, look'd thrice dispirited.

I met a preacher there I knew, and said:
'Ill and o'erwork'd, how fare you in this scene?' —
'Bravely!' said he; 'for I of late have been
Much cheer'd with thoughts of Christ, *the living bread.*'

O human soul! as long as thou canst so
Set up a mark of everlasting light,
Above the howling senses' ebb and flow,

To cheer thee, and to right thee if thou roam —
Not with lost toil thou laborest through the night!
Thou mak'st the heaven thou hop'st indeed thy home.
MATTHEW ARNOLD.

We were eye-witnesses of His majesty.
                    II. PET. i. 16.

IN many respects this story (of the Transfiguration) belongs beside the story of the Temptation.   The two mountains are the complements of one another.   As the Temptation was the typical utterance of the perplexed conditions of human living, so the Transfiguration was the irrepressible utterance of the essential glory of human nature filled with divinity, reclaimed and openly asserted to be the Son of God.   And in the Transfiguration, as in the Temptation, the body has its share. Not merely does the soul enjoy sublime converse with God and with the past.   A sweet and awful gladness shines out from the face and hands, and even pierces from the hidden limbs through the coarse garments which shine "white as the light."   I do not know the meaning of it all, but I know that what came to the spiritual came in some echo to the physical, and the body shared the gladness of the soul.   INFLUENCE, 160.

O God, who on the mount didst reveal to chosen witnesses thine only-begotten Son wonderfully transfigured, in raiment white and glistering; Mercifully grant that we, being delivered from the disquietude of this world, may be permitted to behold the King in his beauty, who with thee, O Father, and thee, O Holy Ghost, liveth and reigneth, one God, world without end.   BOOK OF COMMON PRAYER.

I know how to abound.—PHIL. iv. 12.

TIMES (of great spiritual abundance) have their very deep and subtle dangers. . . . Many a Christian has failed just there. Soon the great light, unused, has faded away and left the soul in darkness. Soon peace which was not vitalized to power has decayed to pride. Something of this kind has come, I think, to whole generations, to whole periods of Christianity. But see! If you lift up your head, if you put out your hand and take your task, which certainly is waiting for you, then instantly your high emotions know their place. They turn themselves to motives. They become the necessary habits of the life. They prove their reality by what they can make you strong to do. . . . Let no spiritual exaltation come to you without your lifting yourself up in its present power, and doing some work for God which in your weaker moments and lower moods has scared you with its difficulty. For duty is the only tabernacle within which a man can always make his home upon the transfiguration mountain.   V. 156.

Hark, hark, a voice amid the quiet intense!
It is thy Duty waiting thee without.
Rise from thy knees, in hope, the half of doubt;
A hand doth pull thee — it is Providence;
Open thy door straightway and get thee hence;
Go forth into the tumult and the shout;
Work, love, with workers, lovers, all about:
Of noise alone is born the inward sense
Of silence; and from action springs alone
The inward knowledge of true love and faith.
                              GEORGE MACDONALD.

TOO often have the minds both of religious and of irreligious men conceived of God as the great hinderer of human knowledge. Even those men who thought they honored Him supremely have talked about Him as if He loved the darkness ; they have dwelt upon mystery as if it were something which God treasured, and which His children were to treasure for itself, as if they did not wish it cleared up and made light. They have imagined Him almost standing guard over whole regions of knowledge and forbidding them to the impatient intellect of man. That is not the idea of David ; that is not the idea of the Bible anywhere. Against all the folly of the Church, and all the ignorance of unbelief which declares that God is darkness, stands up the protest of John, who cries, "God is light, and in Him is no darkness at all ; " and the glowing ascription of the light-loving David, who declares, " In thy light, O Lord, we shall see light."

III. 94. 95.

O Thou, who by the light of nature dost enkindle in us a desire after the light of grace, that by this Thou mayest translate us into the light of glory, — I give Thee thanks, O Lord and Creator, that Thou hast gladdened me by Thy creation when I was enraptured by the work of Thy hands.

JOHN KEPLER.

THE vital principle is too spiritual to be confined to one form. It passes from one form into another which is wholly different, and yet it remains essentially the same. The buried seed and the wheat waving in the sunshine are the same, and yet how different they are ! . . . There is a power of life which pervades the universe. Everywhere it is identical; everywhere it is glorious. It shines in everything. By it sun, moon, and stars are clothed with radiance. But how different is the splendor which it gives to each ! . . . Shall not then this human life, still keeping itself the same human life, be able to go up to heaven and stand in the light of God ?

V. 58.

I was only then
Contented, when with bliss ineffable
I felt the sentiment of Being spread
O'er all that moves and all that seemeth still ;
O'er all that, lost beyond the reach of thought
And human knowledge, to the human eye
Invisible, yet liveth to the heart ;
O'er all that leaps and runs, and shouts and sings,
Or beats the gladsome air ; o'er all that glides
Beneath the wave, yea, in the wave itself,
And mighty depth of waters. Wonder not
If high the transport, great the joy I felt
Communing in this sort through earth and heaven
With every form of creature, as it looked
Towards the Uncreated with a countenance
Of adoration, with an eye of love.

WORDSWORTH

NOW under all outward rebellion and wickedness, there is in every man who ought to be a friend of God, and that means every man whom God has made, a need of reconciliation. To get back to God, that is the struggle. The soul is Godlike and seeks its own. It wants its Father. There is an orphanage, a homesickness of the heart which has gone up into the ear of God, and called the Saviour, the Reconciler, to meet it by His wondrous life and death. I, for my part, love to see in every restlessness of man's moral life everywhere, whatever forms it takes, the struggles of this imprisoned desire. The reason may be rebellious, and vehemently cast aside the whole story of the New Testament, but the soul is never wholly at its rest away from God.

II. 104.

None other Lamb, none other Name,
　None other Hope in heaven or earth or sea,
None other Hiding-place from guilt and shame,
　None beside Thee.

My faith burns low, my hope burns low,
　Only my heart's desire cries out in me;
By the deep thunder of its want and woe,
　Cries out to Thee.

Lord, Thou art Life, tho' I be dead,
　Love's Fire Thou art however cold I be:
Nor heaven have I, nor place to lay my head,
　Nor home, but Thee.

CHRISTINA ROSSETTI.

I therefore, the prisoner of the Lord, beseech you, that ye walk worthy of the vocation wherewith ye are called.

Till we all come in the unity of the faith, and of the knowledge of the Son of God, unto a perfect man, unto the measure of the stature of the fulness of Christ. — EPH. iv. 1, 13.

MEAN to be something with all your might. Do not add act to act and day to day in perfect thoughtlessness, never asking yourself whither the growing line is leading. But at the same time do not dare to be so absorbed in your own life, so wrapped up in listening to the sound of your own hurrying wheels, that all this vast pathetic music, made up of the mingled joy and sorrow of your fellow-men, shall not find out your heart and claim it and make you rejoice to give yourself for them. And yet, all the while, keep the upward windows open. Do not dare to think that a child of God can worthily work out his career or worthily serve God's other children unless he does both in the love and fear of God their Father. Be sure that ambition and charity will both grow mean unless they are both inspired and exalted by religion. Energy, love, and faith, those make the perfect man.

II. 126.

Great Universe — what dost thou with thy dead !
  Now thinking on the myriads that have gone
  Into a seeming blank oblivion,
  With here and there a most resplendent head, —
Eyes of such trancing sweetness, or so dread,
  That made the soul to quake who looked thereon, —
  All utterly wiped out, dismissed and done :
  Lost, speechless, viewless, and forever fled !
Myriad on myriad, past the power to count, —
  Where are they, thou dumb Nature? Do they shine,
  Released from separate life, in summer airs,
On moony seas, in dawns : — or up the stairs
  Of spiritual being slowly mount
  And by degrees grow more and more divine?
RICHARD WATSON GILDER.

THERE are so many souls. What world can hold them all ? What care can recognize, and cover, and embrace them all ? If there only were not so many of us ! The thought of one's own immortality sinks like a tired soldier on a battle-field, overwhelmed and buried under the multitude of the dead. Have not many of you felt this bewilderment ? . . . What can we say to it? How can we grasp and believe in this countless army of immortals who come swarming up out of all the lands and all the ages ? There is only one way. Multiply numbers as enormously as you will, and the result is finite still. Then set the finite, however large, into the presence of the infinite, and it is small. Its limitations show. There is no finite, however vast, that can overcrowd the infinite ; none that the infinite cannot most easily grasp and hold. . . . Here must be the real solution of our difficulty, in the infinity of God.
IV. 69, 70.

Deep calleth unto deep. — Ps. xlii. 17.

THE words of David suggest to me also that there is such a thing as deep calling unto shallow, — by which I mean, of course, the profound and sacred interests of life crying out and finding nothing but the slight and foolish and selfish parts of a man ready to reply.   There are a host of men who . . . have perception enough to hear the great questions and see the great tasks; but they have not earnestness and self-control enough to answer them with serious thought and strong endeavor; so they sing their answer to the thunder, which is not satisfied or answered.   That is what I mean by deep calling unto shallow.

V. 243.

But ye who have seemed to know us, have seen and
    heard;
  Who have set us at feasts and have crowned with
    the costly rose;
  Who have spread us the purple of praises beneath
    our feet;
Yet guessed not the word that we spake was a living
    word,
  Applauding the sound, — we account you as worse
    than foes!
  We sobbed you our message; ye said, " It is song
    and sweet " !

HELEN GRAY CONE.

Gird up the loins of your mind, be sober.
I. PET. i. 13.

A merry heart doeth good like a medicine.
PROV. xvii. 22.

GRAVITY . . . I mean simply that grave and serious way of looking at life which, while it never repels the true lightheartedness of pure and trustful hearts, welcomes into a manifest sympathy, the souls of men who are oppressed and burdened, anxious and full of questions which for the time at least have banished all laughter from their faces. . . . Gravity has a delicate power of discrimination. It attracts all that it can help and it repels all that could harm it or be harmed by it. It admits the earnest and simple with a cordial welcome. It shuts out the impertinent and insincere inexorably.

The gravity of which I speak is not inconsistent with the keenest perception of the ludicrous side of things. It is more than consistent with — it is even necessary to — humor. Humor involves the perception of the true proportions of life. . . . It has softened the bitterness of controversy a thousand times. You cannot encourage it too much. You cannot grow too familiar with the books of all ages which have in them the truest humor, for the truest humor is the bloom of the highest life. Read George Eliot and Thackeray, and, above all, Shakespeare. They will help you to keep from extravagances without fading into insipidity. They will preserve your gravity while they save you from pompous solemnity.
PREACHING. 54-58.

THE mountains to the Hebrew were always full of mystery and awe. They stood around the sunlit level of his daily life robed in deep clouds, the home of wandering winds, flowing down with waters, trembling, as it seemed, with the awful footsteps of God.

They made indeed for him the background of all life, as they make the background of every landscape in which they stand. . . . The foreground of the plain-land rests upon the background of the hills. From them it gains its lights and shadows. The two depend on one another. . . . To most men the actual immediate circumstances of life are so pressing that they forget the everlasting truths and forces by which those circumstances must be made dignified and strong. Then must come something like the cry of Amos the Prophet, " Lo, He that formeth the mountains, and createth the wind, and declareth unto man what is His Thought, that maketh the morning darkness and treadeth upon the high places of the earth." Is there not in these words, dimly but very grandly and majestically set forth, the great suggestion of the divine background of all life ? It is the same which Tennyson has pictured in the Vision of Sin:

" At last I heard a voice upon the slope
   Cry to the summit, ' Is there any hope?'
   To which an answer pealed from that high land,
   But in a tongue no man could understand ;
   And on the glimmering limit far withdrawn
   God made Himself an awful rose of Dawn."

V. 106, 108.

THINK of sin as a mistake, or as an inconvenience, and you stand in great danger, first, of compromising with it, and second, of using low and even sinful methods of opposing it. But think of sin as a frightful wrong in itself, a blot and curse in the universe of God, and you grow at once absolutely intolerant of it, and at the same time watchfully anxious about the nature of the weapons which you shall use to fight it with. . . . Only when pity for it joins with horror at it in our hearts, as they join in the heart of God, each keeping the other strong and pure, only then can we go out to meet it with a perfect determination, bound never to lay down our arms so long as there is any sin left in the world; and at the same time, with an absolute conviction that no impatience to rid the world of sin must tempt us for a moment to use any means for its destruction which are not pure and just; an absolute conviction that it is better that sin should be left master of the field, than that it should be fought with sin.   IV. 271, 272.

But if we strove to stand in battle line like soldiers
    true,
Above us we should see God's help descending from
    the sky.
Ready is He to help all those that fight,
And build their hopes upon His kindliness.
He *makes* for us chances to fight — that we may win.
THOMAS À KEMPIS.

NEVER, no matter how long exclusion from the presence of God may seem to last, though it go on year after year and you are growing old in your seeming orphanhood; never accept it, never make up your mind to it that it is right; never cease to expect that the doors will fly open and you will be admitted to all the joy of your Father's felt love and of unhindered communion with Him.   Never lose out of your soul's sight the seat which is set for you in the very sanctuary of divine love. And what beside?   Seek even more deeply the satisfaction which is in your consecration itself; and that you may find it, consecrate yourself more and more completely.   I. 30, 31.

And should the twilight darken into night,
   And sorrow grow to anguish, be thou strong;
   Thou art in God, and nothing can go wrong
Which a fresh life-pulse cannot set aright.
That thou dost know the darkness, proves the light.
   Weep if thou wilt, but weep not all too long;
   Or weep and work, for work will lead to song.

GEORGE MACDONALD.

IT is a strange perplexing fact of life, this fact that as a being or a work, which has seemed perfect in some lower region, goes up to some higher region, it seems to grow imperfect; at least it manifests its imperfection. We can see at once what a temptation it must offer to the human powers to linger in some lower sphere, in which they seem to be equal to their work, instead of going freely up into a loftier world where they shall learn their limitations and their feebleness. There is reason enough to fear that man's power of thought, revelling to-day in the clearness with which it seems to see the lower world of physical existence, will refuse some of the higher duties which belong to it, the duties which most tax its capacity and show its feebleness, the duties of understanding the soul of man and reaching after the comprehension of God. Sad will it be if it is so; if studious humanity, delighted with its achievements in the mere region of physical research, shall turn its back on the lofty tasks in which man's intellect finds its greatest glory as well as its most complete humility — the struggle to know God.

III. 206, 207.

Thou art so great, that the greatest powers and minds, which Thou couldest create, would all together contain but a little of Thee. And yet Thou willest that such as I should adore Thee and know Thee, and in all eternity love Thee.   PUSEY.

" Because we are sons, God has sent the spirit of His Son into our hearts."

BECAUSE we are sons, His Son Himself could take our nature upon Him. The more truly we believe in the Incarnate Deity, the more devoutly we must believe in the essential glory of humanity, the more earnestly we must struggle to keep the purity and integrity and largeness of our own human life, and to help our brethren to keep theirs. It is because the divine can dwell in us that we may have access to divinity.   I. 240, 241.

Lord, carry me. — Nay, but I grant thee strength
To walk and work thy way to Heaven at length. —

Lord, why then am I weak? — Because I give
Power to the weak, and bid the dying live. —

Lord, I am tired. — He hath not much desired
The goal, who at the starting-point is tired. —

Lord, dost thou know? — I know what is in man ;
What the flesh can, and what the spirit can. —

Lord, dost thou care? — Yea, for thy gain or loss
So much I cared, it brought me to the Cross. —

Lord, I believe ; help Thou mine unbelief. —
Good is the word ; but rise, for life is brief.
The follower is not greater than the Chief :
Follow thou Me along My way of grief.
                              CHRISTINA ROSSETTI.

REST in expectation we may all have now if we believe in God and know we are His children. Every taste of Him that we have ever had becomes a prophecy of His perfect giving of Himself to us. It is as when a pool lies far up in the dry rocks, and hears the tide and knows that her refreshment and replenishing is coming. How patient she is. The other pools nearer the shore catch the sea first, and she hears them leaping and laughing, but she waits patiently. She knows the tide will not turn back till it has reached her. And by and by the blessed moment comes. The last ridge of rock is overwashed. The stream pours in ; at first a trickling thread sent only at the supreme effort of the largest wave ; but by and by the great sea in its fulness. It gives the waiting pool itself and she is satisfied. So it will certainly be with us if we wait for the Lord, however He delays, and refuse to let ourselves be satisfied with any supply but Him.

II. 286.

As torrents in summer,
Half dried in their channels,
Suddenly rise, though the
Sky is still cloudless,
For rain has been falling
Far off at their fountains ;

So hearts that are fainting
Grow full to o'erflowing,
And they that behold it
Marvel, and know not
That God at their fountains
Far off has been raining !

LONGFELLOW.

"LO, I am with you alway," Christ declares. And souls to-day, many and many of your souls, my friends, have found the rich fulfilment of His promise. Sometimes it comes to us with a strange surprise When we are living on as if we lived alone, when we are sitting working silently in some still room which we think is empty but for our own presence, when we are busy in some work which seems as if it were our work, to be done as we should please; slowly, sweetly, surely we become aware of a richer presence which is truly with us, of a love which enfolds us, and an authority which controls us. We are not alone. The work is not our work but His. The strength to do it with is not to be called up out of the depths of ourselves, but taken down from the heights of Him. The room is full, the world is full of Jesus. He is doing what He said He would do. He is with us as He said He would be.

III. 297.

Thy calmness bends serene above,
　My restlessness to still;
Around me flows Thy quickening life
　To nerve my faltering will;
Thy presence fills my solitude:
Thy providence turns all to good.

SAMUEL LONGFELLOW.

IF you must pass through what is even a desert to get to fertile, smiling lands beyond, still it is not good to count even the desert a mere necessary evil to be got through and forgotten as soon as possible. It is good as you plod through the sand to feed your eyes with the vastness and simplicity of the world which the monotony of sky and sand can most impressively display to you. So if God has appointed to any of us times of solitude and friendlessness, — perhaps times of unpopularity and neglect, — let us pray that we may not pass through them, however dreary they may be, without bringing out from them greater conceptions of Him and of our fellow-men and of ourselves.   V. 172, 173.

> A dreary desert dost thou trace,
>   And quaff a bitter bowl?
> The desert make thy Holy Place;
>   Sing as thou drinkest, Soul!
> Or walkest thou 'neath shining skies,
>   A garden all the road?
> Sing, Soul, and make thy paradise
>   The Paradise of God!
>
> T. H. GILL.

Oh, my young friends, prosperous and happy, with life all full of hope and chance and light, . . . no lot is too rich for a soul that enters into it full of humility before God, and love for fellow-men, and a deep desire for holiness.

V. 156.

And I saw as it were a sea of glass mingled with fire, and them that had gotten the victory over the beast . . . stand on the sea of glass, having the harps of God. — REV. XV. 2.

"THEY who have gotten the victory over the Beast" are they who have come out of sin holy, and out of trial pure, and out of much tribulation have entered into the kingdom of heaven.

These are to walk upon "a sea of glass, mingled with fire." What does that imagery mean? The sea of glass, the glassy sea, with its smooth transparency settled into solid stillness without a ripple or the possibility of a storm, calm, clear, placid — evidently that is the type of repose, of rest, of peace. And fire, with its quick, eager, searching nature, testing all things, consuming what is evil, purifying what is good, never resting a moment, never sparing pain; fire, all through the Bible, is the type of active trial of every sort, of struggle. "The fire shall try every man's work of what sort it is." "The sea of glass," then, "mingled with fire," is repose mingled with struggle. It is peace and rest and achievement, with the power of trial and suffering yet alive and working within it. It is calmness still pervaded by the discipline through which it has been reached.   IV. 112.

Though He slay me, yet will I trust in Him.
JOB xiii. 15.

TO stand with the good things of life all stripped away, to stand beaten and buffeted by storms of disaster and disappointment, to stand with all our brethren saying, "Behold, how God hates him," and yet to know assuredly in our own hearts that God loves us, to know it so assuredly, with the intercourse that lies between our heart and His, that we can freely let go the outward tokens of His love, as the most true and trusty friends do not need to take gifts from one another for assurance of their affection, — this surely is the perfection of a faithful life. It is the gathering up of all happinesses into one happiness which is so rich that it can live without them all, and yet regally receives them into itself as the ocean receives the rivers.

V. 320.

Thou, Lord, alone, art all Thy children need,
    And there is none beside ;
From Thee the streams of blessedness proceed,
    In Thee the blest abide, —
Fountain of life, and all-abounding grace,
Our source, our centre, and our dwelling-place.
MADAME GUYON.

With brain o'erworn, with heart a summer clod,
With eye so practised in each form around, —
And all forms mean, — to glance above the ground
Irks it, each day of many days we plod,
Tongue-tied and deaf, along life's common road.
But suddenly, we know not how, a sound
Of living streams, an odour, a flower crowned
With dew, a lark upspringing from the sod,
And we awake.   O joy and deep amaze !
Beneath the everlasting hills we stand,
We hear the voices of the morning seas,
And earnest prophesyings in the land,
While from the open heaven leans forth at gaze
The encompassing great cloud of witnesses.

EDWARD DOWDEN.

LIFE is always opening new and unexpected things to us.   There is no monotony in living to him who walks even the quietest and tamest paths with open and perceptive eyes. The monotony of life, if life is monotonous to you, is in you, not in the world. . . . It is God, and the discovery of Him in life, and the certainty that He has plans for our lives and is doing something with them, that gives us a true, deep sense of movement, and lets us always feel the power and delight of unknown coming things.

V. 288, 289.

THE Church has in herself the very doctrine of tradition. She teaches the child a faith that has the warrant of the ages, full of devotion and of love. She calls on him to believe doctrines of which he cannot be convinced as yet. The tradition, the hereditation of belief, the unity of the human history, are ideas very familiar to her, of which she constantly and beautifully makes use. And yet she does not disown her work of teaching and arguing and convincing. She cannot, and yet be true to her mission. She teaches the young with the voice of authority ; she addresses the mature with the voice of reason. Let her give up the first function, and her assemblies would turn into mere societies of debate. Let her abandon the second, and they must be blighted with some doctrine of infallibility.

I. 67.

We beseech Thine Omnipotence, Holy God, Father Almighty, that Thou wouldst fill us with the gift of Thine Only-begotten Son, and the ineffable blessing, visitation, and life-giving power of Thine and His Holy Spirit, whereby Thy Church, enkindled with His fire, may hold the true faith in Him from Whom she receives all truth.

ANCIENT COLLECTS. BRIGHT.

THE world does say to us, " Enjoy ; " and it is good for us to hear her invitation. But for the world to say, and for us to hear, nothing better or deeper than " Enjoy " is to turn the relation between the world and man into something hardly better than that which exists between the corn-field and the crows. It is clothing one's self with cobwebs. Only when the deeper communion, rich and full and strong, is going on below, between the depths of life and the depths of man, — only then is the surface communion healthy and natural and good. He who is always hearing and answering the call of life to be thoughtful and brave and self-sacrificing, — he alone can safely hear the other cry of life, tempting him to be happy and enjoy.

V. 242.

And the dreamer saw the sorrow and he heard the
    bitter cries,
And he left his dreams of morning, and his Earthly
    Paradise ;

And he changed his lyre of music for the bugle of the
    fight,
And he sounded forth his challenge to the myrmidons
    of Night,

To the tyrant and oppressor who had done the people
    wrong,
While he led the marching millions with the summons
    of his song.

ALLEN EASTMAN CROSS.

WITH our modern, half-personal, unlocalized ideas of Jesus, it must always be striking — sometimes it is startling — to remember that there was one little district of a few miles square upon the surface of this earth, which was known as "His own country." That little group of hills with the quiet valleys among them which lies between Nazareth and the Sea of Tiberias, He loved as we love the streets or farms where we were born. And not very far off to the southward lay the great city of His race, where His feet never seemed to enter except solemnly.

INFLUENCE, 130.

This is the earth he walked on ; not alone
   That Asian country keeps the sacred stain ;
   'Tis not alone the far Judaean plain,
   Mountain and river ! Lo, the sun that shone
On him shines now on us ; when day is gone
   The moon of Galilee comes forth again
   And lights our path as his : an endless chain
   Of years and sorrows makes the round world one.
The air we breathe, he breathed, — the very air
   That took the mold and music of his high
   And godlike speech. — Since then shall mortal dare
With base thought front the ever-sacred sky, —
   Soil with foul deed the ground whereon he laid
   In holy death his pale, immortal head.

RICHARD WATSON GILDER.

"WHY cannot I follow thee now? Why this delay of the divinest life? Why so much duty with so little strength? Why only the journey and the hunger and the thirst, without the brook of refreshment by the way?" No man can wholly answer these questions, but multitudes of saints, if they could speak, would tell you how in their hindered lives God kept them true to such experience as they had attained; and so it was that, by and by, either before or after the great enlightenment of death, the hindrance melted away, and they who had been crying for years, "Lord, why cannot we follow thee now?" passed forth into the multitude of those who "follow the Lamb whithersoever He goeth."

I. 31, 32.

> For who that leans on His right arm
> Was ever yet forsaken?
> What righteous cause can suffer harm
> If He its part has taken?
> > Though wild and loud
> > And dark the cloud
> > Behind its folds
> > His hand upholds
> The calm sky of to-morrow.
>
> . . . . . .
>
> > God give us grace
> > Each in his place
> > To bear his lot,
> > And murmuring not
> Endure and wait and labor.

LUTHER.

Gamaliel said unto them . . . Refrain from these men and let them alone : for if this counsel or this work be of men, it will come to nought : but if it be of God, ye cannot overthrow it. — ACTS v. 38.

THERE are some men whose whole influence is to keep history open, so that whatever good thing is trying to get done in the world can get done; not the doers of great things, but the men who help to keep the world so truly poised that good forces shall have a chance to work. These words of Gamaliel seem to point him out as being such a man. . . . Such men in our community, in our family circles, in our own little groups, whatever they are, any of us may be — men who shall do something to hold the soul of our little group in such ex-pectancy and readiness, in such unwillingness to settle down upon the imperfect present as a finality, that when the inspired word or deed shall come, as it is sure to come some time, it shall find the atmosphere ready to receive it and transmit it. We cannot make the wind to blow — it bloweth where it listeth; but we can keep the windows open, so that when it blows the chambered life about us shall not fail to receive its freshness.   III. 253, 255.

YOU have your cross, my friend. You do not serve your Lord without surrender. There is pain in the duty which you do. But if in all your pain you know that God's love is becoming a dearer and plainer truth to you, and that you are finding the pleasure of obeying God; and that the vision of the world's redemption is growing more certain and bright, then you can be more than brave; you can triumph in every task, in every sacrifice. Your cross has won something of the beauty and glory of your Lord's. Rejoice and be glad, for you are crucified with Christ.   I. 208.

As flames that consume the mountains, as winds that
    coerce the sea,
Thy men of renown show forth Thy might in the
    clutch of death :
Down they go into silence, yet the Trump of the Jubi-
    lee
Swells not Thy praise as swells it the breathless pause
    of their breath.

What is the flame of their fire, if so I may catch the
    flame ;
What is the strength of their strength, if also I may
    wax strong ?
The flaming fire of their strength is the love of Jesu's
    Name,
In Whom their death is life, their silence utters a song.
CHRISTINA ROSSETTI.

W^E look forward into the opening months
and . . . if we have no religion (or do
not use the religion which we have, as many
religious men do not) we think of what will
happen as the falling of accidents or as the ma-
turing of self-ripening processes.   If we think
of it at all religiously, we talk about God sending messages to us.   If our religion is a real live
thing, we feel God actually coming to us Himself, in all the unknown things which are to
happen. . . . Ah, after all, that is everything.   To know that there is no accident.   To
know that indeed there is no such thing as a
mere message of God.   To know that He is
always coming to us, to know that there is
nothing happening to us which is not His coming.   To know all that, is to find the most trivial
life made solemn, the most cruel life made kind,
the most sad and gloomy life made rich and
beautiful.   IV. 365, 366.

From East to West, the God unshrined
Is still discovering me.
                              EDWARD DOWDEN.

Jesus said unto them, I am the bread of life.

JOHN vi. 31.

THE Lord's Supper, the right and need of every man to feed on God, the bread of divine sustenance, the wine of divine inspiration offered to every man, and turned by every man into what form of spiritual force the duty and the nature of each man required, how grand and glorious its mission might become! No longer the mystic source of unintelligible influence; no longer certainly the test of arbitrary orthodoxy; no longer the initiation rite of a selected brotherhood; but the great sacrament of man! . . . There is no other rallying-place for all the good activity and worthy hopes of man. It is in the power of the great Christian Sacrament, the great human sacrament, to become that rallying-place. Think how it would be, if some morning all the men, women, and children in this city who mean well, from the reformer meaning to meet some giant evil at the peril of his life to the school boy meaning to learn his day's lesson with all his strength, were to meet in a great host at the table of the Lord, and own themselves His children, and claim the strength of His bread and wine, and then go out with calm, strong, earnest faces to their work. How the communion service would lift up its voice and sing itself in triumph, the great anthem of dedicated human life! Ah, my friends, that, nothing less than that, is the real Holy Communion of the Church of the living God.   IV. 46, 47, 48.

I T seems very certain that the world is to grow better and richer in the future, however it has been in the past, not by the magnificent achievements of the highly-gifted few, but by the patient faithfulness of the one-talented many. If we could draw back the curtains of the millennium and look in, we should see not a Hercules here and there standing on the world-wasting monsters he had killed; but a world full of men each with an arm of moderate muscle, but each triumphant over his own little piece of the obstinacy of earth or the ferocity of the brutes. It seems as if the heroes had done almost all for the world that they can do, and not much more can come till common men awake and take their common tasks. I do believe the common man's task is the hardest. The hero has the hero's aspiration that lifts him to his labor. All great duties are easier than the little ones, though they cost far more blood and agony.

I. 141.

Is Heroism dead in this our day?
No more rides forth in shining mail the knight,
To do brave deeds in battle for the right,
Or glitter in the tournament's array;
But has the noble heart burned out for aye
Which kindled in those breasts such living fire?
Nay, Virtue's flame may but more straight aspire
With every breath of glory shut away.
Who keep, 'mid bosom foes, their souls alive,
Who furnish other's need at cost untold,
With young hopes wounded. unapplauded strive,—
Are they no knights? A Master said of old
That Honor but from Service doth derive;
From Him their title comes, their rank they hold.
HARRIET WARE HALL.

Whatsoever ye do in word or deed, do all in the name of the Lord Jesus, giving thanks to God and the Father by Him.   Knowing that of the Lord ye shall receive the reward of the inheritance : for ye serve the Lord Christ.— Col. iii. 17, 24.

MAKE your business the centre and fountain of your joy, and then life will be healthy and strong.   Then you will not be running everywhere to find some outside pleasure which shall make up to you for your self-sacrificing toil ; but the scenes of your self-sacrificing toil itself, your store or your office or your work-bench, shall be bright with associations of delight, and vocal with your thankfulness to the God who has given you, in them, the most radiant revelations of Himself.   This is the only true transfiguration and success of labor and of life.

II. 33.

The mountain that the morn doth kiss
　Glad greets its shining neighbor ;
Lord, heed the homage of our bliss, —
　The incense of our labor.

Now the long shadows eastward creep,
　The golden sun is setting ;
Take, Lord ! the worship of our sleep, —
　The praise of our forgetting.

RICHARD WATSON GILDER.

BE interested in some pursuit which will take you into quite unfamiliar fields. Make yourself at home in the Public Library, that great organ-forest of sweet and solemn and inspiring sounds, which will speak to us if we come and sit and are hungry for its music. Let the country, when you can, scatter the cobwebs of the city out of your brain and send you back to its richer life refreshed and simplified. Above all, let the peace of God, the peace of trust and love, the peace of religion, flow in upon your consciousness the moment that business care gives it a moment's freedom. Whenever necessary thought of self gives way for an hour, O how good it is if the thought of the Father instantly, without waiting to be summoned, takes possession of the child. IV. 235.

Calm soul of all things ! make it mine
To feel, amid the city's jar,
That there abides a peace of thine,
Man did not make, and cannot mar !

The will to neither strive nor cry,
The power to feel with others give !
Calm, calm me more ! nor let me die
Before I have begun to live.
MATTHEW ARNOLD.

All things are yours; whether Paul, or Apollos, or Cephas, or the world, or life, or death, or things present, or things to come; all are yours; and ye are Christ's; and Christ is God's. In Whom are hid all the treasures of wisdom and knowledge. — I. Cor. iii. 22, 23. Col. ii. 3.

THE man who has gone on his way, as most of us have to do, with little learning, but has also gone on his way doing duty faithfully, developing all the practical skill that is in him, and sometimes, just because their details are so dark to him, getting rich visions of the general light and glory of the great sciences, seen afar off, seen as great wholes, which often seem to be denied to the plodders who spend their lives in the close study of those sciences, — he is the man who knows how to be unlearned. It is a blessed thing that there is such a knowledge possible for overworked, practical men. The man who has that knowledge may be self-respectful in the face of all the colleges. He may stand before the kings of learning and not be ashamed; for his lot is as true a part of life as theirs, and he is bravely holding up his side of that great earth over which the plans of God are moving on to their completeness. V. 169.

My God! My God! Why hast Thou forsaken Me? — MATT. xxvii. 46.

THOUGH I do not understand this cry fully, I know that I come nearest to its meaning when its meaning seems to me most simple. It is pure love, — love thwarted, hindered, and perplexed, but yet pure love, with that triumph which love always carries in its very existence whether it reach its object and call back response or not. Jesus does not beg for release. He does not even ask for vindication. He only utters love.

And that cry after His Father lets us look down into His heart and see that in loving His Father and being loved by Him was His perpetual joy. INFLUENCE, 177.

O Lord Jesus Christ, Who didst cry from the Cross to Thy Father, My God, My God, why hast Thou forsaken Me? and Who didst say to Thine Apostles, It is expedient for you that I go away: grant that, when we are forsaken for a while by Thee, we may not despair; vouchsafe that, when we cannot see Thee to be with us, we may not utterly faint; but possessing our souls in patience, may follow Thee in the night of Thy tribulation, till at length we behold the day of Thy glory. BOOK OF LITANIES. NEALE.

IT may be that God used to give you plentiful chance to work for Him. Your days went singing by, each winged with some enthusiastic duty for the Master whom you loved. . . . You can be idle for Him, if so He wills, with the same joy with which you once labored for Him. The sick-bed or the prison is as welcome as the harvest-field or the battle-field, when once your soul has come to value as the end of life the privilege of seeking and of finding Him.

V. 321, 322.

O Lord, fulfil Thy Will
Be the days few or many, good or ill :
Prolong them, to suffice
For offering up ourselves Thy sacrifice ;
Shorten them if Thou wilt,
To make in righteousness an end of guilt.
Yea, they will not be long
To souls who learn to sing a patient song :
Yea, short they will not be
To souls on tiptoe to flee home to Thee.
O Lord, fulfil Thy Will :
Make Thy Will ours, and keep us patient still
Be the days few or many, good or ill.

CHRISTINA ROSSETTI.

The Word was made flesh and dwelt among us.

JOHN i. 14.

THEN were the capacities of our human flesh declared. Then in the strong and healthy life of Jesus it was made known to what divine uses a strong body might be given. And since everything in this world properly belongs to the highest uses to which it may possibly be put, the strong human body was there declared to belong to righteousness and God. Thenceforward after Jesus and His life, wherever human flesh appeared at its best, wherever a human body stood forth specially strong, specially perfect and beautiful, it had the mark and memory of the Incarnation on it. It might be totally perverted. It might be given to the Devil. But, since the work that Jesus did, the life that Jesus lived in a human body, the human body in its fullest vigor has belonged to the high work which He did in it, the service of God and help of fellow-man. Its vigor is His mark upon it. Feel this, and then how sacred becomes the body's health and strength. It is no chance, no luxury. God means that in it you should do work for Him. By it He claims you for His own. He to whom God has given it, is bound to have strong convictions, a live conscience, and intense earnest purposes of work.

II. 366, 367.

Far better never to have heard the name
Of zeal and just ambition, than to live
Baffled and plagued by a mind that every hour
Turns recreant to her task ; takes heart again,
Then feels immediately some hollow thought
Hang like an interdict upon her hopes.
This is my lot ; for either still I find
Some imperfection in the chosen theme,
Or see of absolute accomplishment
Much wanting, so much wanting, in myself,
That I recoil and droop, and seek repose
In listlessness from vain perplexity,
Unprofitably travelling toward the grave,
Like a false steward who hath much received
And renders nothing back.

WORDSWORTH.

ANY man who is good for anything, if he is always thinking about himself, will come to think himself good for nothing very soon. It is only a fop or a fool who can bear to look at himself all day long, without disgust. And so the first thing for a man to do, who wants to use his best powers at their best, is to get rid of self-consciousness, to stop thinking about himself and how he is working, altogether.

l. 142.

Do you dare to be
Of the great majority?
To be only as the rest,
With Heaven's common comforts blessed;
To accept, in humble part,
Truth that shines on every heart;
Never to be set on high,
Where the envious curses fly;
Never name or fame to find,
Still outstripped in soul and mind;
To be hid, unless to God,
As one grass-blade in the sod,
Under foot with millions trod?
If you dare, come, with us be
Lost in Love's great unity?   E. R. Sill.

If I feel God behind all existence, then there
is a great identity established between all the
utterances of Him throughout the length and
breadth of human life. The volcanoes know
each other, — Etna crying out to Vesuvius
across the sea, — because of the oneness of the
central fire from which they all proceed. Let
me know God, the source of all that man does
anywhere, and then, O poet, sing your song!
O sculptor, carve your statue! O builder, build
your house! O engineer, roll out your railroad
on the plain! O sailor, sail your ship across the
sea! They are all mine. I am glad; I am proud
of them all.   Is it not what Paul wrote so
triumphantly to his disciples,— " All things are
yours, and you are Christ's, and Christ is
God's"?   V. 70, 71.

Jesus said, Make the men sit down.

JOHN vi. 10.

THE disciples as well as the stragglers from Capernaum — perhaps the busy disciples more than anybody else in all the crowd — must have needed Christ's call to sit down and be fed. The more earnestly you are at work for Jesus, the more you need times when what you are doing for Him passes totally out of your mind, and the only thing worth thinking of seems to be what He is doing for you. That is the real meaning of the days of discouragement and self-contempt which come to all of us, O fellow laborers for the Lord.

God of all love and pity,
  Thy children gently guide;
With heavenly food supply us,
  All needful good provide.

By waters still, refresh us;
  As patiently we wait,
Till Thou, the Fount of brightness,
  Our souls illuminate.

Our wishes and affections,
  Our impulses and powers,
We yield unto Thy guidance;
  For they are Thine, not ours.

With strong attraction draw us
  Unto Thyself alone,
O King of Saints, and bring us
  Unto Thy sapphire throne.

CAROLINE M. NOEL

MAKE your most simple act complete; do your most common daily duty from its divinest motive, and what a change will come! Still your life will need days of retirement, when it will shut the gates upon the noisy whirl of action and be alone with God. But it will not be upon them that it will mostly depend for spiritual nourishment. They will be like great exceptional banquets and extraordinary feasts of grace. The daily bread of spiritual life, the ordinary feeding of the soul on God, which really makes its sustenance, will be in the perpetual doing of the works of life for Him. The real sitting down to be fed will be mysteriously identical with the most eager and energetic standing on the feet to do His will!

IV. 238.

Nothing remains to say to Thee, O Lord,
    I am confessed,
All my lips' empty crying Thou hast heard,
    My unrest, my rest.
Why wait I any longer? Thou dost stay,
And therefore, Lord, I would not go away.

Then when Thou seekest Thy way, and I, mine,
    Let the World be
Not wide and cold after this cherishing shrine
    Illum'd by Thee,
Nay, but worth worship, fair, a radiant star,
Tender and strong as Thy chief angels are.
EDWARD DOWDEN.

Father, I will that they also, whom Thou hast given me, be with me where I am. — JOHN xvii. 24.

THAT was Christ's prayer. He prayed it at the Passover table. The next day He prayed it in all the silent appeal of His suffering upon the Cross. "I, if I be lifted up, will draw all men unto me." The cross was Christ's supreme utterance of His longing that all men might be rescued out of sin and brought to holiness. As we stand and see Him suffer, one thought, one cry alone arises in our hearts. Oh, how He must have wanted to save us! How terrible sin must have seemed to Him! How glorious holiness must have seemed, that such a prayer as this sacrifice of Himself should thus have gone up to God for our salvation!

I. 313, 314.

Be merciful, be gracious; spare him, Lord.
Be merciful, be gracious; Lord, deliver him.

.   .   .   .

From all that is evil;
From power of the devil;
Thy servant deliver,
For once and forever.

By Thy birth, and by Thy Cross,
Rescue him from endless loss;
By Thy death and burial,
Save him from a final fall;
By Thy rising from the tomb,
By Thy mounting up above,
By the Spirit's gracious love,
Save him in the day of doom.

JOHN HENRY NEWMAN.

UNDER every discouragement, untouched by any scepticism or contempt of scornful friend or foe, there has lain at the bottom of the soul a conviction too deep for reason to give an account of, that this which seemed so impossible could be done. The soul could break through its selfishness, could despise danger and pain, could enter into communion with God. . . . But now what happened — one of the things which happened — at the Incarnation was that this assurance, which had lain at the bottom of the human heart, came forth and was a living, manifest Being. It put on human flesh. It spoke with human lips. It worked with human hands. Christ was what man had felt in his soul that he might be. Christ did what man's heart had always told him that it was in his humanity to do. The new man which the old manhood had always felt struggling within itself came forth, and men knew themselves, their true selves, for the first time manifest in Him. This was what made man's hope thenceforth another thing. The stars at which men had guessed, knowing with what they called certainty that they were there, lo! in the Incarnation they burned out visibly.

IV. 281, 282.

Shine, my only Day-star, shine:
So mine eyes shall wake by Thine;
So the dreams I grope-in now
To clear visions all shall grow;
So my day shall measured be
By Thy Grace's clarity;
So shall I discern the Path
Thy sweet Law prescribéd hath;
For Thy ways cannot be shown
By any light but by Thine own.

JOSEPH BEAUMONT.

HOW every truth attains to its enlargement and reality in this great truth, — that the soul of man carries the highest possibilities within itself, and that what Christ does for it is to kindle and call forth these possibilities to actual existence. We do not understand the Church until we understand this truth. Seen in its light the Christian Church is nothing in the world except the promise and prophecy and picture of what the world in its idea is and always has been, and in its completion must visibly become. It is the primary crystallization of humanity. It is no favored, elect body caught from the ruin, given a salvation in which the rest can have no part. It is an attempt to realize the universal possibility. All men are its potential members. The strange thing for any man is not that he should be within it, but that he should be without it. Every good movement of any most secular sort is a struggle toward it, a part of its activity. All the world's history is ecclesiastical history, is the story of the success and failure, the advance and hindrance of the ideal humanity, the Church of the living God. Well may the prophet poet greet it, —

" O heart of mine, keep patience ; looking forth
    As from the Mount of Vision I behold
  Pure, just, and free the Church of Christ on earth, —
    The martyr's dream, the golden age foretold."
                                        V. 15, 16.

IDLENESS standing in the midst of unat-
tempted tasks is always proud. Work is
always tending to humility. Work touches
the keys of endless activity, opens the infinite,
and stands awe-struck before the immensity
of what there is to do. Work brings a man
into the good realm of facts. Work takes the
dreamy youth who is growing proud in his
closet over one or two sprouting powers which
he has discovered in himself, and sets him out
among the gigantic needs and the vast processes of the world, and makes him feel his
littleness. Work opens the measureless fields
of knowledge and skill that reach far out of
sight. I am sure we all know the fine, calm,
sober humbleness of men who have really
tried themselves against the great tasks of life.
It was great in Paul, and in Luther, and in
Cromwell. It is something that never comes
into the character, never shows in the face of
a man who has never worked.   I. 349. 350.

No man is born into the world, whose work
Is not born with him ; there is always work,
And tools to work withal, for those who will ;
And blessed are the horny hands of toil !
The busy world shoves angrily aside
The man who stands with arms akimbo set,
Until occasion tells him what to do ;
And he who waits to have his task marked out
Shall die and leave his errand unfulfilled.
                              JAMES RUSSELL LOWELL.

BEGIN with largeness of thought, and with positiveness of thought. The way in which a man begins to think influences all his thinking to the end of his life. Begin by seeking for what is true, not for what is false, in the thought and belief which you find about you. Be as critical as you will, search as severely as you want to into the belief which offers itself for your acceptance, but let your search and criticism always have for its purpose that you may find what you may believe, not that you may find what you need not believe. Some things which your first thinking accepts, your riper thought may feel compelled to lay aside ; but the habit of believing once established will not be lost out of your life, and the young man's time is the time to make that habit. Scepticism is not merely the disbelief of some propositions. If it were that, there is not one of us but would be a sceptic. It is the habit and the preference of disbelieving. God save us all from that scepticism !

V. 101.

Read much, learn much,
Yet you must always come to one beginning —
I am He
That teaches man knowledge.
I give a clearer understanding to the little ones
Than can be given by man.
I, even I, lift even in a flash the simple mind
To understand more ways of the eternal truth
Than if a man had studied in the schools ten years.

THOMAS À KEMPIS.

The length and the breadth and the height of it are equal. — REV. xxi. 16.

THE life which to its length and breadth adds height, which to its personal ambition and sympathy with man adds the love and obedience of God, completes itself into the cube of the eternal city and is the life complete. Think for a moment of the life of the great apostle, the manly, many-sided Paul. "I press toward the mark for the prize of my high calling;" he writes to the Philippians. That is the length of life for him. "I will gladly spend and be spent for you;" he writes to the Corinthians. There is the breadth of life for him. "God hath raised us up and made us sit together in heavenly places in Christ Jesus;" he writes to the Ephesians. There is the height of life for him. You can add nothing to these three dimensions when you try to account to yourself for the impression of completeness which comes to you out of his simple, lofty story.

Look at the Lord of Paul. See how in Christ the same symmetrical manhood shines yet more complete. See what intense ambition to complete His work, what tender sympathy with every struggling brother by His side, and at the same time what a perpetual dependence on His Father is in Him. "For this cause came I into the world." "For their sakes I sanctify myself." "Now, O Father, glorify Thou me." Leave either of these out, and you have not the perfect Christ, not the entire symmetry of manhood.   II. 124, 125.

THERE is a science of knowledge, as well as a science of fossils, and a science of stars. The sacredness of all knowledge as the gift of God ; the unity of all knowledge as the utterance of God ; the purpose of all knowledge as the food of character in the knower and the helper of humanity through Him — these are the great departments of that science. . . .

Oh, my friends, boys studying at college, men and women reading books and struggling so restlessly for culture, there is no way to win this highest knowledge, — the knowledge of how to know, — but in the service of the God of Light, who is also the God of Love, the God of Character, the God of Man. Any industrious man with a good brain and a good memory can know things if he will ; only the reverent and devoted man can know how to know.

V. 152, 153.

> Who loves not Knowledge? Who shall rail
>   Against her beauty? . . .
>   But she is earthly, of the mind,
> And Wisdom heavenly, of the soul.
>
> TENNYSON.

II. Cor. i. 6.

TO be a true minister to men is always to accept new happiness and new distress, both of them forever deepening and entering into closer and more inseparable union with each other the more profound and spiritual the ministry becomes. The man who gives himself to other men can never be a wholly sad man; but no more can he be a man of unclouded gladness. To him shall come with every deeper consecration a before untasted joy, but in the same cup shall be mixed a sorrow that it was beyond his power to feel before. They who long to sit with Jesus on His throne may sit there if the Father sees them pure and worthy, but they must be baptized with the baptism that He is baptized with. All truly consecrated men learn little by little that what they are consecrated to is not joy or sorrow, but a divine idea and a profound obedience, which can find their full outward expression not in joy, and not in sorrow, but in the mysterious and inseparable mingling of the two. INFLUENCE, 191, 192.

'TO believe, to believe alone is to live. Scepticism as a habit, as a condition, is a sign of deficient vitality. It is a vastly nobler fear which dreads lest it should lose some truth than that which trembles lest it should believe something which is not wholly true. " Seek Truth and pursue it." Of course seeking the Truth, you will hate and avoid the lie, — that goes without saying, — but not to avoid the lie, but to find the Truth. Scepticism only for the sake of Faith, — that is Christ's brave and healthy law of life.

HARVARD MONTHLY, 182.

From doubt, where all is double ;
Where wise men are not strong,
Where comfort turns to trouble,
Where just men suffer wrong ;
Where sorrow treads on joy,
Where sweet things soonest cloy,
Where faiths are built on dust,
Where love is half mistrust,
Hungry, and barren, and sharp as the sea ---
Oh ! set us free.
O let the false dream fly,
Where our sick souls do lie
Tossing continually !
O where thy voice doth come
Let all doubts be dumb,
Let all words be mild,
All strifes be reconciled,
All pains beguiled !
Light bring no blindness,
Love no unkindness,
Knowledge no ruin,
Fear no undoing !
From the cradle to the grave
Save, oh ! save.

MATTHEW ARNOLD.

THERE is in you a power of loving awe which needs infinite perfection and mercy to call it out and satisfy it.   There is an affection which you cannot exercise towards any imperfect being.   It is that mixture of admiration and reverence and fear and love, which we call worship. . . . If this power is not utterly to die within you, do you not need God ?   If you are not to lose that highest reach of love and fear where, uniting, they make worship, must you not have God ?   Lo! before this expiring faculty the personal God comes and stands, and it lifts up its dying hands to reach after Him ; it opens its dying eyes to look upon Him ; as when a man is perishing of starvation, the sight of bread summons him back to life.   He need not die, but live, for here is his own life-food come to him.

II. 102, 103.

Trembling before Thee we fall down to adore Thee,
   Shamefaced and trembling we lift our eyes to Thee :
O First and with the last ! annul our ruined past,
   Rebuild us to Thy glory, set us free
   From sin and from sorrow to fall down and worship
      Thee.
Full of pity, view us, stretch Thy sceptre to us,
   Bid us live that we may give ourselves to Thee :
O Faithful Lord and true ! stand up for us and do,
   Make us lovely, make us new, set us free,
Heart and soul and spirit to bring all and worship
      Thee.

CHRISTINA ROSSETTI.

JOY or delight in what we are doing is not a mere luxury ; it is a means, a help for the more perfect doing of our work.   Indeed it may be truly said that no man does any work perfectly who does not enjoy his work.   Joy in one's work is the consummate tool without which the work may be done indeed, but without which the work will always be done slowly, clumsily, and without its finest perfectness. Men who do their work without enjoying it are like men carving statues with hatchets.   The statue gets carved perhaps, and is a monument forever of the dogged perseverance of the artist ; but there is a perpetual waste of toil, and there is no fine result in the end.

II. 31.

A man's joy in what he has to do is the heart and soul of his relation to it ; or rather it is the relation of his heart and soul to it.   Faithfulness to one's work may be only an outside bondage, but joy in it is a relationship of heart to heart, — of the heart of the man to the heart of his task.

V. 325.

Then a voice that came not from moon or star,
From the sun, or the wind roving afar,
Said, " Man, I am with thee — hear my voice."
And man said, " I rejoice."

GEORGE MacDONALD.

IT is in the silences of Nature that we are often sensible of being most near to Nature's heart. Not when the thunder is roaring, nor when the winds are sighing, but in some hour of the morning or the evening when even the distant song of a bird seems an intrusion, when the silence of Nature grows a transparent veil which reveals and does not hide her loveliness, — then is the time when you know how lovely Nature is !   V. 137, 139.

Love, now an universal birth,
From heart to heart is stealing,
From earth to man, from man to earth,
— It is the hour of feeling.

One moment now may give us more
Than fifty years of reason :
Our minds shall drink at every pore
The spirit of the season.

Some silent laws our hearts will make,
Which they shall long obey :
We for the year to come may take
Our temper from to-day.

And from the blessed power that rolls
About, below, above,
We'll frame the measure of our souls :
They shall be tuned to Love.

WORDSWORTH.

SILENCE has as various moods as speech, and its moods are far more subtle. . . . The completest joy and the profoundest sorrow, both are silent.   It is as different in men as it is in Nature.   There is the silence of sunrise, all tremulous with hope, and the silence of sunset, wrapped in the stillness of its memories.   There is the stillness of the snake slipping unseen through the grass, the silence of the war-horse waiting for the signal of the battle.   How different they are from one another, yet all alike are silent.

V. 125.

What is the saddest, sweetest, lowest sound
   Nearest akin to perfect silence?   Not
   The delicate whisper sometimes in the hot
Autumnal morning heard the cornfields round;
Nor yet to lonely man, now almost bound
   By slumber, near his house a murmuring river
   Buzzing and droning o'er the shores for ever.
Not such faint voice of Autumn oat-encrowned,
And not such liquid murmur, O my heart!
   But tears that drop o'er graves, and sins, and fears,
   A sound the very weeper scarcely hears,
A music in which silence hath some part.
—O Thou, all gentle, Who all-hearing art,
   Hold not Thy peace, sweet Saviour, at my tears!

WILLIAM ALEXANDER.

I NEVER think of the silences of God without thinking how great is the delight which comes when any man discovers that God really has been answering him all the time when he thought that his prayers were all unheard. That must be one of the most exquisite joys of heaven. Among the vials which in the Book of Revelation held the prayers of saints, there must be some which, when the saints who prayed them find them in their vision-time, shine with a brilliancy supremely precious. They are the prayers which seemed as if they were not answered, but which really did bring down their blessing.

V. 132.

Wilt thou not ope the heart to know
What rainbows teach, and sunsets show?
Verdict which accumulates
From lengthening scroll of human fates,
Voice of earth to earth returned,
Prayers of saints that inly burned, —
Saying : ·· *What is excellent,*
As God lives is permanent ;
Hearts are dust, hearts' loves remain.
Heart's love will meet thee again.

EMERSON.

THE suffering Saviour inly known, and through His wounds letting out His life into the starved lives of those who hold Him fast, that is the Gospel. It is not what church you belong to or what work you do, but what you know of, how deeply you are fed by Him — the suffering Saviour. That is the question for the soul.

Before His cross the lesson must be learned. Stand there until you are grateful through and through for such a love so marvellously shown. Let gratitude open your life to receive His Spirit ; let it make you long and try to be like Him ; let love bring Him into you so that you shall do His will because you have His heart. That entrance of His life into you shall give you strength and nourishment you never knew before.

II. 251.

When temptation sore is rife,
When we faint amidst the strife,
Thou, whose death hath been our life,
    Save us, Holy Jesu.

While on stormy seas we toss,
Let us count all things but loss,
But Thee only on Thy Cross :
    Save us, Holy Jesu.

So, with hope in Thee made fast,
When death's bitterness is past
We may see Thy Face at last :
    Save us, Holy Jesu.

LITANY OF THE PASSION.

Seraphic intellect and force
    To seize and throw the doubts of man;
    Impassion'd logic, which outran
The hearer in its fiery course;

High nature amorous of the good,
    But touch'd with no ascetic gloom;
    And passion pure in snowy bloom
Thro' all the years of April blood;

And manhood fused with female grace
    In such a sort, the child would twine
    A trustful hand, unask'd, in thine,
And find his comfort in thy face;

All these have been, and thee mine eyes
    Have look'd on: if they look'd in vain,
    My shame is greater who remain,
Nor let thy wisdom make me wise.

TENNYSON.

THESE are the qualities which we have seen in the choice young man, — purity of body, mind, and soul; simple integrity, and a dignity which will not have what is not his, no matter under what specious form of game or wager it has come into his hands; tenderness, sympathy, sentiment, — call it what name you will, a soul that is not cynical, or cruel; and positive, broad thought and conviction. . . . It is always sad not to feel the choiceness of anything which has in it wonderful and fine capacities, — to be content with the ordinariness and coarseness of that which is capable of being exquisite and great. Oh, that there could thrill through the being of our young men some electrical sense that they are God's sons, that so they might make themselves the servants of His Christ, and live the life and attain the nature which are rightly theirs.

V. 102, 105.

Give attendance to reading, to exhortation, to doctrine. . . . Take heed unto thyself, and unto the doctrine ; continue in them : for in doing this thou shalt both save thyself, and them that hear thee.

I. TIM. iv. 13, 16.

THE truth is, no preaching ever had any strong power that was not the preaching of doctrine. The preachers that have moved and held men have always preached doctrine. No exhortation to a good life that does not put behind it some truth as deep as eternity can seize and hold the conscience. Preach doctrine, preach all the doctrine that you know, and learn forever more and more ; but preach it always, not that men may believe it, but that men may be saved by believing it. So it shall be live, not dead. So men shall rejoice in it and not decry it. So they shall feed on it at your hands as on the bread of life, solid and sweet, and claiming for itself the appetite of man which God made for it.   PREACHING, 129.

To decry dogma in the interest of character, is like despising food as if it interfered with health. Food is not health. The human body is built just so as to turn food into health and strength. And truth is not holiness. The human soul is made to turn, by the subtle chemistry of its digestive experience, truth into goodness. And this, I think, is just what the Christian, as he goes on, finds himself doing under God's grace.   II. 43.

IS it success in the struggle of life simply to get through with decency and die without disgrace or shame ? Is it success in the struggle of life just to have so laid hold on God's mercy, to have so made our peace with Him, that we know we shall not be punished for our sins ? Is it success in the struggle of life even to have so lived in His presence that every day has been bright with the sense that He was taking care of us ? These things are very good ; but if the purpose of God's government of the world and of us is what I said, then the real victory in the struggle can be nothing less than the accomplishment in us of that which it is the object of all His government to accomplish in the world. When, truly obedient, we have been made like Him whom we obey, then, only then, we have overcome in the struggle of life.   II. 70, 71.

And will not, then, the immortal armies scorn
The world's poor, routed leavings? or will they,
Who fail'd under the heat of this life's day,
Support the fervors of the heavenly morn?
No, no! the energy of life may be
Kept on after the grave, but not begun!
And he who flagg'd not in the earthly strife,
From strength to strength advancing — only he,
His soul well-knit, and all his battles won,
Mounts, and that hardly, to eternal life.
                              MATTHEW ARNOLD.

The light will never open sightless eyes,
It comes to those who willingly would see;
And every object — hill, and stream, and skies —
Rejoice within th' encircling line to be.
'Tis day — the field is filled with busy hands,
The shop resounds with noisy workmen's din,
The traveler with his staff already stands
His yet unmeasured journey to begin;
The light breaks gently, too, within the breast, —
Yet there no eye awaits the crimson morn,
The forge and noisy anvil are at rest,
Nor men nor oxen tread the fields of corn,
Nor pilgrim lifts his staff, — it is no day
To those who find on earth their place to stay.

JONES VERY.

THE spiritual nature of the world; that all this mass of things and events is fitted for and naturally struggles towards the education of character; the spiritual nature of man; . . . and God; . . . these are the before unseen realities which come pressing into your intelligence, tempting, demanding your recognition when your conscience is once open, when you have once begun to live in the desire and struggle to do right. Do you not see then what I mean when I say that the conscience stands between man's power of knowledge and the spiritual world, just as the eye stands between man's power of knowledge and the world of visible nature. It is the opened or unopened window through which flows the glorious knowledge of God and heaven; or outside of which that knowledge waits, as the sun with its glory or the flower with its beauty waits outside the closed eye of a blind or sleeping man.

II. 80, 81.

THE things that are spiritual bring their own sidelong testimonies of themselves. They touch my sense of beauty. They make me feel how good it would be for the world if they were true. I hear their movement in the depths of history. . . . Yet there stands the separate glory of the revelation of that day when to me, at last beginning to try to do right, the God whose faint reports have come to me pours in upon my opened soul the glorious conviction of His righteousness and love; and my soul, in which I have half believed, becomes the centre of my life; *becomes* my life, that for which all the other parts of me are made. Then, in the knowledge which pours through my opened conscience, then I know with an assurance which makes all the knowledge that I had before seem but a guess and dim suspicion.   II. 82.

> Ah, there is something here
> Unfathomed by the cynic's sneer,
> Something that gives our feeble light
> A high immunity from Night,
> Something that leaps life's narrow bars
> To claim its birthright with the hosts of heaven;
>
> .   .   .   .
>
> A conscience more divine than we,
> A gladness fed with secret tears,
> A vexing, forward-reaching sense
> Of some more noble permanence;
> A light across the sea,
> Which haunts the soul and will not let it be,
> Still glimmering from the heights of undegenerate years.

JAMES RUSSELL LOWELL.

Mine eyes have seen the King, the Lord of Hosts.
                                        Is. vi. 5.

WHEN one declares that through the conscience man arrives at the knowledge of unseen things, and conceptions of God and spiritual force and immortality reveal themselves to the intelligence, at once the suggestion comes from some one who is listening, " Can we be sure of the reality of what thus seems to be made known ? How can we be sure that what the conscience sends in to the understanding are not mere creations of its own ; things which it thinks exist because it seems to need them ; mere forms in which it has been led to clothe with outward and substantial life its own emotions? " . . . Are not then the questions which haunt the conscience the same as those which haunt the eye ? And as the eye deals with its questions, so will the conscience always deal with its. A conviction of the reality of what it sees, which is a part of its consciousness that no suspicion can disturb ; a use of its knowledge, which brings ever a more and more complete assurance of its trustworthiness, — these are the practical issue of every such question with regard to what the brain sees through the eye ; and the same will be the practical issue of every question with regard to what the soul sees through the conscience. At least we may say this, that it would be a very deep confidence indeed if the soul felt as sure of God as the mind feels of nature.   II. 82, 83.

Looking unto Jesus, the author and finisher of our faith ; who, for the joy that was set before Him, endured the cross, despising the shame, and is set down at the right hand of the throne of God.

HEB. xii. 2.

AS Jesus was, so may we be, seeking an end so great, so constant, so eternal that every change may come to us and be our minister and not our conqueror ; that even our cross may come as His came, and men may gather round it and say, " Alas, then this is all !   Alas, that finally it should all come to this ! "   While we who hang upon the cross cry, " It is finished," with a shout of triumph, counting the finishing but a new beginning, and looking out beyond the cross to richer growth in character, and braver and more fruitful service of our Lord !   V. 372, 373.

Was it not great? did he not throw on God,
    (He loves the burthen) —
God's task to make the heavenly period
    Perfect the earthen ?

  .   .   .   .

He ventured neck or nothing — heaven's success
    Found, or earth's failure :
" Wilt thou trust death or not ? " He answered, " Yes.
    Hence with life's pale lure."

BROWNING.

EVERY emotion has its higher and its lower forms. It means but little to me if I know only that a man is happy or unhappy, if I do not know of what sort his joy or sorrow is. But all the emotions are certainly tempted to larger action if it is realized that the world in which they take their birth is but for a little time, that its fashion passes away, that the circumstances of an experience are very transitory. That must drive me down into the essence of every experience, and make me realize it in the profoundest and the largest way. . . . (Our grief exalted to its largest form) grows unselfish. It is perfectly consistent with a triumphant thankfulness for the dear soul that has entered into rest and glory. It dwells not on the circumstances of bereavement, but upon that mysterious strain in which love has been stretched from this world to the other, and, amid all the pain that the tension brings, is still aware of joy at the new knowledge of its own capacities which has been given it.

I. 325, 326.

My love involves the love before;
  My love is vaster passion now;
  Tho' mixed with God and Nature thou,
I seem to love thee more and more.

Far off thou art, but ever nigh;
  I have thee still, and I rejoice;
  I prosper, circled with thy voice;
I shall not lose thee tho' I die.

TENNYSON.

CHRIST comes and puts His essential life into our human form.   In that form He claims the truest brotherhood with us.   He shares our lot.   He binds His life with ours so that they never can be separated.   What He is we must be; what we are, He must be forever.   Finally by the cross of love, He entering into our death takes us completely into His life.   And when He had done all this He rose.   Out of His tomb, standing there among human tombs, He comes, and lo, before Him there rolls on the unbroken endlessness of Being.   And not before Him alone, — before those also whom He had taken so completely to Himself.   His resurrection makes our resurrection sure.   Our earthly life, like His, becomes an episode, a short, special, temporary thing, when it is seen like His against an immortality.

I. 331.

Earth breaks up, time drops away,
In flows Heaven, with its new day
Of endless life, when He who trod,
Very Man and very God,
This earth in weakness, shame and pain,
Dying the death whose signs remain,
Up yonder on the accursed tree, —
Shall come again, no more to be
Of captivity the thrall,
But the one God, All in all,
King of kings, Lord of lords,
As His servant John received the words,
"I died, and live forevermore!"

BROWNING.

THERE is somewhere in the human mind an image of human character in which all wayward impulses are restrained, not by outside compulsion, but by the firm grasp of a power which holds everything into obedience from within by the central purpose of the life. This character dreads fury and excitement as signs of feebleness. It shrinks from self-display just in proportion as it accepts the responsibilities of selfhood. It is patient because it is powerful. It is tolerant because it is sure. It is this character, I think, which St. Paul calls by his great word moderation. It is self-possession. It is the self found and possessed in God. It is the sweet reasonableness which was in Jesus.

IV. 367, 368.

Whose high endeavors are an inward light
That makes the path before him always bright:

More skilful in self-knowledge, even more pure,
As tempted more; more able to endure,
As more exposed to suffering and distress;
Thence, also, more alive to tenderness.

But who, if he be called upon to face
Some awful moment to which Heaven has joined
Great issues, good or bad for human kind,
Is happy as a lover; and attired
With sudden brightness, like a man inspired;
And, through the heat of conflict, keeps the law
In calmness made, and sees what he foresaw;
Or if an unexpected call succeed,
Come when it will, is equal to the need.

WORDSWORTH.

IN our own little sphere, it is not the most
active people to whom we owe the most.
Among the common people whom we know
it is not necessarily those who are busiest, not
those who, meteor-like, are ever on the rush
after some visible change and work. It is the
lives, like the stars, which simply pour down
on us the calm light of their bright and faithful
being, up to which we look and out of which
we gather the deepest calm and courage.

i. 105.

QUIET WORK.

One lesson, Nature, let me learn of thee,
One lesson, which in every wind is blown,
One lesson of two duties kept at one,
Though the loud world proclaim their enmity —

Of toil unsever'd from tranquillity !
Of labor, that in lasting fruit outgrows
Far noisier schemes, accomplish'd in repose —
Too great for haste, too high for rivalry !

Yes, while on earth a thousand discords ring,
Man's senseless uproar mingling with his toil,
Still do thy quiet ministers move on,

Their glorious tasks in silence perfecting !
Still working, blaming still our vain turmoil,
Laborers that shall not fail, when man is gone.

MATTHEW ARNOLD.

SOLITUDE makes the consciousness ; society develops, multiplies, and confirms it. That which would have remained only a quality in Jesus, if He had stayed in the desert, becomes a life when He goes forth into the world. What Goethe wisely says of all men does not lose its truth when we are thinking of the Son of Man : " A talent shapes itself in stillness, but a character in the tumult of the world." This is Christ's balance between solitude and society. Each makes the other necessary. With us they often lose this value, because they are not set in any relation to each other. Solitude is barren, and so society is frivolous. Solitude creates no consciousness for society to ripen. Solitude is like an unfertile seed, and society is like an unplanted ground.   INFLUENCE, 105, 106.

By all means use sometimes to be alone.
Salute thyself : see what thy soul doth wear.
Dare to look in thy chest ; for 'tis thine own :
And tumble up and down what thou find'st there.
Who cannot rest till he good fellows find,
He breaks up house, turns out of doors his mind.
GEORGE HERBERT.

Open innumerable doors
To heaven where unveiled Allah pours
The flood of truth, the flood of good,
The Seraph's and the Cherub's food.
Those doors are men : the Pariah hind
Admits thee to the perfect Mind.
RALPH WALDO EMERSON.

IF you look back to the men who have taught you most, and in the fuller light where you now stand, study their character, you will surely find that the real secret of their power lay here, in the harmonious blending of the knowing and the loving powers in their nature ; in the opening of their nature on both sides, so that truth entered in freely here and you entered in freely there, and you and truth met, as it were, familiarly in the hospitality of their great characters. The man who has only the knowing power active, lets truth in, but it finds no man to feed. The man who has only the loving power active, lets man in, but he finds no truth to feed on. The real teacher welcomes both. . . Grace and Truth ! These are exactly the two elements of which we have been speaking, and it must have been in the perfect meeting of those two elements in Jesus that His mediatorship, His power to transmute the everlasting truths of God into the immediate help of needy men consisted. He was no rapt self-centred student of the abstract truth ; nor was he the merely ready sentimental pitier of the woes of men. But in His whole nature there was finely wrought and combined the union of the abstract and eternal with the special and the personal.

IV. 10, 12.

One poor day! —

Remember whose and not how short it is!
It is God's day, it is Columbus's.
A lavish day! One day, with life and heart,
Is more than time enough to find a world.

JAMES RUSSELL LOWELL.

ONE year God lifted the curtain from a hidden continent, and gave His children a whole new world in which to carry out His purposes. Another year He revealed to them a strange, simple little invention which made the treasured knowledge of the few to be the free heritage of all. Another year He touched the solid frame of a great spiritual despotism, and it trembled and quaked, and thousands of its slaves came forth free men. Another year, in our own time, in our own land, He sent the message of liberty to a nation of bondmen, and the fetters fell off from their limbs. We call these events of history. They have a right to be called the comings of the Lord. They all are echoes and illustrations of that great coming of the Lord from which they who have known of it agree by instinctive consent to date their history, the birth of the child of Bethlehem, the Man of Nazareth and Calvary into the world.

IV. 363, 364.

"BRETHREN, the time is short." There is the fact, then, forever pressing on us, and these are the consequences which it ought to bring to those who feel its pressure. Behold, it is no dreary shadow hanging above our heads and shutting out the sunshine. It is an everlasting inspiration. It makes a man know himself and his career. It makes him put his heart into the heart of the career which he knows to be his. It makes the emotions and experiences of life great and not petty to him. It makes life solemn and interesting with criticalness; and it makes friendship magnanimous, and the desire to help our fellow-men real and energetic. It concentrates and invigorates our lives. In the brightest, freshest, clearest mornings, it comes to us not as a cloud, not as a paralysis, but as a new brightness in the sunshine and a new vigor in the arm. "Brethren, the time is short." Only remember the shortness of life is not a reality to us, except as it shows itself against a true realization of eternity.

I. 330.

Up, my drowsing eyes!
  Up, my sinking heart!
Up to Jesus Christ arise!
  Claim your part
In all rapture of the skies.

Yet a little while,
  Yet a little way,
Saints shall reap and rest and smile
  All the day: —
Up! let's trudge another mile.

CHRISTINA ROSSETTI.

Phillips Brooks consecrated Bishop, 1891.

THE SHEPHERD OF THE PEOPLE ! He fed us faithfully and truly. He fed us with counsel when we were in doubt, with inspiration when we sometimes faltered, with caution when we would be rash, with calm, clear, trustful cheerfulness through many an hour when our hearts were dark. He fed hungry souls all over the country with sympathy and consolation. He spread before the whole land feasts of great duty and devotion and patriotism, on which the land grew strong. He fed us with solemn, solid truths. . . . He made our souls glad and vigorous with the love of liberty that was in his. He showed us how to love truth and yet be charitable — how to hate wrong and all oppression, and yet not treasure one personal injury or insult. . . . He spread before us the love and fear of God just in that shape in which we need them most, and out of his faithful service of a higher Master who of us has not taken and eaten and grown strong ?

SERMON ON ABRAHAM LINCOLN.

Therefore to thee it was given
Many to save with thyself ;
And, at the end of thy day,
O faithful shepherd ! to come,
Bringing thy sheep in thy hand.

MATTHEW ARNOLD.

CHRISTIANITY, or the change of man's life by Christ, has three different aspects in which it appears — three ways in which it makes its power known. It appears either as Truth, as Righteousness, or as Love. Every soul which is really redeemed by Christ will enter into new beliefs, higher ways of action, and deeper affections towards fellow-men. . . . All spiritual character must reside ultimately in single souls ; but still I think that it is manifestly true that an aggregate of individuals may possess in its own peculiar way the spiritual character which the individual possesses, and a city, like a man, have and exhibit Christian faith and Christian righteousness and Christian love.

III. 139, 140.

I dream'd in a dream I saw a city invincible to the attacks of the whole of the rest of the earth,
I dream'd that was the new city of Friends,
Nothing was greater there than the quality of robust love, it led the rest,
It was seen every hour in the actions of the men of that city,
And in all their looks and words.

WALT WHITMAN.

You're my friend —
What a thing friendship is, world without end !
How it gives the heart and soul a stir-up,
As if somebody broached you a glorious runlet !
BROWNING.

THERE is nothing so bad for man or woman as to live always with their inferiors. It is a truth so important, that one might well wish to turn aside a moment and urge it, even in its lower aspects, upon the young people who are just making their associations and friendships. Many a temptation of laziness or pride induces us to draw towards those who do not know as much or are not in some way as strong as we are. It is a smaller tax upon our powers to be in their society. But it is bad for us. I am sure that I have known men, intellectually and morally very strong, the whole development of whose intellectual and moral life has suffered and been dwarfed, because they have only accompanied with their inferiors, because they have not lived with men greater than themselves. Whatever else they lose, they surely must lose some culture of humility. If I could choose a young man's companions, some should be weaker than himself, that he might learn patience and charity ; many should be as nearly as possible his equals, that he might have the full freedom of friendship ; but most should be stronger than he was, that he might forever be thinking humbly of himself and be tempted to higher things. I. 339, 340.

IF in doing (your work), the principal blessing of it all was that it permitted you to
look into God's soul and see how self-complete
and perfect and supreme He was; how, after
all His workings, it was not in His works but in
His nature, not in His doing but in His being,
that God's true glory lay; if as you worked
with Him, you really looked into His nature
and discerned all this, — then when He takes
your work away and bids you no longer to do
good and obedient things but only to be good
and obedient, surely that is not the death of
faith.   That may be faith's transfiguration.

V. 322.

Lord, I had planned to do Thee service true,
To be more humbly watchful unto prayer,
More faithful in obedience to Thy Word,
More bent to put away all earthly care.

I thought of sad hearts comforted and healed,
Of wanderers turned into the pleasant way,
Of little ones preserved from sinful snare,
Of dark homes brightened with a heavenly ray;

Of time all consecrated to Thy Will,
Of strength spent gladly for Thee, day by day, —
When suddenly the heavenly mandate came,
That I should give it all, at once, away.

. . . .

And was it loss, to have indulged such hopes?
Nay, they were gifts, from out the Inner Shrine, —
Garlands, that I might hang about Thy Cross,
Gems, to surrender at the call Divine.

CAROLINE M. NOEL.

Luke the beloved physician. — COL. iv. 14.

MAY we not say this of the two works (theology and medicine), that, first, they above all others demand, as of fundamental importance, character in the men who do them; and that, second, the element of merciful feeling and readiness for self-sacrifice which are incidental to most other occupations are essential and indispensable in these two? These are what really mark how divine they are, and how they belong together. . . . I add to this that both live constantly in the immediate presence of awful and mysterious forces; that both are always, while they see before them human need, feeling behind them that which, call it by what name they will, is Divine Power — is God; and so are always pressed on by the demand for reverence and piety.

I add again that while each has its immediate appeal to make to terror and the fear of pain, the ultimate address of each must be to ardent courage and enthusiastic hope. I put all these together and then the figures of Paul and Luke walking together through history as the ministers of Christ, — the images of theology and medicine laboring in harmony for the redemption of man, for the saving of body, soul, and spirit, — become very sacred and impressive. May their fellowship become more generous and hearty as the years go on! May each gain greater honor for the other, and both become more humbly and transparently the ministers of Christ!

V. 232, 233.

AS you grow better . . . you sweep up out of the grasp of money, praise, ease, distinction. You sweep up into the necessity of truth, courage, virtue, love, and God. The gravitation of the earth grows weaker, the gravitation of the stars takes stronger and stronger hold upon you. And on the other hand, as you grow worse, as you go down, the terrible opposite of all this comes to pass. The highest necessities let you go, and the lowest necessities take tighter hold of you. Still, as you go down, you are judged by what you can do without and what you cannot do without. You come down at last where you cannot do without a comfortable dinner and an easy bed, but you can do without an act of charity or a thought of God.

I. 293.

Oh, good, gigantic smile o' the brown old earth,
This autumn morning! How he sets his bones
To bask i' the sun, and thrusts out knees and feet
For the ripple to run over in its mirth;
Listening the while, where on the heap of stones
The white breast of the sea-lark twitters sweet.

That is the doctrine, simple, ancient, true;
Such is life's trial, as old earth smiles and knows.
If you loved only what were worth your love,
Love were clear gain, and wholly well for you:
Make the low nature better by your throes!
Give earth yourself, go up for gain above!

BROWNING.

HE who comes into the presence of any powerful nature, whose power is at all of a spiritual sort, feels sure that in some way he is coming into the presence of God. But it would be melancholy if only the great men could give us this conviction. The world would be darker than it is if every human spirit, so soon as it became obedient, did not become the Lord's candle. . . . There is no life so humble that, if it be true and genuinely human and obedient to God, it may not hope to shed some of His light. There is no life so meagre that the greatest and wisest of us can afford to despise it. We cannot know at all at what sudden moment it may flash forth with the life of God.

II. 8, 9.

Our little systems have their day ;
They have their day and cease to be :
They are but broken lights of Thee,
And Thou, O Lord, art more than they.

TENNYSON.

Jesus said unto him, Thou shalt love the Lord thy God . . . with all thy mind. — MATT. xxii. 37.

GOD, the Father of men, is not satisfied if His children give Him simply gratitude for His mercies or the most loyal obedience to His will ; He wants also, as the fulfilment of their love to Him, the enthusiastic use of their intellects, intent to know everything that it is possible for men to know about their Father and His ways. That is what is meant by loving God with the mind. And is there not something sublimely beautiful and touching in this demand of God that the noblest part of His children's nature should come to Him ? " Understand me ! understand me ! " He seems to cry ; "I am not wholly loved by you unless your understanding is reaching out after my truth, and with all your powers of thoughtfulness and study you are trying to find out all that you can about my nature and my ways."   III. 32.

Vouchsafe then, O Thou most Almightie Spright !
From whom all gifts of wit and knowledge flow,
To shed into my breast some sparkling light
Of Thine eternall Truth, that I may show
Some litle beames to mortall eyes below
Of that immortall beautie, there with Thee,
Which in my weake distraughted mynd I see.
                                        SPENSER.

IT is the continuity of life, the continuity of nature, that is our salvation. " Nothing from nothing " is the first law of her household, and her dullest children must learn it, for it is written on the walls that shelter them, on the ground they tread, on the table from which they eat, and on the tools with which they work.

And her law of economy is just as clear. Profusion, but no waste; this is the lesson that Nature reads us everywhere. The dead leaves of this autumn are worked into next year's soil. The little stream that has watered the greenness of many meadows goes afterwards to do duty in the great sea. The vast surrounding atmosphere is made efficient over and over again for the breath of living men. Everywhere profusion, but no waste. For men who need to be trained to reasonableness and care, God has built just the home they needed for their training, and sent us to live in this star which shines among His other stars steadily and soberly with its double light of continuity and economy.

II. 132, 133.

Mother she is and cradle of our race,
   A depth where treasures lie,
The broad foundation of a holy place,
   Man's step to scale the sky.

Earth may not pass till heaven shall pass away,
   Nor heaven may be renewed
Except with earth; and once more in that day
   Earth shall be very good.

CHRISTINA ROSSETTI.

CONTINUITY and economy ; these are the laws of Him who is leading us, the Captain of our salvation.   He always binds the future to the past, and He wastes nothing. O, there are some here who want to get away from all their past; who, if they could, would fain begin all over again.   Their life with Christ seems one long failure.   But you must learn, you must let God teach you, that the only way to get rid of your past is to get a future out of it.   God will waste nothing. There is something in your past, something, even if it only be the sin of which you have repented, which, if you can put it into the Saviour's hands, will be a new life for you.

II. 145.

'Forsake the Christ thou sawest transfigured, Him
Who trod the sea and brought the dead to life?
What should wring this from thee? '— ye laugh and
    ask.
What wrung it?   Even a torchlight and a noise,
The sudden Roman faces, violent hands,
And fear of what the Jews might do !   Just that,
And, it is written, ' I forsook and fled ':
There was my trial and it ended thus.
Ay, but my soul had gained its truth, could grow.

BROWNING.

YOU are a star and not a sun. Your place in life is not in the forefront of things; it is subordinate and secondary. What then? Can you learn this truth, — that if you do your work with complete faithfulness and with the most absolute perfectness with which it is capable of being done, you are making just as genuine a contribution to the substance of the universal good as is the most brilliant worker whom the world contains? You are setting as true a fact here between the eternities as he. You are doing what he cannot do. It is Emerson's fable of the Mountain and the Squirrel, —

> "If I cannot carry forests on my back,
> Neither can you crack a nut."

"There is one glory of the sun, and another glory of the stars."

All our works, even the greatest, are so little in relation to the world's need; all our works, even the least, are so great in relation to the doer's faithfulness. There is the secret of self-respect. Oh, go take up your work and do it. Do it with cheerfulness and love. So shall you shine with a glory which is all your own, — a glory which the great heaven of universal life would be poorer for missing.

V. 68, 69.

> "Like as a star,
> That maketh not haste,
> That taketh not rest,
> Be each one fulfilling
> His God-given best."

A bruised reed shall He not break,
And the smoking flax shall He not quench :
He shall bring forth judgment unto truth.

Is. xlii. 3.

TO say "well-done" to any bit of work that has embodied good effort, is to take hold of the powers which have made the effort and confirm and strengthen them. But if you have nothing to say to your child or to your scholar except (what may be perfectly true) that much of his work is badly done, that he is wasting opportunities and losing the value of his life, then you are coming to him not to fulfil but to destroy.

I beg you to think of this, you who are set in positions of superintendence and authority. Make a great deal more of your right to praise the good than of your right to blame the bad. Never let a brave and serious struggle after truth and goodness, however weak it may be, pass unrecognized. Do not be chary of appreciation. Hearts are unconsciously hungry for it. There is little danger, especially with us in this cold New England region, that appreciation shall be given too abundantly.   IV. 214, 215.

And he said unto Jesus, Lord, remember me when Thou comest into Thy kingdom. And Jesus said unto him, Verily I say unto thee, To-day shalt thou be with Me in Paradise.

LUKE xxiii. 42, 43.

WITH silent, soft, and mighty pressure, the sight of the Sufferer's holiness, and the gratitude for the Sufferer's pity, as one complete power, one perfect love, has drawn the depths of men's lives on to the nature of the Sufferer, and there their oneness to Him has become known to them, and they, in and through Him, have been renewed into the image of their Father, and His Father. The robber who was crucified with Him felt that power first. It was a baptism of blood, and the power which our baptisms re-echo found its first utterance in Him. " Being by nature, born in sin and the child of wrath," there by the fellowship of suffering, there by the power of love, in which admiration and gratitude met, he was made the " child of grace."

INFLUENCE. 53.

O Jesus, Who lovest us all, stoop low from Thy
    Glory above :
Where sin hath abounded make grace to abound and
    superabound,
  Till we gaze on Thee face unto Face, and respond to
    Thee love unto Love.

CHRISTINA ROSSETTI.

I have finished my course, I have kept the faith.
II. TIM. iv. 7.

MEN lose their love and trust and hope, as they grow old. Here was a man [St. Paul] who kept them all fresh to the last. Men cease to have strong convictions, and grow cynical or careless. Here was a man who believed more, and not less, as he knew more of God, and of himself, and of the world. His old age did not come creeping into port, a wreck, with broken masts and rudder gone, but full-sailed still, and strong for other voyages in other seas. We are sure that his was the old age God loves to see; that the careless and the hopeless and the faithless are the failures. To such men as Paul alone is God's promise to David fulfilled: " With long life will I satisfy him and show him my salvation."
II. 77.

Youth ended, I shall try
My gain or loss thereby;
Be the fire ashes, what survives is gold:
And I shall weigh the same,
Give life its praise or blame:
Young, all lay in dispute; I shall know being old.
BROWNING.

OUR creed, our credo, anything which we call by such a sacred name, is not what we have thought, but what our Lord has told us. The true creed must come down from above and not out from within. Have your opinions always, but do not bind yourself to them. Call your opinions your creed, and you will change it every week. Make your creed simply and broadly out of the revelation of God, and you may keep it to the end. This is the difference between the hundreds of long, detailed confessions of many differing sects, overloaded with the minute speculations of good men, which take in and dismiss their believers like the nightly lodgers of an eastern caravansary, and the short scriptural creed of the church universal, into which souls come seeking rest and strength, and live in it as in a home, and go no more out forever.   I. 71, 72.

O Almighty God, who hast built Thy Church upon the foundation of the Apostles and Prophets, Jesus Christ Himself being the head corner-stone ; Grant us so to be joined together in unity of spirit by their doctrine, that we may be made an holy temple acceptable unto Thee ; through Jesus Christ our Lord.

BOOK OF COMMON PRAYER.

While Peter thought on the vision, the Spirit said unto him, Behold, three men seek thee.

ACTS X. 19.

EVERY man has visions, glimpses clearer or duller, now bright and beautiful, now clouded and obscure, of what is absolutely and abstractly true; and every man also has pressing on him the warm, clear lives of fellow-men. There is the world of truths on one side, and there is the world of men upon the other. Between the two stands man; and these two worlds, if man is what he ought to be, meet through his nature.

.   .   .   .

Truth is vague and helpless until men believe it. Men are weak and frivolous till they believe in truth. To furnish truth to the believing heart, and to furnish believing hearts to truth, certainly there is no nobler office for a human life than that. . . . How can we better tell the story of you who first believe in God yourself and then are drawn out to make your fellow-men believe in Him, and in making them believe in Him find your own belief grow steadier and clearer — how shall we better depict this human life which never learns anything without hearing other human lives clamoring to share the blessings of its knowledge than by recurring to the story of Peter, to whom, "as he thought on the vision, the Spirit said, Behold, three men seek thee."

IV. 2, 4.

I am the . . . Truth. — JOHN xiv. 6.

THE great fact concerning (the intellectual life of Jesus) is this, that in Him the intellect never works alone. You never can separate its workings from the complete operation of the whole nature. He never simply knows, but always loves and resolves at the same time. Truth which the mind discovers becomes immediately the possession of the affections and the will. It cannot remain in the condition of mere knowledge. Indeed, knowledge is no word of Jesus. Solomon in the Book of Proverbs is always talking about knowledge. Jesus, in the Gospel of John, is always talking about truth. So genuine is the unity of His being, that what comes to Him as knowledge is pressed and gathered into every part of Him, and fills His entire nature as truth. The rays of intellectual light are absorbed into the whole substance of the spontaneous affections and the unerring will. The right and the true, the wrong and the false, are not separable from one another. The life is simple because of its completeness. It is the true unity of a man.

INFLUENCE, 219.

> O Father of Truth,
>   Have mercy upon us.
> O Express Image of the Father,
>   Change us into Thy likeness.
> O Ineffable Truth,
>   Guide us into all truth.

BOOK OF LITANIES. NEALE.

If any man will do His will, he shall know of the doctrine. — JOHN vii. 17.

If a man love me, he will keep my words: and my Father will love him, and we will come unto him, and make our abode with him.

JOHN xiv. 23.

THOSE, I think, are the two critical passages in which Jesus gives us His doctrine of the intellectual life. They are as clear and definite as if they were written in a book of science. They both declare that in the highest things the intellect can never work alone for the discovery of truth. Truth, when it is won, is the possession of the whole nature. By the action of the whole nature only can it be gained. The king must go with his counsellors at his side and his army at his back, or he makes no conquest. The intellect must be surrounded by the richness of the affections and backed by the power of the will, or it attains no perfect truth.

INFLUENCE, 247.

Happy the man taught by the truth itself;
Not by the shapes and sounds that pass across his life
But by the very truth.
Our thoughts and senses often lead us wrong;
They see one side alone.

 . . . .

  O God of truth
Make me one with Thee in eternal love.
Oft am I weary, reading, listening,
But all I wish and long for is in Thee.
Then silent be all teachers, hushed be all creation at the
  sight of Thee:
Speak Thou to me alone.

THOMAS À KEMPIS.

YOU go to your saint and find God working and manifest in him. He got near to God by some saint of his that went before him, or that stood beside him, in whom he saw the Divine presence. That saint again lighted his fire at some flame before him; and so the power of the sainthoods animates and fills the world. So holiness and purity, and truth and patience, daring and tenderness, hope and faith, are kept constant and pervading things in our humanity. Each man has not to begin and work them out from the beginning for himself. So there is a church of God as well as souls of God in the earth. This is the truth of All Saints.

I. 122, 123.

Then sudden silence made a little space
For the One Voice that fills the universe,
And Christ's own roll-call swept the white camp
    through.
And lo! the faithful noiseless moved as thought
Responsive, yet unconscious of response,
Their rapt eyes lifted to the shining morn,
As seeing Him who is invisible.
He named them, clan by clan, His chosen ones:
The poor in spirit, and the souls that mourn,
The meek, and those for righteousness athirst,
The merciful, the pure in heart, the just,
The valiant, the forbearing, named He thus.
For every clan a benediction sweet,
And sweeter promises of victory.

HARRIET McEWEN KIMBALL.

THE Church is the union of believers, out-wardly manifested by the sacraments, but having its essence in the personal union of each believer's soul with Christ. . . . This Jesus must be a true Lord of men. This power which draws His disciples to each other must be a genuine power. These sacraments must be in-trinsically natural utterances of what they try to express ; for, lo, everywhere the Church has built itself ! In every age, in every land she stands, her single life pulsating with the multi-tudinous life of which she is composed, the ul-timate pulsation coming from the living life of her Master, to which every particle of her being immediately responds ; the two jewels on her breast-plate burning with ever-deepening and accumulating richness, and making together the clasp which holds about her essential nature the robe of her outward form.　　　　　　V. 180.

> Lord, grant us eyes to see and ears to hear
>   And souls to love and minds to understand,
>   And steadfast faces toward the Holy Land,
> And confidence of hope, and filial fear,
> And citizenship where Thy saints appear
>   Before Thee heart in heart and hand in hand,
>   And Alleluias where their chanting band
> As waters and as thunders fill the sphere.
> Lord, grant us what Thou wilt, and what Thou wilt
>   Deny, and fold us in Thy peaceful fold :
>   Not as the world gives, give to us Thine own :
> Inbuild us where Jerusalem is built
> With walls of jasper and with streets of gold,
>   And Thou Thyself, Lord Christ, for Corner-Stone.
>   CHRISTINA ROSSETTI.

WE have sometimes known some men or women, helpless so that their lives seemed to be all dependent, who yet, through their sickness, had so mounted to a higher life and so identified themselves with Christ that those on whom they rested found the Christ in them and rested upon it. Their sick-rooms became churches. Their weak voices spoke gospels. The hands they seemed to clasp were really clasping theirs. They were depended on while they seemed to be most dependent. And when they died, when the faint flicker of their life went out, strong men whose light seemed radiant, found themselves walking in the darkness; and stout hearts, on which theirs used to lean, trembled as if the staff and substance of their strength was gone.

II. 365.

What is this psalm from pitiable places
  Glad where the messengers of peace have trod
Whose are these beautiful and holy faces
  Lit with their loving and aflame with God?

Eager and faint, empassionate and lonely,
  These in their hour shall prophesy again:
This is His will who hath endured, and only
  Sendeth the promise where He sends the pain.

Ay unto these distributeth the Giver
  Sorrow and sanctity, and loves them well,
Grants them a power and passion to deliver
  Hearts from the prison-house and souls from hell.

F. W. H. MYERS.

THE Holy Catholic Church, the Communion of Saints! Wherever men are praying, loving, trusting, seeking, and finding God, it is a true body with all its ministries of part to part. Nay, shall we stop at that poor line, the grave, which all our Christianity is always trying to wipe out and make nothing of, and which we always insist on widening into a great gulf? Shall we not stretch our thought beyond, and feel the life-blood of this holy church, this living body of Christ, pulsing out into the saints who are living there, and coming back throbbing with tidings of their glorious and sympathetic life. It is the very power of this truth of ours to-day, that it lays hold on immortality.

I. 133.

Light is our sorrow for it ends to-morrow,
Light is our death which cannot hold us fast;
So brief a sorrow can be scarcely sorrow,
Or death be death so quickly past.

One night, no more, of pain that turns to pleasure,
One night, no more, of weeping, weeping sore;
And then the heaped-up measure beyond measure,
  In quietness forevermore.

Our sails are set to cross the tossing river,
Our face is set to reach Jerusalem;
We toil awhile, but then we rest forever,
Sing with all Saints and rest with them above.

CHRISTINA ROSSETTI.

CORRUPTION in political life is really scepticism. It is a distrust, a disuse which has lasted so long that it has grown into disbelief of political principles, of the first fundamental truths of the sacredness of government and the necessity of righteousness. And where has such a disbelief come from ? We all know well enough. It is from the narrow view which has looked at machineries, and magnified them till they have hid from view the great purposes for which all machineries exist. If a man tells me that it is absolutely necessary that such or such a political party should be maintained whether its acts and its men are righteous or unrighteous, or else the government will fall, that man is an unbeliever. He has lost his faith in the first principles of government, and he has lost it by persistently tying down his study and his soul to second causes, to the mere machinery of party. I. 161.

Our fathers to their graves have gone ;
Their strife is past — their triumph won ;
But sterner trials wait the race
Which rises in their honored place —
A moral warfare with the crime
And folly of an evil time.

So let it be. In God's own might
We gird us for the coming fight,
And, strong in Him whose cause is ours
In conflict with unholy powers,
We grasp the weapons He has given, —
The Light, and Truth, and Love of Heaven.

WHITTIER.

IS there a greater call than that which comes out of the depths of a nation's needs? "Tell me what this means, and that, in my experience. Tell me how I shall get rid of this corruption and that danger. Tell me how I can best be governed. Help me to self-control." These are the appeals which come out of the nation's heart of hearts. And what is it that they find to cry to ? In part, at least, are they not answered back by personal ambitions, by party spirit, by the trickery of selfishness, and by the base love of management? This is the misery of politics, — the disproportion between the interests which are at stake and the men and machineries which deal with them. Those interests need the profoundest thought and the most absolute devotion. In some degree they get it; but how often what they get is only prejudice and passion, — the lightest, least reasonable, most superficial action of our human nature.

V. 243, 244.

Life or death then, who shall heed it, what we gain or
    what we lose?
Fair flies life amid the struggle, and the Cause for each
    shall choose.

Hear a word, a word in season, for the day is drawing
    nigh,
When the Cause shall call upon us, some to live and
    some to die !

WILLIAM MORRIS.

ALL prohibitory measures are negative. That
they have their use no one can doubt.
That they have their limits is just as clear. He
who thinks that nothing but the moral methods
for the prevention of intemperance and crime
can do the work is a mere theorist of the closet
and knows very little about the actual state of
human nature. But, on the other hand, the
man who thinks that any strictest system of
prohibition, most strictly kept in force, could
permanently keep men from drink, or any other
vice, knows little of human nature either. That
nature is too active and too live to be kept right
by mere negations. You cannot kill any one
of its appetites by merely starving it. You
must give it its true food, and so only can you
draw it off from the poison that it covets. Here
comes in the absolute necessity of providing
rational and cheap amusements for the people
whom our philanthropists are trying to draw
off from the tavern and the gambling-house.
Pictures, parks, museums, libraries, music, a
healthier and happier religion, a brighter, sun-
nier tone to all our life, — these are the positive
powers which must come in with every form
of prohibition and restraint before our poorer
people can be brought to live a sensible and
sober life.

I. 356, 357.

WHAT is more dreadful than irreverent art which paints all that it sees, because it sees almost nothing, and yet does not dream that there is more to see; which suggests nothing because it suspects nothing profounder than the flimsy tale it tells, and would fain make us all believe that there is no sacredness in woman, nor nobleness in man, nor secret in Nature, nor dignity in life? Irreverence everywhere is blindness and not sight. It is the stare which is bold because it believes in its heart that there is nothing which its insolent intelligence may not fathom, and so which finds only what it looks for, and makes the world as shallow as it ignorantly dreams the world to be. V. 250.

In the old days of awe and keen-eyed wonder,
   The poet's song with blood-warm truth was rife;
He saw the mysteries which circle under
   The outward shell and skin of daily life.
Nothing to him were fleeting time and fashion,
   His soul was led by the eternal law;
There was in him no hope of fame, no passion,
   But with calm, godlike eyes he only saw.

   .   .   .   .

Awake, then, thou! we pine for thy great presence
   To make us feel the soul once more sublime,
We are of far too infinite an essence
   To rest contented with the lies of Time.
JAMES RUSSELL LOWELL.

THE higher, soberer, spiritual optimism to which they come who are able to believe that all things work together for good to the man or the people that serve Him. . . . That was the optimism of Jesus. There was no blindness in His eyes, no foolish indiscriminate praise of humanity upon His lips. He saw the sin of that first century and of Jerusalem a thousand times more keenly than you see the sins of this nineteenth century and of America. But He believed in God. Therefore He saw beyond the sin, salvation. He never upbraided the sin except to save men from it. He never beat the chains except to set the captive free ; never, as our cynics do, for the mere pleasure of their clanking. "Not to condemn the world, but to save the world," was His story of His mission. And at His cross the shame and hope of humankind joined hands.   II. 161.

Grant us hope from earth to rise,
And to strain with eager eyes
Towards the promised heavenly prize :
We beseech Thee, hear us.

Grant us love Thy love to own,
Love to live for Thee alone,
And the power of grace make known :
We beseech Thee, hear us.

Lead us daily nearer Thee
Till at last Thy face we see,
Crowned with Thine own purity.
We beseech Thee, hear us.

LITANY OF PENITENCE

WE can, and I think we ought to, earnestly assert, when men praise it most loudly, that secularism, however we may accept it cheerfully, as the only expedient for the present time, is not the highest nor the eternal type of government. We may strive, by that devotion to the spiritual element in national life which even pure secularity of public methods still leaves possible, to hasten the day, which must come if Christ be what we know He is, when the idea of Jesus shall be the shaping and moving power of the Christian State; and among the happy sons of God the Son of God shall evidently reign, as the old phrase describes, "King of nations as King of saints."

INFLUENCE, 136, 137.

Thy kingdom come, O God!
  Thy rule, O Christ, begin!
Break with Thine iron rod
  The tyrannies of sin!

Where is Thy reign of peace,
  And purity, and love?
When shall all hatred cease,
  As in the realms above?

We pray Thee, Lord, arise,
  And come in Thy great might;
Revive our longing eyes,
  Which languish for Thy sight.

LEWIS HENSLEY.

The letter killeth, but the spirit giveth life.
II. Cor. iii. 6.

THE Christian Church has her symbols and her ordinances, and she has her true and inner life. Her outward ways of living really belong with her inward power. In a perfectly harmonious world there never could be any conflict. In Heaven the outward and the inward church shall absolutely correspond; but here and now the church may be so set upon her symbols and her regularities that she shall fail of doing her most perfect work and living her most perfect life. The Christian may be so bound to rites and ceremonies that he loses the God to whom they ought to bring him near. The congregation may be so jealous for its liturgy that it loses the power of prayer. The church at large may make so much of its apostolic ministry that it loses the present ministry of Christ Himself. Here it certainly is true that no symbol is doing its true work unless it is educating those who use it to do without itself if need be. The Christian is misusing his rites and ceremonies, unless they are bringing him more personally and immediately near to God. The congregation is not using its liturgy aright if it is getting more and more unable to worship except in just that form and order; and the church is suffering and not thriving by her ancient ministry if she is making it exclusive and mechanical, and calling none the ministers of Christ who have not that ordination.

I. 291, 292.

WHEN Jesus met the woman of Samaria at the well He honored her ; He valued and reverenced her soul. When He met Pontius Pilate, He honored him. When He dealt day after day with the ripening treachery of Judas Iscariot, He honored him. When He found John the Baptist making the door ready through which He was to enter on His work, He honored him. The spiritual nature, the special humanity, of each of them seemed to Him, not in any mere fiction but in simple truth, to be a beautiful and precious thing. His honor for that was the soul of His courteousness. And then the special words He said, whether of sympathy or of rebuke, might be just what the special occasion bade them be. Different as they were, they were all courteous alike because of this personal honor and value that filled them all. There is no complete courtesy that has not such a soul and such a body, — a soul of honor for the individual, living in and uttering itself through the intelligent recognition of the class condition.

INFLUENCE, 116, 117.

Man he loved

As man ; and to the mean and the obscure,
And all the homely in their homely works,
Transferred a courtesy which had no air
Of condescension.   WORDSWORTH.

THERE is something so sublimely positive in
Nature.   She never kills for the mere sake
of killing ; but every death is but one step in
the vast weaving of the web of life.   She has
no process of destruction which, as you turn it
to the other side and look at it in what you
know to be its truer light, you do not see to be
a process of construction.   She gets rid of her
wastes by ever new plans of nutrition.   This is
what gives her such a courageous, hopeful, and
enthusiastic look, and makes men love her as a
mother and not fear her as a tyrant.   They see
by small signs, and dimly feel, this positiveness
of her workings which it is the glory of natural
science to reveal more and more.   I. 359.

Verily now is our season of seed,
Now in our Autumn ; and Earth discerns
'Them that have served her, in them that can read,
Glassing where under the surface she burns
Quick at her wheel, while the fuel, decay,
Brightens the fire of renewal ; and we?
Death is the word of a bovine day
Know you the heart of the springing To-be.
GEORGE MEREDITH.

GOD is infinitely various. His great arms can hold the infant like a mother, and build a strong wall about the mature man who is fighting the noonday fight of life, and lay the bridge of sunset over which the old man's feet may walk serenely into the eternal day. . . . How shall the soul carry with it the sense of safety and assurance in God, which it has won within His earthly care, forth into this unknown, untrodden vastness whither it now must go? Only in one way; only by deepening as deeply as possible its assurance that it is God — not accident, not its own ingenuity, not its brethren's kindness — that it is God who made this earthly life so rich and happy. God is too vast, too infinite for earth. He is too vast for time, and needs eternity. Wrapped into Him the soul may be not merely resigned; it may be even impatient to explore those larger regions where the power which has made itself known to it here shall be able to display to it all the completeness of its nature and its love. . . . The child of God may wish for eternity, sure that there upon the vaster fields he shall see vaster exhibitions of that power and grace which he has learned completely to believe in here.

II. 326, 327.

A little longer still — patience, beloved :
  A little longer still, ere heaven unroll
The glory, and the brightness, and the wonder,
  Eternal and divine, that waits thy soul.

A little longer, and thy heart, beloved,
  Shall beat forever with a love divine ;
And joy so pure, so mighty, so eternal,
  No mortal knows, and lives, shall then be thine.
HYMNS OF THE AGES.

DELIGHT, enthusiasm, hope, content, — these are the true conditions of a Christian life, just as song is the true condition of the bird, or color of the rose. But just as the bird is still a bird although it cannot sing, and the rose is still a rose although its red grows dull and faded in some dark, close room where it is compelled to grow, — so the Christian is a Christian still, even although his soul is dark with doubt, and he goes staggering on, fearing every moment that he will fall, never daring to look up and hope.

V. 173.

Shadows to-day, while shadows show God's Will.
   Light were not good except He sent us light.
   Shadows to-day, because this day is night
Whose marvels and whose mysteries fulfil
Their course and deep in darkness serve Him still.
   Thou dim aurora, on the extremest height
   Of airy summits wax not over bright ;
Refrain thy rose, refrain thy daffodil.
Until God's Word go forth to kindle thee
   And garland thee and bid thee stoop to us,
     Blush in the heavenly choirs and glance not down :
     To-day we race in darkness for a crown,
In darkness for beatitude to be,
   In darkness for the city luminous.

CHRISTINA ROSSETTI.

Behold, God himself is with us for our captain.
II. CHRON. xiii. 12.

ST. PAUL has a noble verse which says that "experience worketh hope." It must, if it is full of Christ. The soul that is getting deeper and deeper into the certain knowledge of Him must be learning that it has no right to fear; that however hopeless things look there can be nothing but success for every good cause in the hand of Christ. It is a noble process for a man's life that gradually changes the cold dogma that "truth is strong and must prevail" into a warm enthusiastic certainty that "my Christ must conquer." It is terrible to see a man calling himself a Christian who despairs more of the world the longer he lives in it. It shows that he is letting the world's darkness come between him and his Lord's light. It shows that he is not near enough to Christ.

And with the growing hopefulness there comes a growing courage. How timid we are at first! I become a Christian, and it seems as if just to get this soul of mine saved were all that I could dare to try; but as the Saviour's strength becomes more manifest to me, as I know Him more, I see that He is able to do much more than that. I begin to aspire to have a little part in the great conquest of the world in which He is engaged. And so the Soldier of the Cross at last is out in the very thick of the battle, striking at all his Master's enemies in the perfect assurance of his Master's strength.

II. 57.

I HOPE that many of you have read the interesting book which gives an account of the *Personal Life of David Livingstone*. It is a noble record of a noble history. But the great beauty of his life as it comes out there is in the centralness of his religion. Two of the greatest interests of the human mind and soul were always with him — science and philanthropy. He opened the desert and traced the mysterious rivers, and watched the wanderings of the stars. He trampled out the slave trade in whole regions of its worst brutality ; but, at the heart of them, the man's science and philanthropy both got their light from his religion. He was first, last, and always and above all things the Christian and the Christian Missionary, carrying the glorious Gospel of the grace of God to the most miserably benighted of His children. He refuses to be called the mere scientist or the mere philanthropist. In the light of God he sees light, and he makes light in the mystery and sin of the Dark Continent. Therefore his fame has among the scientists and the philanthropists its own peculiar beauty.

III. 109, 110.

My times are in Thy Hand, O Lord! Go Thou with me and I am safe. And above all make me useful in promoting Thy cause of peace and goodwill among men.

DAVID LIVINGSTONE.

THE missionary idea that man is God's child gives birth to two enthusiasms: one for the Father, one for the child ; one for God, one for man. . . . Who can tell, as the missionary stands there preaching the salvation to his dusky congregation, which fire burns the warmest in his heart ? Is it the love for God or for his brethren ? Is it the Master who died for him, or these men for whom also He died, from whom his strongest inspiration comes ? No one can tell. He cannot tell himself. The Lord Himself in His own parable foretold the noble, sweet, inextricable confusion. " Inasmuch as ye have done it unto one of these ye have done it unto Me." But surely in the blended power of the two enthusiasms there is the strongest power of magnanimity. All that the mystic feels of personal love of God, all that the philanthropist knows of love for man, these two, each purifying and deepening and heightening the other, unite in the soul of him who goes to tell the men whom he loves as his brethren, about God whom he loves as his Father.

II. 179, 180.

Why they have never known the way before —
Why hundreds stand outside Thy mercy's door —
I know not: but I ask, dear Lord, that Thou
    Wouldst lead them now !

Why in the hard and thorny way they press
Unloved, uncomforted, with none to bless,
In living death, I know not: but spare Thou,
    And lead them on.

C. C. FRASER TYTLER.

If we believe that Jesus died and rose again, even so them also which sleep in Jesus will God bring with Him.—I. THESS. iv. 14.

IT is a beautiful connection, one whose mysterious beauty we are always learning more and more, that the deeper our spiritual experience of Christ becomes, the more our soul's life really hangs on His life as its Saviour and continual Friend, the more real becomes to us the unquenched life of those who have gone from us to be with Him.

I. 226.

Lord, make me one with Thine own faithful ones,
    Thy saints who love Thee and are loved by Thee;
    Till the day break and till the shadows flee
At one with them in alms and orisons:
At one with him who toils and him who runs,
    And him who yearns for union yet to be;
    At one with all who throng the crystal sea
And wait the setting of our moons and suns.
Ah, my beloved ones gone on before,
    Who looked not back with hand upon the plough!
    If beautiful to me while still in sight,
    How beautiful must be your aspects now;
    Your unknown, well-known aspects in that light
Which clouds shall never cloud forevermore.

CHRISTINA ROSSETTI.

NOWHERE is it more necessary that the Church should realize the largeness of her life, should know that she is not the Clergy only but the total people, than where she hears herself called upon to take interest in, and give her help for, the solution of the pressing social and economical problems of the day. Those calls are growing constant and urgent. To these calls she must not close her ears. The Church of Christ must be a leader in the adjustment of the relations of mankind and the building of the better society which is to come. Only, what is the Church, and how shall she do this work? Not merely by Ministers studying in their libraries and preaching from their pulpits — though the earnest thought and helpful word must not be lacking, — but by Christian men and women in their shops and homes, growing more rich in sympathy, and dealing in larger daily justice with their fellow-men. The great questions which are bewildering us are to find their solution quite as largely in the fields of active work as in the laboratories of the scholars. The Church is dealing with these questions wherever Churchmen are trying to do their duty with the fullest light. There is much hope in the Christian Social Union, which has been organized for the study of the theory of social questions. I invite to it your attention and regard. There is still more hope in the growing desire of all men to be just and fair, and to live with their fellow-men as brethren in the family of God. Convention Address.

And there came a traveller unto the rich man, and he spared to take of his own flock, and of his own herd, to dress for the wayfaring man that was come unto him. —II. SAM. xii. 4.

YOU cannot do your duty to the poor by a society. Your life must touch their life. You try to work solely by a society, and what does it come to? Is it not the old story of the book of Samuel? The traveller appeals to you, and you spare to take of your own thought and time and sympathy to give to the wayfaring man that is come to you. They are too precious. You say: "There is thought, time, sympathy, down at the charity bureau to which I have a right by virtue of the contribution I have made. Go down and get a ticket's worth of that."

II. 354.

My brother, I am hungry: give me food
Such as my Father gives me at his board;
He has for many years been to thee good,
Thou canst a morsel, then, to me afford.
I do not ask of thee a grain of that
Thou offerest when I call on thee for bread;
This is not of the wine nor olive fat,
But those who eat of this like thee are dead.
I ask the love the Father has for thee,
That thou should'st give it back to me again;
This shall my soul from pangs of hunger free,
And on my parchèd spirit fall like rain;
Then thou wilt prove a brother to my need,
For in the Cross of Christ thou, too, canst bleed.
                              JONES VERY.

Hereby perceive we the love of God, because He laid down His life for us : and we ought to lay down our lives for the brethren.

I. JOHN iii. 16.

THE wayfarers come to us continually, and they do not come by chance.   God sends them.   And as they come, with their white faces and their poor scuffling feet, they are our judges. Not merely by whether we give, but by how we give and by what we give, they judge us. One man sends them entirely away.   Another drops a little easy, careless, unconscientious money into their hands.   Another man washes and clothes them.   Another man teaches them lessons.   Thank God there are some men and women here and there, full of the power of the Gospel, who cannot rest satisfied till they have opened their very hearts and given the poor wayfaring men the only thing which really is their own, themselves, their faith, their energy, their hope in God.   Of such true charity-givers may He who gave Himself for us increase the multitude among us every day !   II. 354.

And the voice that was calmer than silence said,
  " Lo it is I, be not afraid !

.   .   .   .

The Holy Supper is kept, indeed,
In whatso we share with another's need ;
Not what we give, but what we share, —
For the gift without the giver is bare ;
Who gives himself with his alms feeds three, —
Himself, his hungering neighbor, and me."
JAMES RUSSELL LOWELL.

WHEN I suffer or when I enjoy, — when down these nerves the quick agony shoots and leaves me trembling like a poor tree which the blast has shivered, or when through the healthy blood peace runs like the sunlight on a flowing river, — when, in the aggregate of life, beneath affections, thoughts, dreams, memories, desires, there is always felt this human body with its pangs and blisses, what a noble meaning there is in it all as it lies open to the influence of Jesus! "Lo, I am human!" And all the dignity and pathos of humanity surrounds me. "Behold in what a disturbed and struggling world I live!" And hope and fear, — twin captains of the soul, — patience and expectation spring to life. "See here, touching this very flesh of mine, the fingers of the hand whose heart is my Father's," and through the passions which the body feels opens a way into the deepest woes and loftiest pleasures, which can belong only to the sons of God.

INFLUENCE, 173, 174.

But when the sharp strokes flesh and heart run through,
For thee and not another; only known,
In all the universe, through sense of thine;
Not caught by eye or ear, not felt by touch,
Nor apprehended by the spirit's sight,
But only by the hidden, tortured nerves,
In all their incommunicable pain, —
God speaks Himself to us, as mothers speak
To their own babes, upon the tender flesh
With fond familiar touches close and dear; —
Because He cannot choose a softer way
To make us feel that He Himself is near,
And each apart His own beloved and known.

UGO BASSI. SERMON IN THE HOSPITAL.

THE construction of life is everywhere the same. Wherever the background is lost, the foreground grows false and thin. What is this foolish realism in our literature but the loss of the background of the ideal, without which every real is base and sordid ? In how many bright books there is no God treading on the high places of the earth ; nay, there are no high places of the earth for God to tread upon. What is the practical man's contempt for theory ? What is the modern man's contempt for history ? What is the ethical man's contempt for religion ? All of them are the denials of the background of life. All of them therefore are thin and weak.

V. 122.

Yet is it just
That here, in memory of all books which lay
Their sure foundations in the heart of man,
Whether by native prose. or numerous verse ;

   .   .   .   .

'Tis just that in behalf of these, the works,
And of the men that framed them, whether known,
Or sleeping nameless in their scattered graves,
That I should here assert their rights, attest
Their honors, and should, once for all, pronounce
Their benediction ; speak of them as Powers
For ever to be hallowed ; only less,
For what we are and what we may become,
Than Nature's self, which is the breath of God,
Or His pure Word by miracle revealed.

WORDSWORTH.

THE great procession of the year, sacred to our best human instincts with the accumulated reverence of ages, — Advent, Christmas, Epiphany, Good Friday, Easter, Ascension, Whitsunday, — leads those who walk in it, at least once every year, past all the great Christian facts, and, however careless and selfish be the preacher, will not leave it in his power to keep them from his people. The Church year, too, preserves the personality of our religion. It is concrete and picturesque. The historical Jesus is forever there. It lays each life continually down beside the perfect life, that it may see at once its imperfection and its hope.

PREACHING, 91.

O God, of unchangeable power and eternal light, look favorably on Thy whole Church, that wonderful and sacred mystery; and, by the tranquil operation of Thy perpetual Providence, carry out the work of man's salvation; and let the whole world feel and see that things which were cast down are being raised up, and things which had grown old are being made new, and all things are returning to perfection through Him from whom they took their origin, even through our Lord Jesus Christ.

ANCIENT COLLECTS. BRIGHT.

I take pleasure in infirmities, in reproaches, in necessities, in persecutions, in distresses, for Christ's sake : for when I am weak, then am I strong. — II. COR. xii. 10.

THERE is a noble dignity about those words. They are not the words of one who is merely trying to console himself for the lack of comfort, and to hold out till comfort shall bestow itself upon him. They are the words of a man whom circumstances, which he knows to be the hands of God, have led into a certain life. He has not led himself there ; he has not chosen poverty ; he has not tried to be poor ; but being in that land of poverty, he looks about, and lo ! it is not barren. It has pleasures, revelations, cultivations of its own. It has its own peculiar relationships to God. It is not necessary to say whether it is poorer or richer than the other land, the land of profusion and abundance. It is a true land by itself ; and Paul, who lives there, honors and respects it, and so it honors him and gives him freely its own peculiar strength ; and he stands in the midst of it and cries, "When I am weak, then am I strong."

V. 162.

YOU cannot see the distant heaven. You cannot hear the songs of angels. You cannot even say assuredly that you know the love of God, — but you do know that to be brave and true and pure is better than to be cowardly and false and foul. You do know that there are men and women all about you suffering, some of them dying, for sympathy and help. You do know that whether God loves you or not, right is right! Oh, how these great simple assurances come out when the higher lights of the loftier experiences grow dark! I will not say, I dare not say, that God lets the heavenly light be darkened in order that these earthly duties may appear. I only say that when the cloud stretches itself across the heavens, then, underneath the cloud and shut out from the sunshine, the imprisoned soul still finds for itself a rich life of duty, a life of self-control, a life of charity, a life of growth.

V. 174, 175.

Who knows? God knows: and what He knows
  Is well and best.
The darkness hideth not from Him, but glows
Clear as the morning or the evening rose
  Of east or west.

CHRISTINA ROSSETTI

A MAN has no right to give to the tint on his parlor walls that anxiety of thought which belongs only to the justification of the ways of God to man. And why ? Mainly, I suppose, because the man who has expended his highest powers upon the lightest themes has no new, greater seriousness to give to the great problems when they come, and so either avoids them altogether or else, by a strange perversion, turns back and gives them the light consideration which was what he ought to have given to his headache or the color of his walls.   V. 247, 248.

High above these things that change is the wise man
    with spirit well taught,
Who cares not what he feels,
Nor from what quarter blows the shifting breeze,
If but the holy motive of his mind go onward to the
    due and longed-for end.
For thus will he be able to remain the same, unshaken,
Pointing the simple eye of motive
Through many changing chances straight at Me.
The purer that his eye of motive is,
The straighter sails the vessel through the many
    storms.

———

By two wings man is lifted from the things of earth —
Simplicity and purity.
Simplicity must be the keynote to his motive ;
Purity the keynote to his love.
His motive aims at God ;
His love embraces and enjoys Him.

THOMAS À KEMPIS.

LET us give thanks to God upon Thanksgiving Day. Nature is beautiful, and fellow-men are dear, and duty is close beside us, and He is over us and in us. What more do we want, except to be more thankful and more faithful, less complaining of our trials and our time, and more worthy of the tasks and privileges He has given us. We want to trust Him with a fuller trust, and so at last to come to that high life where we shall "Be careful for nothing, but in everything, by prayer and supplication, with thanksgiving, let our request be made known unto God," for that and that alone is peace.

I. 173

For flowers unsought, in desert places
Flashing enchantment on the sight;
For radiance on familiar faces
As they passed upward into light;

For blessings of the fruitful season,
For work and rest, for friends and home,
For the great gifts of thought and reason, —
To praise and bless Thee, Lord, we come.

And when we gather up the story
Of all Thy mercies flowing free,
Crown of them all, that hope of glory,
Of growing ever nearer Thee.

ELIZA SCUDDER.

I BELIEVE so fully that the Christian ministry in the next fifty years is to have a nobler opportunity of usefulness and power than it has ever had in the past, that I would gladly call, if I could, with the voice of a trumpet to the brave, earnest, cultivated young men who are to live in the next fifty years to enter into it, and share the privilege of that work together.

And the word with which I would summon them should be that great word "service." "Whosoever will be chief among you, let him be your servant," Jesus said. . . . And then He stretched out His arms, and with that self-assertion which no other son of man has ever dared to make, He bade them see the illustration of what He had just told them in Himself. "Even as the Son of Man came not to be ministered unto but to minister," He said.   v. 188.

Almighty God, who didst give such grace unto Thy holy Apostle Saint Andrew, that he readily obeyed the calling of Thy Son Jesus Christ, and followed Him without delay ; Grant unto us all, that we, being called by Thy holy Word, may forthwith give up ourselves obediently to fulfil Thy holy commandments ; through the same Jesus Christ our Lord.

BOOK OF COMMON PRAYER.

THE man is weak and useless who, however devoutly, looks only for the repetition of past miracles, good and great as those miracles were in their own time. Solemnly and surely — to some men terribly and awfully, to other men joyously and enthusiastically — it is becoming clear to men that the future cannot be what the past has been. The world of the days to come is to be different from the world that has been. Every interest of life is altered ; government, society, business, education, all is altered, all is destined to alter more and more. Only these two elements remain the same, — God and man ! What then shall we expect ? That God will guide man and supply him as He has in all the times which are past and gone, but that the new government and guidance will be different for the new days. He who believes that, looks forward to changes of faith and changes of life without a fear, for underneath all the changes is the unchangeableness of God.

V. 31, 32.

> For Destiny is but the breath of God
> Still moving in us, the last fragment left
> Of our unfallen nature, waking oft
> Within our thought, to beckon us beyond
> The narrow circle of the seen and known,
> And always tending to a noble end.
>
> .   .   .   .
>
> All things are fitly cared for, and the Lord
> Will watch as kindly o'er the exodus
> Of us His servants now, as in old time.

JAMES RUSSELL LOWELL.

WHAT tender charity and what unsparing scrutiny there must be all over a world that is waiting for the Judgment Day. At last He comes! Where has He been? Not far away. The absence of the Parable is but a figure for the suspended judgment, the holding back ˙of consequences till probation is complete. The king's coming in, what is that then but just the letting loose of consequences that have been held back in His hand, to fly to their causes. Everywhere the reward seeks the goodness, and the misery seeks the sin, and so the world is judged.

Where the good man stands with his eye on God is Heaven. Where the wicked man cowers, is Hell. No longer joy gilds the guilt, and misery no longer vexes the goodness. The setting free of joy and sorrow from their long unnatural attachments to seek their fitness of character, that is the coming in of the King, that is the Judgment Day. Mss.

Gather you, gather you, angels of God—
   Freedom, and Mercy, and Truth;
Come! for the Earth is grown coward and old,
   Come down and renew us her youth,
Wisdom, Self-Sacrifice, Daring and Love,
Haste to the battle-field, stoop from above,
   To the Day of the Lord at hand.

CHARLES KINGSLEY.

Above it stood the seraphim : each one had six wings ; with twain he covered his face, and with twain he covered his feet, and with twain he did fly. — Is. vi. 2.

ISAIAH says of the seraphim not merely that their eyes were covered, but that they were covered with their wings. Now the wings represent the active powers. It is with them that movement is accomplished and change achieved and obedience rendered ; so that it seems to me that what the whole image means is this, — that it is with the powers of action and obedience that the powers of insight and knowledge are veiled. . . . The mystery and awfulness of God is a conviction reached through serving Him. . . .

Behold, what a lofty idea of reverence is here ! It is no palsied idleness. The figure which we see is not flung down upon the ground, despairing and dismayed. It stands upon its feet ; it is alert and watchful ; it is waiting for commandments ; it is eager for work ; but all the time its work makes it more beautifully, completely, devoutly reverent of Him for whom the work is done. The more work the more reverence. So man grows more mysterious and great to you, oh, servant of mankind, the longer that you work for him. Is it not so ? So Nature grows more mysterious to you, oh, naturalist, the longer that you serve her. Is it not so ? So God grows more sublime and awful as we labor for Him in the tasks which He has set us. Would you grow rich in reverence ? Go work, work, work with all your strength ; so let life deepen around you and display its greatness.

V. 259, 260.

Ye know neither the day nor the hour wherein the Son of Man cometh. — MATT. xxv. 13.

LET us do what we ought and what we can for our own souls at once.   For the judgment is coming not only at the last day, but all the time.   Every day the power that we will not use is failing from us.   Every day the God whose voice speaks through all the inevitable necessities of our moral life is saying of the men who keep their talents wrapped in napkins, "Take the talent from him;" and since' he will not enter into the perfect light he must be "cast into the outer darkness."

I. 156.

Why do we heap huge mounds of years
  Before us and behind,
And scorn the little days that pass
  Like angels on the wind?

Each turning round a small sweet face
  As beautiful as near;
Because it is so small a face
  We will not see it clear:

And so it turns from us, and goes
  Away in sad disdain:
Though we would give our lives for it,
  It never comes again.

DINAH MULOCH CRAIK.

THE real question everywhere is whether the world, distracted and confused as everybody sees that it is, is going to be patched up and restored to what it used to be, or whether it is going forward into a quite new and different kind of life, whose exact nature nobody can pretend to foretell, but which is to be distinctly new, unlike the life of any age which the world has seen already. . . . It is impossible that the old conditions, so shaken and broken, can ever be repaired and stand just as they stood before. The time has come when something more than mere repair and restoration of the old is necessary. The old must die and a new must come forth out of its tomb.

V. 30, 31.

What is this, the sound and rumor? What is this
    that all men hear,
Like the wind in hollow valleys, when the storm is
    drawing near,
Like the rolling on of ocean in the eventide of fear?
    'Tis the people marching on.

"On we march then, we, the workers, and the rumor
    that ye hear
Is the blended sound of battle and deliv'rance drawing
    near ;
For the hope of every creature, is the banner that we
    bear."
    And the world is marching on.

WILLIAM MORRIS.

*For we must all appear before the judgment seat
of Christ; that every one may receive the things
done in his body, according to that he hath done,
whether it be good or bad.* — II. COR. v. 10.

OUT of all the lower presences with which
they have made themselves contented;
out of all the chambers where the little easy
judges sit with their compromising codes of
conduct, with their ideas worked over and
worked down to suit the conditions of this
earthly life; out of all these partial and imperfect judgment chambers, when men die they
are all carried up into the presence of the perfect righteousness, and are judged by that. All
previous judgments go for nothing unless they
find their confirmation there.   IV. 63, 64.

O God the Son, Redeemer of the world,
        Have mercy upon us.
O our One Salvation,
        Save us.
O Perfect Holiness,
        Sanctify us.
By Thy sitting on the right hand of the Father,
    where Thou ever makest intercession for us:
        Let Thy servants serve Thee, O Lord, and let
        them see Thy face.
                            BOOK OF LITANIES. NEALE.

IT is our punishment that Jesus shares. It is our woe down into which His love has brought Him. We hang upon our cross and He hangs on His beside us. For our cross we can blame none but ourselves. Our sin has brought us what we suffer, but His cross no sin of His has built. It is the wickedness in which we have so deep a part, which decrees that it shall be a cross and not a throne. There comes, as the result of all, just exactly what is expressed in the strange deep words of the penitent thief to his mocking comrade, — words which the soul may turn and address to itself, invoking from itself a solemn repentance and hate of sin as it sees its Saviour a sharer in the suffering which its sin brings : " Dost not thou fear God, seeing thou art in the same condemnation ? And we indeed justly, for we receive the due reward of our deeds ; but this man hath done nothing amiss."

I. 202.

Beside Thy Cross I hang on my Cross in shame,
My wounds, weakness, extremity cry to Thee:
Bid me also to Paradise, also me
For the glory of Thy Name.

CHRISTINA ROSSETTI.

THE ship looks forward fearlessly to the new ocean with its new stars and new winds, for the same captain will sail her there who has sailed her here, and the fact that he will sail her there otherwise than he sails her here will be only the sign of how sleepless and watchful is his care.

V. 32.

I.

"Friend, why goest thou forth
When ice-hills drift from the north
    And crush together?"

"The Voice that me doth call
Heeds not the ice-hill's fall,
    Nor wind, nor weather."

II.

"But friend, the night is black;
Behold the driving wrack
    And wild seas under!"

"My straight and narrow bark
Fears not the threatening dark,
    Nor storm, nor thunder."

.   .   .   .

IV.

"Hark! Who is he that knocks
With slow and dreadful shocks
    The walls to sever?"

"It is my Master's call,
I go, whate'er befall;
    Farewell forever."

RICHARD WATSON GILDER.

AS the spiritual life with which the Bible deals is the flower of human life, so the Book which deals with it is the flower of human books. But it is not thereby an unhuman book. It is the most human of all books. In it is seen the everlasting struggle of the man-life to fulfil itself in God. All books in which that universal struggle of humanity is told are younger brothers, — less clear and realized and developed utterances of that which is so vivid in the history of the sacred people and is perfect in the picture of the divine Man. I will not be puzzled, but rejoice when I find in all the sacred books, in all deep, serious books of every sort, foregleams and adumbrations of the lights and shadows which lie distinct upon the Bible page. I will seek and find the assurance that my Bible is inspired of God not in virtue of its distance from, but in virtue of its nearness to, the human experience and heart. It is in that experience and heart that the real inspiration of God is given, and thence it issues into the written book :

> " Out of the heart of Nature rolled
> The Burdens of the Bible old.
> The Litanies of nations came
> Like the volcano's tongue of flame ;
> Up from the burning core below
> The Canticles of love and woe."

That book is most inspired which most worthily and deeply tells the story of the most inspired life.

V. 17.

YOU are in God's world; you are God's child. Those things you cannot change; the only peace and rest and happiness for you is to accept them and rejoice in them. When God speaks to you, you must not make believe to yourself that it is the wind blowing or the torrent falling from the hill. You must know that it is God. You must gather up the whole power of meeting Him. You must be thankful that life is great and not little. You must listen as if listening were your life. And then, then only can come peace. All other sounds will be caught up into the prevailing richness of that voice of God. The lost proportions will be perfectly restored. Discord will cease; harmony will be complete.

V. 88.

Long and dark the nights, dim and short the days,
Mounting weary heights on our weary ways,
    Thee our God we praise.
Scaling heavenly heights by unearthly ways,
Thee our God we praise all our nights and days,
    Thee our God we praise.

CHRISTINA ROSSETTI.

THE rich men of our community must be truly rich themselves, or they can have nothing worth giving to the poor; nothing with which they can permanently help their poorer brethren. Only a class of men independent, intelligent, and glorying in struggle themselves, can really send independence, intelligence, and the dignity of struggle, down through a whole city's life. This is the reason why your selfish and idle rich man, who has neither of these great human properties, does nothing for the permanent help of poverty. The money which he gives is no symbol. It means nothing.   O let us be sure that the first necessity for giving the poor man character is that the rich man should have character to give him.

II. 353.

Our gaieties, our luxuries,
　Our pleasures and our glee,
Mere insolence and wantonness,
　Alas! they feel to me.

.　　.　　.　　.　　.　　.　　.

The joy that does not spring from joy
　Which I in others see,
How can I venture to employ,
　Or find it joy for me?

ARTHUR HUGH CLOUGH.

MEN are coming more and more to feel that
the rich man does not do his duty by the
poor man, the rich class does not really take of
its own and give it to the poor class, unless by
some outflow of itself it . . . sends a perpetual stream of independence, intelligence, and
struggle, down through the social mass, making
the spiritual privileges of those who are living
on the heights of life the possession and inspiration of the waiting, unsuccessful, discouraged
souls that lie below.   II. 342.

"Lazarus, come forth!" Out from the gloom,
    Haggard and gaunt and dazed, there came
He who had lain within the tomb
    Until the Blessed One called his name;
But, in death's night, he heard the sound;
    Forth to the shuddering gazer's sight
He staggered, in foul grave-clothes bound,
    And breathed at last in life and light.

"Lazarus, come forth!" The people lies
    With mind in bonds, with soul all dead;
Shall not Christ, through us, bid it rise?
    Through us, shall not His words be said?
Strong in His love — strong with the strength
    He gives, shall we not, in His might,
Call forth our Lazarus at length
    From its dark gloom to life and light?

                          W. C. BENNET.

Phillips Brooks born, 1835.

We, we have chosen our path —
Path to a clear-purposed goal,
Path of advance ! — but it leads
A long steep journey, through sunk
Gorges, o'er mountains in snow !

MATTHEW ARNOLD.

HOW large a part of our godward life is travelled not by clear landmarks seen far off in the promised land, but as travellers climb a mountain peak, by putting footstep after footstep slowly and patiently into the prints which some one going before us, with keener sight, with stronger nerves, tied to us by the cord of saintly sympathy, has planted deep into the pathless snow of the bleak distance that stretches up between humanity and God.

I. 123.

I am He that made all saints ;
I gave them My good influence,
I showed them glory.
I called them by My favour,
I drew them by My pity,
I led them on through many a temptation,
I poured upon them wondrous consolations,
I gave them strength unto the end,
I crowned their suffering,
I know them first and last,
I throw My arms, with love past telling, round them,
I must be praised in all My saints.

THOMAS À KEMPIS.

CHRIST'S powerful death is the great renewing spectacle of human life. When men look at it, there comes up out of their hearts the pattern of divinity which is there, their sonship to the Holy One; and to attain that holiness, to realize it perfectly, becomes the passion of their lives. And it is love for the Sufferer which makes that passion, — love with its two perfect elements perfectly combined. It is admiration for what He is doing, the unselfishness, the heroism, the godlike patience. And it is gratitude because He is doing it for us. It is these two which blend into the passionate devotion with which a man, in the great phrase of the Gospels, "follows after Christ," — seeks, that is, with his own essential sonship, to realize in himself, the sonship of the Son of God.   INFLUENCE, 52.

THE SONG OF A HEATHEN.

(Sojourning in Galilee, A.D. 32.)

'If Jesus Christ is a man, —
    And only a man, — I say
That of all mankind I cleave to him,
    And to him will I cleave alway.

If Jesus Christ is a God, —
    And the only God, — I swear
I will follow Him through Heaven and hell,
    The earth, the sea, and the air!

RICHARD WATSON GILDER.

ST. PAUL would have men live here on earth,
yet conscious of their capacity of Heaven.
He would have earth real, clear, definite, distinct, shining with its own color, holding us
with its own grasp ; and yet he would have
man so conscious of his larger self that the very
definiteness of what he is to-day makes real to
him the greater thing that he will be in the vast
world beyond.

Is not that what we want ? The life of earth
now, the life of heaven by and by, — each clear
with its own glory ! And our humanity capable
of both, capable of sharp thinking, timely hard
work here and now, capable also of the super-
nal, the transcendent splendor there when the
time shall come ! The glory of the star, the
glory of the sun ! We must not lose either in
the other ; we must not be so full of the hope
of heaven that we cannot do our work on earth ;
we must not be so lost in the work of earth that
we shall not be inspired by the hope of heaven.
God grant us all the contentment and the hope
which come to those who live in Him who
covers all yesterday, to-day, and forever with
Himself.   IV. 72.

The earth may gain by one man the more,
And the gain of earth shall be heaven's gain too.
BROWNING.

Now it is high time to awake out of sleep: for now is our salvation nearer than when we believed. — ROMANS xiii. 11.

THOSE words which once came from the apostle's lips, expressed the feeling and the power which was always in all the apostles' hearts.

And it has been this expectation of the coming of the Lord which, ever since the time of the apostles, has always been the inspiration of the Christian world. The noblest souls always have believed that humanity was capable of containing, and was sure sooner or later to receive, a larger and deeper infusion of divinity. The promise of Christianity is as yet but half fulfilled. All that has been done yet in all the Christian centuries is only the sketch and prelude of what is yet to be done. . . . And as the noblest souls have thought of the world's history, so the most earnest men and women have always thought of their own lives. The power of any life lies in its expectancy. "What do you hope for? What do you expect?" The answer to these questions is the measure of the degree in which a man is living. He who can answer these questions by the declaration, "The Lord is at hand: I am expecting a higher, deeper, more pervading mastery of Christ" — we know that he is thoroughly alive.　　　　IV. 354, 355.

Wisdom crieth aloud . . . The Lord possessed me in the beginning of His way, before His works of old. I was set up from everlasting, . . . or ever the earth was. . . . Before the mountains were settled, before the hills was I brought forth.

PROV. viii. 22, 23, 25.

WHEN the Hebrew used the word "wisdom" of man, it covered the whole range of spiritual life, either in its moral or its mental aspects. . . . There are two layers of power in life; the one that lies upon the top is carnal. It is material, inert. It has no power to shape itself. The other that lies below is spiritual. It is full of force and movement. Skill, judgment, affection, duty, knowledge, these are its elements. Out of it force comes to move the dead mass that cannot move itself. The world of things is moved by the world of character. Perhaps this word, "character," in its spirituality, and comprehensiveness, and variety, most nearly expresses the idea of the old "wisdom." . . .

It shines in many a work of man. Wherever it appears it is excellent and beautiful. But its true glory is seen back where the thought of God first touches the gross chaos with intention and a world is born. Its Epic is that first chapter of Genesis. There where the Spirit of God moves upon the face of the lifeless waters and a divine voice summons the light and creates order, there is Creation, there is the Eternal Wisdom moving into visibility. . . . All the wisdom and skill that is in the world is to be traced home to one devising and ordering mind that sits above and issued into all our life.

OXFORD REVIEW.

Christ Jesus, who of God is made unto us wisdom and righteousness and sanctification and redemption. — I. COR. i. 30.

REMEMBER what Christ is called in St. John's Gospel, " The Word." A word is wisdom in utterance. Remember what St. Paul calls Christ, " The power of God and the wisdom of God." Remember what is said of the Word in that first chapter of St. John, "In the beginning was the Word. He was with God and He was God." " He was in the beginning with God." " All things were made by Him." " In Him was life, and the life was the light of men." It is just exactly what is said of Wisdom in . . . Proverbs. " The Lord possessed me in the beginning of His way." " When He prepared the Heavens, I was there." " Whoso findeth Me, findeth Life." See how the Word was just the *Wisdom* at last uttering Itself to a needy world. This divine love and grace and truth which we have been tracing in Creation and in Providence, at last coming, that men might know them perfectly, and putting on humanity and becoming incarnate in Jesus Christ.

OXFORD REVIEW.

O Wisdom, Which camest forth out of the Mouth of the Most High, and reachest from one end to the other, mightily and sweetly ordering all things : Come and teach us the way of prudence.   WISDOM. viii. 1, 7.

SURELY this is the most terrible and ghastly thing about all sorrow, the sense that it must have been prepared for us in all the unconscious days when we never thought of it. This is the thought of fate which takes the pang of suffering and presses it home into the very soul. How old, how everlasting our suffering is! And just then to many a soul Wisdom opens her voice and cries. Wisdom, the divine mind, the divine intention, will, love, she has something to say. "Before the mountains were settled, before the hills was I brought forth." Yes, the sorrow is old, it says, but the plan of God, instinct with love, that made the sorrow possible, is older. . . . More eternal, more fundamental than your suffering is the love, the justice, the thoughtfulness of God. Let your soul rest on them and be at peace.

OXFORD REVIEW

Amid the awe
Of unintelligible chastisement,
Not only acquiescences of faith
Survived, but daring sympathies with power,
Motions not treacherous or profane, else why
Within the folds of no ungentle breast
Their dread vibration to this hour prolonged?
Wild blasts of music thus could find their way
Into the midst of turbulent events ;
So that worst tempests might be listened to.
Then was the truth received into my heart,
That, under heaviest sorrow earth can bring,
If from the affliction somewhere do not grow
Honor which could not else have been, a faith,
An elevation, and a sanctity,
If new strength be not given, nor old restored,
The blame is ours, not Nature's.

WORDSWORTH.

Christ . . . the wisdom of God. — I. COR. i. 24.

WITH this identification in our minds, how clear becomes all that we said before about the wisdom of God being the soul's refuge in affliction and temptation. . . . But now it is not the voice of any abstraction, no merely celestial wisdom that cries out to him and offers to help him, and assures him of its own eternity. But it is the dearer, and closer, and tenderer voice of a man, of a friend, of Christ the Consoler and the Strengthener. He speaks, He assures the soul that He is older than its sorrow, older than its trial, that He has had purposes concerning it that go back behind its birth. He was there when the arrow was launched, and knows what it was sent for. Mounting back along the continuous eternity of Christ, the soul outgoes its sorrow, and gets back to the purpose of its sorrow which it finds folded safe and warm in the hand of the eternal Christ's wise love. The soul's Christ, with His eternity, dwarfs the puny ages of its calamities and makes them seem temporary and insignificant.

OXFORD REVIEW

In Him again
We see the same first, starry attribute,
" Perfect through suffering," our salvation's seal
Set in the front of His Humanity.
For God has other Words for other worlds,
But for this world the Word of God is Christ.

UGO BASSI. SERMON IN THE HOSPITAL.

IT is especially in the great mysterious work of the atonement that Christ is seen to be the wisdom, the conquering spiritual element in the world. . . . When Jesus died, it was as if He lifted up His voice and said: "Sin is old, but I am older than sin ; sin is strong, but I am stronger than sin ; punishment is necessary, but mercy, the forgiveness of the penitent, is a necessity far back behind that, deeper in the Eternal Divinity. The law began its vengeance when man broke it, but 'I was set up from everlasting, from the beginning, or ever the earth was.' Know, O my brethren, that even more original and certain than the truth that God must punish you if you do wrong, is the higher truth that God will forgive you, if you repent."

OXFORD REVIEW.

Blessed be Thou, O Lord,
So good unto Thy servant, according to the great·
　　ness of Thy pity.
What can I say more in Thy presence,
But humbly lay myself before Thee,
Mindful of my iniquity and worthlessness?
For there is none like Thee
'Mid all the wonders of the heaven and earth.
Thy works are very good,
Thy judgments true,
And by Thy foresight all is ruled.
Praise then to Thee and glory,
O Wisdom of the Father ;
Bless and praise Him, O my lips,
My soul and all things that are made.

THOMAS À KEMPIS.

THREE things concerning (the Puritans) are worthy of our notice, — first, that the Puritans, who came direct from England, are always to be distinguished from the Pilgrims, who came by way of Holland and caught some of the broader spirit of that " nursery of freedom and good-will ; " second, that the noblest utterance of hopeful tolerance in all that noble century was in the famous speech in which John Robinson, their minister, bade loving farewell to his departing flock at Leyden, in which occur those memorable words : " I am verily persuaded, I am very confident, that the Lord has more truth yet to break out of His holy Word ; " and thirdly, that somewhere in the bitter heart of Puritanism was hidden the power which, partly by development, and partly by reaction, was to produce the freedom of these modern days.   TOLERANCE, 36, 37.

God of our fathers, Thou who wast,
Art, and shalt be when those eye-wise who flout
Thy secret presence shall be lost
In the great light that dazzles them to doubt,
We, sprung from loins of stalwart men
Whose strength was in their trust,
That Thou wouldst make Thy dwelling in their dust,
And walk with them, a fellow-citizen,
Who build a city of the just,
We, who believe Life's bases rest
Beyond the probe of chemic test,
Still, like our fathers, feel Thee near,
Sure that, while lasts the immutable decree,
The land to Human Nature dear
Shall not be unbeloved of Thee.
                                   JAMES RUSSELL LOWELL.

DEATH is so old in the world. It lies so thick and heavy upon all we do and are. But "Life is older than Death," Christ said, and so, when He, the Master, came, the intruder yielded before Him. He rose from the grave, "because it was not possible that He should be holden of it." And so all that He tells us of our resurrection, all that St. Paul expounds so fully of the power of the spirit, that that which is sown a natural body shall be raised a spiritual body, what is it all, but an assertion that in us, too, the spiritual life is stronger than any law of physical decay, and must come up through them all to meet the issues of the spiritual world? This is the last triumph of that spiritual nature which is older and more fundamental than the mountains and the streams, when the earth and the sea shall give up their dead, because it is not possible that they shall be holden of them.

OXFORD REVIEW.

O quickly come, true Life of all ;
  For Death is mighty all around ;
On every home his shadows fall,
  On every heart his mark is found ;
O quickly come ; for grief and pain
Can never cloud Thy glorious reign.

LAWRENCE TUTTIETT

EVERYWHERE the nature that is conscious of the infiniteness of life longs to believe in a manifested God. Its whole disposition is toward faith; and then if any glimpse is offered of a Son of God, a manifestation of the Invisible Deity who sends happiness and sorrow and who can forgive sin, there is no tendency to disbelieve, there is the hunger of the heart leaping with fearful hope. . . . To one who finds the forces of this life sufficient, an incarnation, a supernatural salvation is incredible. To one who, looking deeper, knows there must be some infinite force which it has not found yet, — some loving, living force of Emmanuel, of God with man, — the Son of God is waiting on the threshold and will immediately come. Christ supposes an element of incompleteness everywhere, making a hungry world, — preparing the whole man not to reject as useless and incredible, but to accept as just what it needs and expects, a mysterious, a supernatural, divine Redemption, preparing the mental nature for faith, and the moral nature for repentance, and the spiritual nature for guidance. To this readiness alone can Christ come.   V. 208, 209.

O little town of Bethlehem!
  How still we see thee lie;
Above thy deep and dreamless sleep
  The silent stars go by;
Yet in thy dark streets shineth
  The everlasting Light:
The hopes and fears of all the years
  Are met in thee to-night.

PHILLIPS BROOKS.

Unto us a Child is born. — Is. ix. 6.

They shall call His Name Emmanuel . . . God with us. — MATT. i. 23.

> How silently, how silently,
>   The wondrous gift is given!
> So God imparts to human hearts
>   The blessings of His heaven.
> No ear may hear His coming,
>   But in this world of sin,
> Where meek souls will receive Him still,
>   The dear Christ enters in.
>
> O holy child of Bethlehem!
>   Descend to us we pray;
> Cast out our sin, and enter in,
>   Be born in us to-day.
> We hear the Christmas angels
>   The great glad tidings tell;
> Oh come to us, abide with us,
>   Our Lord Emmanuel!

PHILLIPS BROOKS.

AND now once more comes Christmas Day. Once more, borne abroad on the words of simple-minded shepherds, runs the story. God and man have met, in visible, actual union, in a life which is both human and divine. . . . Lift up yourselves to the great meaning of the Day, and dare to think of your Humanity as something so sublimely precious that it is worthy of being made an offering to God. Count it a privilege to make that offering as complete as possible, keeping nothing back, and then go out to the pleasures and duties of your life, having been truly born anew into His Divinity, as He was born into our Humanity, on Christmas Day.

CHRISTMAS SERMON.

THE Incarnation opened the spiritual, the supernatural, the eternal. It was as if the clouds were broken above this human valley that we live in, and men saw the Alps above them, and took courage. For, remember, it was a true Incarnation. It was a real bringing of God in the flesh. It was a real assertion of the possible union of humanity and divinity; and by all its tender and familiar incidents, by the babyhood and home life, the hungerings and thirstings of the incarnate Christ, it brought the divinity that it intended to reveal close into the hearts and houses of mankind. It made the supernatural possible as a motive in the smallest acts of men. . . . It brought God so near that no slightest action could hide away from Him; that every least activity of life should feel His presence, and men should not only lead their armies and make their laws, but rise up and go to sleep, walk in the street, play with their children, work in their shops, talk with their neighbors, all in the fear and love of the Lord.

I. 186.

(Stephen) said, Behold I see the heavens opened, and the Son of Man on the right hand of God.

ACTS vii. 56.

It is not death, O Christ, to die for Thee :
   Nor is that silence of a silent land
   Which speaks Thy praise so all may understand :
Darkness of death makes Thy dear lovers see
Thyself Who Wast and Art and Art to Be ;
   Thyself, more lovely than the lovely band
   Of saints who worship Thee on either hand
Loving and loved through all eternity.
CHRISTINA ROSSETTI.

AS we watch Jesus [on the night of the Passover] sitting there and telling the disciples truth after truth about Himself, what words like the old words of the Psalmist describe the scene, He is "clothing Himself with light as with a garment." We can seem to see the lustrous raiment of truth gathered about His familiar form, at once revealing it to, and hiding it from, His amazed disciples; revealing it to their love, hiding it from their understanding, . . . until at last the John who had once questioned Jesus as if he were a scribe or teacher, "Master, where dwellest thou?" is seen writing his reminiscence of it all in words that burn with mysterious reverence, words that make us think he wrote them on his knees. "The Word was made flesh and dwelt among us, and we beheld His glory, the glory as of the only begotten of the Father."

II. 315, 316.

All at once I looked up with terror.
He was there.
He Himself with His human air,
On the narrow pathway, just before.
I saw the back of Him, no more —

No face : only the sight
Of a sweepy garment, vast and white,
With a hem that I could recognize.

Soul of mine, hadst thou caught and held
By the hem of the vesture! — And I caught
At the flying robe, and unrepelled
Was lapped again in its folds full-fraught
With warmth and wonder and delight,
God's mercy being infinite.

BROWNING.

I KNOW that the death of the beggar, the death of the baby, has in it a mystery of force which no wisest man can comprehend. I know that He whose life was one with the baby's and the beggar's, and yet infinitely deeper, vaster, must have had a mystery in His death over which eternity shall keep guard, husbanding its treasures, and giving them forth to the eternally ripening soul as it shall need and shall be able to receive them. He who tells me that he will read to me now the mystery of the death of Jesus, shuts my ears with his very offer. I will not let him tear for me the mystery of the dawn which no hand can hasten as it slowly brightens to the full morning.   INFLUENCE, 51.

[*Holy Innocents' Day.*]

Oh weep not o'er thy children's tomb,
    Oh Rachel, weep not so !
The bud is cropt by martyrdom,
    The flower in Heaven shall blow !

Firstlings of faith ! the murderer's knife
    Has miss'd its deadliest aim :
The God for whom they gave their life,
    For them to suffer came.

Though feeble were their days and few,
    Baptized in blood and pain,
He knows them, whom they never knew,
    And they shall live again.

REGINALD HEBER.

The foundations of the wall of the city were garnished with all manner of precious stones. . . . The glory of God did lighten it. — REV. xxi. 19, 23.

EVERY new experience is a new opportunity of knowing God. Every new experience is like a jewel set into the texture of our life, on which God shines and makes interpretation and revelation of Himself. You hang a great rich dark cloth up into the sunlight, and the sun shines on it and shows the broad general color that is there. Then one by one you sew great precious stones upon the cloth, and each one, as you set it there, catches the sunlight and pours it forth in a flood of peculiar glory. A diamond here, an emerald there, an opal there, the sun seems to rejoice as he finds each moment a new interpreter of his splendor, until at last the whole jewelled cloth is burning and blazing with the gorgeous revelation.

Now a much-living life, a life of manifold experiences, is like a robe which bursts forth of itself to jewels. They are not sewn on from the outside. They burn out of its substance as the stars burn out of the heart of the night. And God shines with new revelation upon every one. And the man who feels himself going out of a dying year with these jewels of experience which have burned forth from his life during its months, and knowing that God in the New Year will shine upon them and reveal Himself by them, may well go full of expectation, saying, " The Lord is at hand."

IV. 359.

LIFE as a part, life set upon the background of eternity, life recognized as the temporary form of that whose substance is everlasting, that is short; we wait for, we expect its end. And remember that to the Christian the interpretation of all this is in the Incarnation of Jesus Christ. "I am He that liveth, and was dead; and behold, I am alive for evermore." The earthly life set against the eternal life, the incorporate earthly form uttering here for a time the everlasting and essential being, those years shut in out of the eternities between the birth and the ascension, that resurrection opening the prospect of the life that never was to end, — these are the never failing interpretation to the man who believes in them of the temporal and eternal in his own experience.

I. 330, 331.

Does the precept run " Believe in Good,
In Justice, Truth, now understood
For the first time "? — or, " Believe in Me,
Who lived and died, yet essentially
Am Lord of Life "?

BROWNING

OH friends, the old year is fast slipping back
behind us. We cannot stay in it if we
would. We must go forth and leave our past.
Let us go forth nobly. Let us go as those
whom greater thoughts and greater deeds
await beyond. Let us go humbly, solemnly,
bravely, as those must go who go to meet the
Lord. With firm, quiet, serious steps, full of
faith, full of hope, let us go to meet Him who
will certainly judge us when we meet Him,
but who loves us while He judges us, and who,
if we are only obedient, will make us, by the
discipline of all the years, fit for the everlasting world, where life shall count itself by
years no longer.   IV. 369.

Time's waters will not ebb, nor stay,
Power cannot change them, but Love may;
  What cannot be, Love counts it done.
Deep in the heart, her searching view
Can read where Faith is fix'd and true,
Through shades of setting life can see Heaven's
    work begun.

O Thou, who keep'st the Key of Love,
Open Thy fount, eternal Dove,
  And overflow this heart of mine,
Enlarging as it fills with Thee,
Till in one blaze of charity
Care and remorse are lost, like motes in light divine;

Till as each moment wafts us higher,
By every gush of pure desire,
  And high-breathed hope of joy above,
By every secret sigh we heave,
Whole years of folly we outlive,
In His unerring sight, who measures Life by Love.
                                    KEBLE.